Mothers' Day

Drawing from her life as a rural midwife, Fiona McArthur shares her love of working with women, families and health professionals in her books. In her compassionate, pacey fiction, her love of the Australian landscape meshes beautifully with warm, funny, multigenerational characters as she highlights challenges for rural and remote families, and the strength shared between women. Happy endings are a must.

Fiona is the author of the non-fiction book *Aussie Midwives* and lives on a farm with her husband in northern New South Wales. She was awarded the Excellence in Midwifery Award for NSW in 2015.

Find her at FionaMcArthurAuthor.com

Mothers' Day

FIONA McARTHUR

MICHAEL JOSEPH
an imprint of
PENGUIN BOOKS

MICHAEL JOSEPH

UK | USA | Canada | Ireland | Australia
India | New Zealand | South Africa | China

Penguin Books is part of the Penguin Random House group of companies
whose addresses can be found at global.penguinrandomhouse.com.

Penguin
Random House
Australia

First published by Penguin Random House Australia Pty Ltd 2018

1 3 5 7 9 10 8 6 4 2

Text copyright © Fiona McArthur 2018

The moral right of the author has been asserted.

Cover design by Louisa Maggio © Penguin Random House Australia Pty Ltd
Cover photograph by Stocksy/Andreas Gradin
Typeset in Sabon by Midland Typesetters, Australia
Printed and bound in Australia by Griffin Press, an accredited ISO AS/NZS 14001
Environmental Management Systems printer.

 A catalogue record for this
book is available from the
National Library of Australia

ISBN 978 0 14378 581 1

penguin.com.au

To all mothers, including those who live in our hearts, and to grandmothers, aunts, sisters, girlfriends and, of course, midwives, who mother others. You are a gift, and those you bless salute you.

Chapter One

Jacinta

Ambulance sirens sucked big time when you lived in a dive near Paddington station. Still, Pedro's crumbling flat beat the heck out of sleeping in the park.

One day, Jacinta McCloud would own a home. And it would be nowhere near an ambulance station. At seventeen she had a way to go, but she was determined it would happen. Her baby would have a safe place to live and play, and no one, ever, no matter what, would be able to evict them onto the street.

The siren wailed again. She thought of her mum every time she heard it and her thin fingers crept to the button on her shirt and tightened around it. Pedro said if you held a button on your shirt until you saw a four-legged animal, then you might, just might, keep something bad from happening to the patient in the ambulance. Jacinta's whip-smart mind disagreed, but her heart couldn't take the risk.

Someone should've done it for her mum.

There were too many sirens. Too many ambulances. Too many people who didn't care. The one person who mattered the most had died and left her sixteen-year-old daughter on Mother's Day last year.

Jacinta's belly kicked and rolled so she moved awkwardly to rest on her knees, slid her free hand down, and rubbed through the shirt. 'Morning, baby. Did that nasty ambulance wake you, too? Let's go find and feed Cat so I can let go of the stupid button.'

The darn cat ate better than she did. She could put on the vegetable soup Pedro liked – all part of the plan to make herself indispensable to a man who had no sexual interest in women, which suited Jacinta just fine. Since moving in, she'd stayed low key, tried to be useful and didn't cry even when she wanted to. Pedro admired her for that. 'Thank God you're not one of those weepy bitches,' he said.

She'd become bigger and more unwieldy in the five months she'd been here – and she needed to make him glad she was here until she'd sorted plan B.

A sudden, loud, *ratta-tap-tap* forced her to stare at the heavy reinforced door Pedro was so proud of. Pedro didn't knock. And his friends used a coded rhythm. Whoever it was, they knocked again.

Like the police knocked.

Like her heart knocked.

'I'm looking for Jacinta McCloud.' It was a male voice. Posh. Firm. And determined. He didn't say *police* . . .

Looking for her?

If she stayed quiet he might go away, but then she'd never know who or why. It's not like she had people knocking on her door every day, *looking for her*. Jacinta edged closer and squinted her eye to the peephole all good doors in Kings Cross cherished.

A man stood there. He was taller than Pedro, over six foot. He didn't look gay. She'd developed skills at telling that, too. This guy reminded her of those jocks who strutted into the gym and came out all sweaty and muscled – except he was clean, and old. Probably mid-thirties or more.

She couldn't see his face because he was staring down at something in his hand. She hoped it wasn't a gun or a knife. She'd seen a few of those since she'd been here.

'What do you want?' Her voice came out sounding impolite, which was better than frightened, but there was a decent door between them so she could afford a bit of bravery. Pedro had paid a lot for that door. She'd be safe.

The man lifted his head and she saw his eyes. Blue. A deep, dynamite blue, like the squares on the police tape. He stared back at the peephole. Back at her. But he couldn't see her like she could see him.

He had thick dark eyebrows and a brick for a chin. With his square-cut hair and long grey coat, he looked like an assassin from the movies.

'I have a letter.' He spoke slowly. 'From her mother. Asking me to find her.'

She froze. *Letter?*

The words hit like an arrow to her chest and she sucked in splinters of air with the pain of grief. 'Filthy liar! My mother's dead.' The words fired out harsh and cracked and staccato; broken bullets from her heart.

Stupid. Stupid. Stupid. She should have stayed quiet. She felt like swearing. She'd learned a lot of crude words since she'd come to the Cross, but she'd sworn off profanity. On that horrible night

3

when her mum had passed, Jacinta had whispered, 'Don't you fucking die!' to her mother.

'Don't swear,' her mum had said. 'Please.' So she didn't. It was the only thing she could do for her mum now.

'Not lies,' the man behind the door said. Conviction rang in his tone. She glared back at the peephole. Back at his eyes. He didn't say anything else. He just stared at her as if he knew she was watching, and something in that look told her he, at least, believed what he said. She knew liars rabbited on to make their case. This guy stayed silent.

The cat rubbed against her legs and she looked down. *Four-legged animal.* Her hand fell away from the button on her shirt. The tactile distraction helped her focus. Her anger returning, she lifted her chin and faced the closed door. 'Why would she write to you?'

'I'm your father, Jacinta. Iain McCloud.'

Jacinta's breath caught in her throat and her world tilted. For a second there she thought she might be sick.

Her last name was McCloud.

No. No. He was lying. He had to be. She didn't have a father. She didn't have anyone except her baby. She was stupid again for even giving him a chance. She turned away from the door. 'My father is dead.'

'No!' His voice stayed calm but determined. Implacable. 'I'm not dead. I didn't know. I'm sorry. I have your mother's letter with me.' He paused. 'I want to help.'

Her heart pounding, Jacinta scooped the cat and held her like a shield. Her eyes began to sting but she willed the tears back. She hadn't cried once since she'd come here.

The cat purred and whirred against her ribs like a small, warm engine, calming her until her brain began to work.

'Jacinta,' he said again. 'I want to help.'

Yeah right. 'That's what they all say.'

Jacinta rubbed one hand across her eyes and fiercely held back a sob. The letter would prove he was lying. 'Slide it under the door.'

A sheet of pale paper pushed into sight and she squeezed the cat. Cat arched and, as if the animal were made of glass, she carefully eased her onto the floor. A ridiculous precaution, she knew, because that was one tough cat. All through the slow-motion action, shock and disbelief shuddered in her rib cage, because even as she bent to pick up the note she could tell.

Her mother's cheap paper.

Her mother's clear handwriting.

Her mother's last letter . . . to him.

Jacinta's throat burst into a hundred tiny needles of emotion and she couldn't swallow.

Thirty minutes later Jacinta stood in the centre of a formal lounge room overlooking Sydney Harbour, while her brain scrambled for a frame of reference. She had a father. Unable to stand still, she walked with agitation across to the huge windows to grip the windowsill. She stared blindly out at the Harbour Bridge from a vantage point so close it felt like she could reach out and touch the metal of the structure. But what she wanted to touch was the folded letter in her pocket.

Her eyes blurred until the green Sydney ferries and even the tall ship with waves creaming off its sides passed unnoticed.

The letter. She could recite what her mother had written, the words burned into her brain.

Jacinta is your child. For the last sixteen years, I've managed without you – but it's different now. I'm not well and I'm worried about her care if anything happens to me.

Her mother had suspected she'd die. And she hadn't told Jacinta.

Jacinta turned back to Iain McCloud. He'd been watching her, but when she returned the scrutiny he shifted his gaze to the envelope that had carried the missive. It lay on the coffee table between them crossed with address changes. It wasn't his fault that he hadn't received it right away. It was nobody's fault. Except now, he knew about her and he'd come. Too late to save her mum.

'I wish your mother had told me. I would have been there for you both,' he said, his voice a quieter version now.

She didn't trust him. She didn't trust anybody. Jacinta scoffed. 'Sure you would. You probably don't even remember her.' She watched him wince with some satisfaction.

'I remember Adele,' he said almost fiercely. With no small degree of shock, Jacinta realised that her voice changed like that when she felt strongly about something. It was weird to hear it come from someone else.

'I remember the summer it must have happened,' he went on. Then he looked at her and again she could see how much he wanted her to believe him. Maybe deep down she did, but she wasn't telling him that. No way.

'Adele was older than me,' he said. 'I thought she was the most beautiful woman I'd ever seen.'

Jacinta flinched, but he didn't see it. She suspected he didn't see anything in this room as he lost himself in the past.

'Not at the end she wasn't,' Jacinta muttered. Her mother's years of hard work and illness had been etched on her face.

His gaze shifted to hers. 'And I want to know that, too. But we have a little time.'

She saw him look at the swell of her belly. He didn't say, 'before the baby', but she knew he was thinking it. The pregnancy had been a shock for him when the door had opened.

It had been a shock for Jacinta when she'd first found out, too. Nick the Nasty had pushed her backwards by her little bulge when he'd realised it was there. 'You're pregnant!' As if she'd done it all by herself to spite him. And she'd looked down and realised it was true. Then he'd said scornfully, 'Get yourself fixed before it gets any bigger. Or get out.' And she'd cupped her stomach and run away.

She pulled herself back to the present. Back to the posh room with its expensive harbour view and the man who was supposed to be dead. She watched him run his hand through his tousled hair. *Not so immaculate now, are you, buddy?*

He was watching her again. 'Let me support you, at least until your baby's born. I'm offering a safe place for both of you at a time when you're vulnerable. Your baby is vulnerable.'

And that was the heart of it.

She couldn't afford to turn him down. Pedro had been skirting the back door of a paddy wagon for a while now and he could go any time. Then she definitely wouldn't be safe. Not with his friends. Not with the other drug dealers. Her baby wouldn't be safe.

'You look like her,' he said softly as his eyes stared through her again.

Jacinta turned her head and dispassionately studied her face in the big gold-framed mirror hanging over the marble fireplace. She looked crumpled, her hair dull and her cheeks prominent in her thin face. Maybe she had her mother's nose. What she couldn't dispute was she had this guy's eyes and eyebrows.

Her hair was light brown, almost blonde like her mother's, but her eyebrows were two dark slashes across her forehead. She'd always wondered where her dark brows had come from. She guessed she should be glad he didn't have a monobrow.

This was all too much to take in.

Then he said something that made her stare. 'What's ironic is that I was the same age as you are now. But I lied to her and told her I was twenty.' He laughed bitterly. 'I would have told her anything to make her see me as a man and not a boy. I was so infatuated with her.' He went on and she turned back to look at this man who evidently did know her mother. Someone who had memories of her when she was young – times Jacinta knew nothing about.

'Until the day she changed.' His voice altered. Flattened. 'When she sent me away.' He looked at her. 'Apparently to hide you.'

Jacinta shrugged. 'Why would she do that? Unless she was scared of you?' Maybe he was meaner than he looked.

He laughed, but it was an odd, humourless noise. 'I was the puppy and she was the mistress. I would have done anything for her. But she always said she was too old for me, that I had my life ahead of me. And she chose to exclude me from your life. I wish I knew why.'

He didn't look like a puppy now. More like a big, square-shouldered guard dog, staring her down. Pretty sure of himself, all decked out in his silk tie. It did put her at a disadvantage to be smelling like Kings Cross and dressed in a grubby man's shirt, with a pair of old bike pants stretched over her belly.

Survival kicked in. If he was her dad, he owed her – and she'd make him pay. 'You got a shirt I can wear? I need a shower.'

'A shirt, please.' He raised one of those dark brows.

She raised her left brow to mimic him. 'Spare me,' she said. She didn't do submissive.

To her surprise he laughed. Like Pedro had.

'So where did you meet this Pedro?'

They were sitting at the dining-room table and her new parent had just made an omelette. A pretty good one. And he also made good coffee, which had improved her mood. As had the crazy shower that fell from the bathroom ceiling like a waterfall from a plate-sized shower rose, and the amazing flower-scented conditioner. She'd never smelled anything like it. And the towels! She could have curled up in the swimming-pool-sized bath in those towels and slept like a baby.

Unfortunately, she had to pay the man and answer the questions.

'Under a park bench. The cops were chasing him and I woke up when he fell down next to me. He pretended to be asleep, as if he'd been there all night. They ran past and after they left, he asked my name. Offered me a place to sleep.' She shrugged. 'So, I said yes.'

Iain closed his eyes and she watched his hand tighten on his mug. She could almost imagine it creaking as his knuckles went white. Interesting. She'd have to watch him. But some instinct told her his anguish was *for* her, not against her.

He gestured to the silver coffee pot. 'More?'

'No.' She shook her head. 'I read in a magazine that too much coffee could be bad for the baby.' It wasn't the worst thing she'd turned down, not by a long shot.

'That's true. The baby can have withdrawals from caffeine after birth,' he said, as if he knew what he was talking about. For a moment he looked as though he was going to ask something else, then changed his mind. Changed the subject back to Pedro.

He studied his long fingers, his face tight. 'Was he good to you?' She didn't pretend not to know what he meant. *It's a bit late to play daddy*, she thought grimly.

'I knew Pedro was gay from the first moment,' she said to comfort him – unsure why she felt she needed to. She'd been fine, and the truth was it could have been way worse. 'That was a plus.'

Iain stared at his hand on the mug, not looking at her. 'How old are you, exactly?'

'Don't you know?' Her voice dripped with sarcasm.

'I mean, when's your birthday? I've worked out that you're seventeen, but I'd like to know the date,' he clarified.

She sighed. Okay, maybe she could stop being a bitch, but it was all a bit much to be 'saved' by her new dad. Excuse her if the fact that she just might have the backup plan she'd been searching for took a bit of getting used to.

She sighed. 'I turned seventeen three weeks ago. Pedro taught me to drive last month.' She didn't say she had the feeling it was so she could be the one behind the wheel of a getaway car. She suspected her new daddy wouldn't like that. Wickedly, she imagined the horrified expression on his face and it almost made her want to say it out loud.

But what if he threw her out like Nick the Nasty had? Then she'd be back on the street. She'd been desperate to figure out what she was going to do when this baby was born. To have actual plans for the future. This was her chance.

'How long ago did you move into that place? How did you buy food?'

'Five months.' *Get over it*, she wanted to tell him. She'd been glad to have a real roof over her head after the park bench.

'I work a few hours at the local drycleaners on weekends, ironing fancy clothes to give myself some cash.' Pedro had said she didn't have to pay rent, but she'd at least started an emergency fund for when baby was born. Just in case she needed to run.

She'd developed impressive skills with an iron at an early age when her mother had first become ill, and that expertise still helped with the bills. Her back had ached, though, lately.

'And the father of your baby?'

'Threw me out when he found out I was pregnant.' When she looked up she blinked at the cold anger in Iain's face. She shrugged. 'It was a good thing, really. Pedro's turned out to be much safer. It's okay. I was ready to leave.'

This time it was she who changed the subject. A little mockingly, but she couldn't help herself. Thinking about her baby's father made her angry. 'So, have you always wanted to be a daddy?'

He looked at her and she refused to shift under his gaze. But it was difficult. Then he looked away with a smile and said, 'Yes.'

That surprised her. 'So why aren't you married with two-point-two private school kids?' She'd seen them, girls with black tunic uniforms and white shirts. Black stockings in the winter and a tie. So up themselves. They always walked by in twos and threes, giving her filthy looks, the street girl. She'd wondered what they talked about. What their homes were like. What their mothers were like.

'My ex-wife didn't want to adopt and was unable to have children herself.'

Jacinta wished she'd had some choices. 'Well, you're not adopting me.'

He sat back, looked at her, and then laughed. 'I don't have to. I have a copy of your birth certificate and my name's on it.' Then he shrugged and smiled. 'We could try to get on for the sake of your baby?'

'You could just pay for a flat and I could stay there,' she countered.

'Or you could stay here.'

Chapter Two

Noni

The antenatal class was held in the grounds of the Burra District Hospital. The grass surrounding the two-storey building was brown from the dry summer, and it crunched underfoot as Noni Frost walked across it. Gums reached for the sapphire-blue sky and the roses were ecstatic, blooming like vivid-pink smiling faces against the white walls. Autumn was here, but the warm breath of wind pretended it wasn't.

The hospital was a long, early-1900s brick edifice painted white and had three large arches at the centre leading to the administration, kitchen and utility sections. Past those arches, up the stairs or the ancient lift, were the wards. At the end of the corridor the sound of a baby crying drifted down the hallway.

The verandah tucked under the corrugated iron roof caught afternoon breezes before it soared into an attic. Somewhere, a switch tripped and the security lights outside came on with the dusk.

Noni glanced at her watch and saw it was six-fifteen. She was late again. She unlocked the door for the new antenatal class and switched on the subtle pan flutes to play in the background. Some of the station hands from the surrounding sheep stations didn't like the flutes, and she wished she could find a decent relaxation album with a more country-music feel. She shrugged. The boys would just have to try a new experience. Maybe she could get some of Aunt Win's muso friends to try a low-key instrumental with banjo and harmonica.

She rolled her right shoulder and grimaced. Trying to bowl overarm in the nets at her son's Kanga cricket practice made her shoulder feel odd. She doubted she'd get elected as bowler or coach of the year. Hopefully, someone else would volunteer there soon – with a town of five thousand, surely someone was waiting in the wings. Maybe one of the new dads in her class would take it on if she asked them. But she couldn't do that the first week.

Actually, she'd prefer to have someone save the maternity service in town, instead. Confirmed today, it was only six weeks until Dr Soams's retirement. That gave them until April to find a new GP obstetrician or Burra District Hospital would close its labour unit. Not only would the birthing women have to drive to the Base Hospital, an hour and a half away, but some of the midwives would have to find new jobs. And as she was the last midwife hired, she'd likely to be the first out. Noni had only just found her feet presenting these classes and she loved them with a passion, but unless a new doctor was found, this could be her last group.

She inhaled the light scent of lavender as it wafted past her towards the screen door of the little outbuilding where she took her classes, and tried to relax. Noni wished she'd started the music in her headphones earlier for her own stress relief. It might have helped the first-night butterflies as well.

The entrance door scraped open and she turned to see a tall, painfully thin woman standing uncertainly in the doorway. Dressed in ripped jeans, heavy black boots and a black singlet top that stretched over her baby belly, she looked like a rapper about to go into labour. Noni didn't recognise her, which was a little unusual, as she'd done all her schooling here, so she knew most families. This woman looked like she was in her late teens or early twenties, so not that far from Noni's age, and she would have remembered those distinctive dark eyebrows under the thick fringe of kinked almost-blonde hair. Noni made a quick calculation based on the size of the girl's stomach and decided the she'd be lucky to finish the classes before her baby was born.

Hopefully, she'd be able to give birth at Burra before the maternity ward closed for births. Noni clamped down on the negative thought and moved towards the newcomer.

'Hello. I'm Noni, the antenatal teacher.' She smiled encouragingly and waited for the woman to offer her name.

'Right place then,' she said, and pushed her protruding stomach past Noni to enter the room until she could lower herself slowly into a chair with a soul-weary sigh. It wasn't a good start. Noni decided the young woman might be younger than twenty.

Noni blinked and turned to follow, intrigued by the way the girl had tied an untidy knot in her long hair to keep the strands at the back away from her face, rather than use a hair tie. Noni had never seen anybody do that before.

'I gather this is the antenatal class?' The deep, rich tones came from behind her, and Noni found herself spinning back towards the new voice. This time, she blinked for another reason. The man in front of her screamed city-slicker, not something they saw a lot of in their working-class town, and he appeared at least ten years older than the girl he followed.

Disconcertingly, he stood a good foot taller than Noni – it made her think of a skyscraper, but they didn't do skyscrapers in Burra. A really tall tree, then. Unconsciously, she straightened her spine and jutted her chin. 'Yes, it is.'

I do not have an attitude about my height, she reminded herself. 'Good evening, I'm Noni. I facilitate the antenatal class.'

She'd made the pretentious introduction coolly on instinct. The guy could stop traffic, if there'd been traffic in town at this time of night, with his carved cheekbones and startling blue eyes. Quite the alpha male – her least-favourite type – and she didn't have a thing for new dads-to-be. Especially older, condescending ones who made her feel like a garden gnome.

She gestured towards the names in the attendance book on the table. 'If you could write your name on the name tags for the first couple of weeks, I should have all your names sorted out in my head by week three.'

She smiled her heck-I'm-blonde smile, but he didn't smile back. *Crash and burn.* She gave a mental shrug. Sense of humour missing there, too.

She watched him add the last two names, Jacinta and Iain McCloud, as late entries – so they *were* married. His writing stood starkly uniform and perfectly positioned on the stick-on label. He took one for his wife.

He carefully placed his own name tag so it sat squarely on his pocket. Clearly, the man was a control freak. Noni smiled to herself and turned to the next couple walking in the door.

Chapter Three

Jacinta

Jacinta surreptitiously scanned the room for anyone, apart from the short chick at the front who seemed to be running the show, who was somewhere near her age. No-one else was. Either this hick town didn't have anyone pregnant under twenty or it had a class somewhere else with normal people, where you didn't take your new freakin' parent. This just got worse and worse.

Her back ached in the stupid chair because they'd driven south-west all day, and once they'd left the city it had been all rocky hills, sheep and brown rivers to this hole of a place. She turned her head and narrowed her eyes at the man who had dragged her here as he sat down. She'd been working herself up all day.

It was all his fault.

His fault her mother had had to slave herself to death.

His fault she'd had to live on the streets until she'd hooked up with Pedro.

It would have been so much more sensible if he'd left them a fortune in his will and died instead. Preferably years ago, like her mum had always told her.

Jacinta's eyes stung and she screwed up her face hard to stop the stupid tears from falling. Since he'd found her, she always seemed to be on the edge of tears. Why now? She'd vowed to stop the blubbering that seemed to engulf her every time she thought of her mum and that horrible breathing before she died. The day when the only person in the world who'd really cared about her had floated away while everyone else had celebrated their mum.

Somewhere inside, she suspected that maybe the floodgates had opened because, despite Iain being the biggest pain in the arse, she did feel safe for the first time since her mum had gone, and she finally had the luxury of grief. But this was ridiculous. She didn't want to cry so she replaced the choked throat with seething anger towards this man beside her and felt her emotion stabilise into fury again.

She wasn't sure why she'd gone with him when he'd turned up at Pedro's door that morning. The opportunity to hear about her mother; to find out what she had seen in this man to begin with; and the possibility of being in a better place when her baby arrived were all factors. Plus there was the worry that Pedro's drug dealings were becoming more dangerous. If he didn't get himself killed he'd end up in jail, and where would she be then? Not as safe as she was under Pedro's protection, that was for sure.

So, when Iain had arrived and promised her a nice flat and food, she'd gone. She almost wished she hadn't because this guy acted like a freakin' school teacher, always watching her in case she ran away. But she wouldn't run. Not yet, not until after the baby was born anyway. She owed her baby that safety at least. She had wanted to visit Pedro and tell him she was fine, but as soon as she'd suggested that, the next thing she'd known she was in Iain's car and they were speeding away from the city.

So here she was at freakin' antenatal classes in the back of woop woop, waiting to fatten up like a turkey for Christmas. Not that she'd ever had a turkey for Christmas.

Jacinta glanced at the poster on the wall of an unborn child nestling inside a Madonna-like mother's uterus, and sighed as her gaze returned to her father. The way he made executive decisions like, 'We are heading to the Riverina for the rest of your pregnancy' annoyed her. With his bossiness, she couldn't see what her mother had seen in him apart from his looks. And his money.

That was the point, wasn't it? If you had money you had control. If you didn't, you were screwed.

That insane apartment on the harbour reminded her of an art gallery, not that she'd let him see it intimidated her. He was already too full of himself. Too much 'my way or the highway'.

How different her life would have been if he'd known the consequences of that one summer he'd had with her mother.

'We'll start soon.' The little blonde at the front had set the chairs out in a complete circle around the room, even across the front whiteboard, and Jacinta tried to settle beside Iain. *Be the good girl in class*, Jacinta thought.

Her father leaned towards her. 'Try to look a little less like you've been sentenced to the gallows, Jacinta. You might even enjoy this.'

She opened her eyes wide. 'Why, thank you, wise one.' *Really?* Who was he kidding?

They stared at each other, clashing looks, and finally Iain looked away.

This sleepy country town was the last place she wanted to be, but she wasn't sure what constituted a better place to be in her disaster of a life. And apparently, her new 'daddy' was terrified she'd run back to the Cross. She'd heard him talking on the phone.

They'd only stayed two nights in his posh flat. And hadn't that been awkward'r'us, with Iain watching her, until some doctor friend of his had suggested they travel out to this quiet country town and disappear until the baby was born. Just as soon as she'd had an ultrasound and some blood tests, which she hadn't realised you could get on such short notice. They'd also done some shopping because her clothes weren't up to his standard. She'd rather have banked the money if he wanted to spend it, but the next best thing to do was to buy what she wanted and he hadn't blinked at the cost.

It appeared that her pregnancy care would be good with this Dr Greg Soams. Considering she hadn't had any till now, theoretically it could only improve.

From the moment they hit the long stretch of country road, Jacinta could feel the loss of her freedom; the familiarity of the city slipping away. The brown hills, the gum trees everywhere, the heat of summer still in the air despite the fact that it was autumn weather in Sydney. It had taken five hours to arrive at the big white guesthouse on the hill this afternoon. Her room overlooked an old-fashioned town, apparently a thriving goldrush centre in the past, but now the wide empty streets echoed and strange bird and animal sounds closed in on her. Then, once unpacked, they'd been strong-armed in the nicest possible way by their hostess, to enrol for tonight's course.

Jacinta had never been outside Sydney and here even the cars were different. Bullbars full of headlamps on the glut of utes and men wearing cowboy boots made her feel like she'd woken up in a country music festival. And those never-ending brown paddocks with sheep. Sheep? She was no Little Bo Peep, though the lambs were cute. But what the heck was she doing here?

She watched her father smile politely at a couple as they sat down next to them. The man, dressed in his RM Williams shirt and elastic-sided riding boots, produced a small soft pillow and nestled it in the small of his wife's back. Jacinta suppressed a groan and looked cynically towards the door to see how many more doting couples were coming, when she noticed her father's gaze caught again on the little blonde educator.

The chick was running through her book-and-nametags spiel again, and Iain's eyes seemed glued to her face. Jacinta tried to see what he was seeing. The educator's eyes and mobile mouth seemed too large for her heart-shaped face. Dressed in hospital purple scrub trousers and a gumnut baby T-shirt, she looked young and short. The top of her head would be lucky to reach up to Iain's shoulders. She was no supermodel, that was for sure.

Jacinta sighed again and hoped the classes weren't going to be too airy-fairy.

Chapter Four

Noni

'Welcome, everyone. As I said when you came in, my name is Noni
Frost and I'm one of the midwives in the maternity unit here. You
all have nametags, so we'll skip the "who I am and why I'm here"
bit. Most of us know each other, anyway.' She smiled at the sighs
of relief from the room.

'Unlike school, everyone is here because they want to be.' Noni
found herself looking at the McCloud couple. The girl studied the
cracked linoleum floor and the man stared right back at her with
a sardonic lift of one black eyebrow. *Maybe not you, buster, but
we'll pretend it's true.* She looked away to the eager faces in the
class and felt herself relax.

'It's great to see you all here. Tonight, we'll start with some dis-
comforts of pregnancy and suggestions for relief your doctor may
not have suggested.'

The odd guy lifted his eyebrow again. Noni ignored him.

'We call these symptoms the common complaints of pregnancy.
It's useful to remember that most symptoms of discomfort usually

appear as a by-product of something good your body is doing for your baby.'

Paul, a thin man in his late twenties, and Suzie, his much larger wife, consulted before he put up his hand.

'What good thing is your body doing when your missus has cramps in the legs every night?' He looked around at the other men. 'She wakes up in the night and hops around the bed. I can't catch her to try to help.' The class laughed and several of the men nodded.

'Does anybody else have leg cramps?' Two of the women put up their hands and Noni smiled. 'Lack of calcium is one cause. Your baby is using up your stores and that's a pretty worthy cause. If you increase the calcium in your food that can help. More milk, fish, kelp, sesame and sunflower seeds, along with the dark-green leafy vegetables.'

She glanced around to check she still had their interest. 'Other reasons are hormone changes. The release of progesterone and relaxin prepares your body for stretching and changing shape in pregnancy and labour, so that's good for later pregnancy and birth. Everything,' Noni stressed the word, 'is more elastic . . .'

'Even her temper,' another man murmured.

Noni smiled but stuck to the topic and resisted a comeback. 'Including the stretch in your blood vessels. When your body increases blood volume this leads to the pooling of blood in your legs. The best way to get that blood back to your heart is to use your calf muscles as a pump. Make sure you keep your calf pumps working. Rotate and work your calves when you're sitting or standing for long periods.' Some of the women obediently rolled their ankles.

She grinned cheekily. 'Of course, a pleasant way to assist is to have your partner massage your legs regularly.' She smiled as the men shifted in their seats. 'What about it, fellas?'

She saw Jacinta McCloud scowl at the man beside her and she muttered, 'No way.'

Her husband gave a short, sharp laugh and stared up at the ceiling, and Noni frowned. She suspected something really weird going on between these two.

There were a few half-hidden smiles and strange looks from the class and Noni purposefully shifted the focus from the McClouds. 'Another good way of preventing cramps is to have a warm foot bath containing a few drops of lavender oil before bed.'

That brought Mr McCloud's eyes down from their contemplation of the ceiling. He stared at her and she could feel his attitude across the room. She knew the sharing of his dubious wisdom hung imminent. Noni resisted the urge to sigh. There was one in every class – but she wouldn't let him get to her.

'How much research has been done with oils in pregnancy?'

So, the wisdom has begun, Noni thought, as she assembled her thoughts. He'd have her on her toes over the next weeks, she guessed.

'Don't you have to be careful with essential oils and the pregnant woman?' He effortlessly drew the attention of the room without raising his voice. She had to admit there was something a little mesmerising about his presence. Something she had little experience of in Burra, and the presence kept everyone's attention focused on him.

Noni offered a noncommittal nod. This was her show, not his. 'That's very true. Some oils are contraindicated during different stages of pregnancy and you should check with an aromatherapist if you want to blend oils during this time. Remember the concept of less is more.' She smiled kindly at him. 'Lavender is safe in pregnancy if you use small amounts. The book that mentioned lavender foot baths suggested six drops – I'd suggest half that at the most. If you use too much you can reverse the response you're looking for.'

He sat back. She tagged him silently as the type to be muttering, 'Mumbo-jumbo'. Usually, it didn't worry her, but this guy had an aura of arrogance that Noni found hard to ignore. But she would.

'Is it true the birthing unit might have to shut in a couple of months?' The question was from Suzie, Paul's wife. Suzie worked at the local hairdresser's so she'd be one of the first to find out new information. Noni guessed these women and their partners had the right to know, even though she'd been practising positive thinking. Maternity would find someone to save them.

'It's true that Dr Soams is retiring, but we're hoping to find a replacement obstetrician before that happens, Suzie.'

Suzie nodded, but Paul said with a worried glance at his wife, 'What happens to the women who haven't had their babies before it shuts?'

'They'd have to go to Wagga Wagga. In the long term, if the birthing unit does close then we could look at setting up a midwifery practice, but that would take time. The best thing is to convince a new doctor's family to settle in our beautiful town and combine the two like we do now.' She infused a positive note in her voice with some difficulty and Iain McCloud gave her a disbelieving look. Yep, she disliked him intensely.

The two-hour class passed quickly for Noni, and after some last-minute questions everybody dribbled out the door in twos and fours, already chatting between each pair in a friendly fashion.

She mused over the night as she put away her charts. It was interesting to see the way people interacted. In some groups all her jokes fell flat. This group seemed lovely, except maybe for the McCloud couple. She didn't like to speculate about her clients, but heck, the girl would be beautiful if she'd only stop glaring, and if she ate more. She looked way too young for him. With his looks, Iain McCloud didn't need to cradle-snatch either.

She decided she definitely didn't like him. Iain McCloud's ideas on childbirth left a lot to be desired if the repetitive lift of his eyebrow revealed much about his thoughts. Every time she'd mentioned something about birth choices and faith in natural instincts she'd seen the sceptical movement. An old-schooler. Probably had a baby from a previous relationship, most likely a private hospital caesarean the woman had been steered towards, and this guy thought he knew it all. Then again, maybe she was being unfair and he had a congenital twitch. She shrugged, unusually glad the class had finished, and locked the last window.

As it was only the beginning of March, it was still warm even at this time of night. That's what she liked about southern New South Wales – the extension of summer and the quiet peace of the meandering creeks that flowed down into the Murrumbidgee River. There was a special bend in the Burra creek that she loved where white-trunked river gums glistened on full moon nights like this. In fact, she could do with some calm contemplation by moonlight tonight – but her aunt would be waiting for her.

Noni zipped up her leather jacket and pulled the door shut behind her. Tomorrow would bring more junior cricket and her first day as coach of the under-sixes. Out of twelve boys, how come she scored as the only parent able to spare the time to coach?

She glanced around a little uneasily as she crossed the dim car park, and jumped as a terrified rabbit ran past her ankle. 'That startled both of us, bunny,' she murmured. She reached her one indulgence, unclipped her helmet and climbed on. Noni pressed the ignition, gunned the big motorbike and grinned at the powerful response of the engine. The growl of power never failed to lift her spirits. She flipped up the stand and accelerated into the corner as she left the hospital grounds.

The wind in her face blew the first-night tension into the ether. The air brushed her skin like warm velvet in the early night as she burbled along, raising her mood back to its usual buoyant optimism.

Ten minutes later her fingers eased the throttle as she pulled into her driveway and the bike settled to a quieter rumble. All the lights were on in the guesthouse. So, Aunt Win's new lodgers had arrived.

Under the five-vehicle carport, a sleek Lexus sat disdainfully next to Aunt Win's dusty table-top utility truck. Noni rolled the bike over to the V-shaped ledge she'd made to save having to wrestle the bike onto its stand every night. That could be an issue when little women had big bikes. If the bike started to fall over it usually meant strain, struggle, and then that embarrassingly irreversible slide to the ground.

As she walked past the twin white columns at the entrance and pushed open the front door to go in, the ambience from her pleasant ride fell like a saddlebag breaking its strap and going plonk onto the ground.

'Noni!' Luckily, Aunt Win enfolded her in her usual hug and she had a moment to lift her jaw from the timber floor.

Aunt Win, with her long, white braided hair swinging, was dressed as usual in pastel-coloured cheesecloth. Win revelled in being a sixties child, had been to Woodstock, listened to Marianne Faithfull, and wore the colours of the rainbow in soft skirts and flat sandals. Her rosy-cheeked aunt reminded Noni of a bygone fairy godmother in technicolour, and her twinkling blue eyes seemed to derive pleasure out of thin air. Her skin had been tanned an even brown. To Noni, Win embodied peace and tranquillity. And home. She mothered Noni while Noni mothered the mothers.

The faint drift of rose oil settled over Noni and she hugged her aunt in return. Perhaps a little harder than usual, and with eyes shut.

Win patted her back. 'You've met Iain and Jacinta McCloud, of course.'

Noni reluctantly drew away and opened her eyes. She should have had that moonlight meditation down at the river because she wasn't relaxed enough to deal with this. Still, she plastered a smile on her face and turned to face them. 'Hello again.'

'They'll be staying with us for the next few weeks,' Win supplied. 'Maybe even staying on to have her baby here if Jacinta decides she wants to.'

She's got six weeks until we shut, Noni thought dismally. Jacinta's scowl didn't change and Noni wondered if her face got tired from holding the fierce expression.

'Did you enjoy tonight's class?' Noni directed her question at Jacinta.

The girl yawned and her face did relax a little then. 'Yeah, it was okay. I'm going to bed.' The lack of enthusiasm prickled a warning to the midwife in Noni and she glanced at Aunt Win. Despite her usual smile, her aunt's eyes shone with concern. It seemed they both agreed that this young woman was in for a difficult couple of months ahead. Noni watched the girl turn to the stairs. For a young woman away from her friends, late pregnancy, labour and new motherhood were all lonely places if you didn't let people in.

Jacinta pulled herself up the stairs with the rail and when she disappeared Noni turned back to the man beside her aunt. She guessed she'd have to say something to him. 'And you?'

'I found the class very interesting.' He sounded sincere and looked much more comfortable than earlier, which seemed reassuring. Aunt Win had that influence on people.

His blue eyes spiked with humour, an unexpected facet of him, and Noni felt an uncomfortable tug of attraction in her stomach before she stamped it down. She'd spent the last five years clawing her way back to respectability in a small town that loved to talk; she wasn't about to become attracted to a dad-to-be.

'I'm glad there were chairs and not the pillows and mats I expected.' His smile encouraged Noni to join him in being amused.

She half smiled back before she realised the guy appeared to be actually flirting with her. Cold settled over her with the thought. *The slime.* No wonder Jacinta was unhappy.

'That's week three when the physiotherapist comes. Well, nice meeting you.' Her tone said otherwise. 'I'm for bed, too.' She turned her back on him to face her aunt.

Win had her small smile on her face as if she knew something

Noni didn't. Her aunt was a big believer in people learning their own life lessons and Noni's heart sank a little. Now what?

She shrugged it off. All she said was, 'Big day at cricket tomorrow. Harley and I should be out of here by about eight-fifteen. I'll be back before one, so you can still get away by twelve-thirty. Is that okay?' They'd come to that arrangement years ago. Win's rules.

'Fine. I'll leave a couple of quiches out and you can make a salad and sweets for our guests for tea. We need to fatten Jacinta up. That girl is all baby.'

Noni laughed, her good humour restored. 'You said the same thing about me when I turned up on your doorstep.' She hadn't thought about that time for a while. Maybe it would help her connect with Jacinta. It wasn't that long ago.

She hugged her aunt again and nodded to Iain before half jogging up the stairs on the way to her son's bedroom.

Chapter Five

Win

Winsome Frost noted her guest watching her niece's bottom bob up the stairs, and if she wasn't mistaken, he'd forgotten to breathe. She tried not to grin. Poor guy was having a wild week.

When he dragged his eyes back to her he exhaled a sigh. 'I'll never sleep. I don't often go to bed before midnight. May I use the library you showed me earlier, please, Miss Frost?'

Win patted his arm. The muscles were so tense under her fingers she wondered when was the last time someone had actually patted him. 'Call me Win, and the house is yours except for the east wing where Noni and Harley have their own quarters.' She watched his shoulders ease a fraction. He was strained tighter than her front fence.

'Thanks, Win. I appreciate you taking us in at such short notice. It's true what they say about the hospitality of country people.'

Win laughed. 'I'm sure there're guesthouses in the city where they like having guests, too. It's what we do. But any friend of Greg Soams is a friend of mine. We'll go the extra mile to help you two sort it out.'

'Thank you. It's been a big week.'

'I'll bet it has. For both of you. Greg said you had no idea about Jacinta prior to this. That would be a shock for any man to find her at seventeen.'

Iain looked at her with sincerity in his eyes. 'I always wanted children. But I admit teenage-daughter negotiation is a skill set I haven't mastered.'

Win smiled at him. 'Yet.' She suspected Iain McCloud wasn't used to situations out of his control.

'I want this to work out very much. Not just for me but for Jacinta. I owe her that.'

Win thought that Jacinta didn't know if she was relieved she had someone to take care of her or angry that Iain threatened her independence. She suspected it was a mixture of both. There was adjustment needed on both sides and they only had these few weeks until the baby was born. At least they'd come to Burra. It was a safe place.

'You strike me as an intelligent man. You'll get the hang of it.' She shooed him with her hand. 'Go through into the library and I'll get you some coffee – or would you like a glass of whisky?'

'Can I have both?'

She grinned at him and decided her new lodger could charm without even trying. *Interesting.* She'd seen the look of dislike her niece had sent him. Her mouth twitched. He must have been out of line in the antenatal classes, which wasn't surprising. Greg Soams had told her the man was a doctor and at sixes and sevens, and not recovered from discovering he had a daughter, let alone one who was seventeen and pregnant.

Win would help as much as she could. She'd do anything for Greg. Not for personal reasons though; she'd recovered from her infatuation of the man all those years ago when he'd married the wrong woman. He'd paid the price for that one and now had a daughter pretty much like the deceased mother to deal with, instead. Her thoughts shied away from wishing she didn't dislike Greg's daughter.

Win turned her thoughts to her own home and the sparks that would fly when Iain's arrogance rubbed up against Noni's stubbornness. She chuckled as she headed into the kitchen. She'd like to be a fly on the wall when they started pushing each other around. Still, she enjoyed her time with her weekend friends way too much to stay home.

And it looked like glorious weather this weekend, which was a bonus if you were going to enjoy nature to the fullest. They were going kayaking this week. It was a shame she'd miss Harley's cricket, but she'd decided years ago that Harley and his mum needed time to themselves, and twenty-four-seven support wasn't beneficial to her niece in the long run. Most weekends she left early and played away Saturday night, and came home Sunday afternoon.

Win thought about Jacinta, the young woman upstairs, barely a child bearing a child. Noni had come to her like Jacinta had, but she'd been a little older. Nearly twenty. Win had never tried to be the parents Noni had lost, because she'd had no experience of parenthood. Just the fullness of life and knowing things didn't always work out the way you hoped they would. But she knew how to love her niece and later her great-nephew, and she was thankful for the day Noni had come into her life.

She bustled around to prepare the tray, heard Noni coming down the stairs, and suppressed a smile as she set the glasses.

'Noni, dear. Could you carry this tray through to our guest, please.'

Chapter Six

Noni

Great, Noni thought, as she tried not to rattle the glass and the whisky decanter against each other. Iain McCloud sat in the big wing chair and looked as though he suffered from troubled thoughts.

The sound of the tray setting down beside him made him shift, but he continued to stare into the empty fireplace as if searching for answers just out of range of his vision.

'Thank you. Am I the right person for her at this time? Do you think she'll ever forgive me for not knowing about her?'

Noni had no idea what he was talking about so she didn't answer.

He turned around, and his head jerked up in surprise. 'I'm sorry, I thought you were your aunt.'

'I had to go back to the kitchen and she asked me to bring this in.' She looked down at him sitting erect in what should have been a comfy chair. His strong thighs looked taut in the expensive trousers, and the worry on his face was a far cry from his earlier humour.

Noni's thoughts began to drift and scatter, a little like leaves in a breeze, and she realised she felt sorry for him. Why feel sorry for him? He'd been a jerk in class. She should just drop the tray and run.

'Can I help you?' she found herself saying, though she had no idea why.

He looked up at her with genuine relief in his face, as if he really didn't want to be alone with his thoughts. 'I'm worried about Jacinta. My daughter doesn't like me and I'm hoping she won't run away before she has the baby.'

Daughter? Daughter? Noni stifled a laugh. Oops. Why hadn't she realised that herself instead of jumping to conclusions? He'd seemed older, but not old enough to be her father. And the longer the class had gone on, the younger she'd suspected Jacinta was. She must have made a small sound because he looked at her, and she had no doubt he'd see the tide of colour that crept up her cheek.

He frowned and raised an eyebrow in question. *May as well get it out*, she thought with an inner cringe. 'Um, I thought she was your wife.'

'Thank you.' Iain laughed a little uncomfortably. 'I mustn't look as old as I feel.'

Noni closed her eyes and this time didn't hide her wince. How could she have been so wrong about someone? She'd sensed there were undercurrents she hadn't understood between the two. She hoped that other sensation she could feel wasn't relief. Relief that she could be attracted to him without flaying herself. Relief that . . . umm, she didn't want to think about!

Noni refocused. Was he struggling not to laugh? Great. Now, she'd provided a source of amusement. When he stopped biting his lip and finally grinned, that smile did strange things to her stomach. *Sheesh.*

'Well, thanks for the vote of confidence.' His voice shook a little when he spoke. 'You think I'd want to entice a seventeen-year-old girl into my bed?' He rolled his eyes. 'Did everyone else in the class think that tonight?'

Noni didn't like to say she'd be pretty sure they did. But seventeen? Good grief. 'She looks older than that. And yes, you look younger than you must be to have a seventeen-year-old daughter!'

He didn't look appeased. 'It's a worry that I even looked like a cradle snatcher. It's not my style, though.'

'So, tell me about it,' She said sympathetically.

His mouth curved again. 'What? My style?'

Out went the sympathy. 'No.' Her voice came out so dry it nearly crumbled. 'I could probably work that one out for myself. You must have had your style for a while if you have a seventeen-year-old daughter.'

That damn gleam in his eyes returned. Then just as quickly his face changed and the humour disappeared as if it had never been. 'I fibbed to her mother about my age.' The brilliant blue of his eyes leached cooler as he thought about it.

'Please.' He gestured for her to sit opposite him.

Invitation or order? It didn't matter at this point. She was curious enough to agree. She lowered her butt into the chair, curled her feet up under herself, and waited.

'My ex-wife and I divorced last year. We didn't have children. Recently, when she remarried, she forwarded me a letter. The letter said I had a daughter.' His voice flattened.

Noni spread her hands. He'd said he and his wife hadn't had any children, so how was Jacinta his daughter?

'That letter came from Jacinta's mother, Adele, an old and

dear friend . . .' He hesitated over the word 'friend', before continuing. 'A good friend, I thought, from a very long time ago, who informed me of my daughter's existence and asked for desperate assistance.' The shock echoed in his voice.

'When they weren't at the address on the envelope I hired a private investigator to find them.' He ran his hand through his hair. 'Eventually, we discovered that Adele had died not long after she sent the letter. Then after some anxious false trails the detective managed to track Jacinta down at a hovel in Kings Cross.' He looked up and shook his head and then his gaze lowered again as his voice dropped down. 'By then, she'd spent nearly a year on the streets.

'Jacinta's mother's life wasn't easy, from what I've gathered, and since Jacinta turned ten, Adele had been plagued with illness.' His eyebrows drew together. 'I've yet to discover what the problem was.' His fingers tightened on the small whisky glass. 'Thankfully she put the surname McCloud on Jacinta's birth certificate, though God knows I don't deserve any recognition. It may have been the saving of us all. Adele died not long after my divorce and Jacinta moved in with a very dubious character and fell pregnant.'

He looked up again. 'I'm telling you this in the hope it may help you understand where Jacinta's biggest needs lie.'

His fingers squeezed until they were white around the glass and Noni crossed her fingers it wouldn't break. Win liked those glasses.

'When she started to show signs of pregnancy, the boyfriend told her terminate the pregnancy or get out. I'm telling myself that was a good thing. Except she hooked up with more dubious characters she'd met while sleeping under a park bench. One of whom, a drug dealer, has been "looking out for her".'

He regarded his glass. Noni considered the expression on his face as his brows drew together again. 'I really hope I never meet the father of her child.' His voice held an edge more dangerous for that. Noni shivered in the warmth of the room.

He sucked in a breath and let it out slowly. 'So, I brought my heavily pregnant daughter to my apartment and tried to connect with her on some level, any level, but it was fraught with just the two of us.' He laughed without humour. 'The first night alone together in Sydney progressed to sheer hell and I thought she'd run away.' His mouth twisted. 'I couldn't say the right things. She stopped talking and started looking longingly at the door. I began to think we should get away, in case her friends found her or she went looking for them. Then she suggested dropping in on the drug dealers. Your Dr Soams happened to ring me out of the blue and, when I told him what was going on, suggested we come here, perhaps even stay until the baby was born. I jumped at the idea.'

Noni wondered how he knew their local doctor. But he'd moved on. She'd ask Aunt Win.

'Jacinta carries a lot of emotional baggage from her mother's death, which she won't talk about, and we needed a buffer until we can begin to understand each other. Greg suggested this guest-house might work since there are other people here to talk to, that it would be somewhere I could concentrate on fostering a relationship with my daughter without my life – or, my biggest fear, her other life – intruding. The squat she lived in . . .' He shuddered. 'I wouldn't let a dog stay there, and I'm pretty sure it was physically and legally dangerous for her.' He huffed out a breath. 'I'm hoping we'll have enough time to form some sort of connection before the baby is born.' He grimaced. 'Maybe that's too ambitious, but at least I can try. We'll stay a month, and see where we are after that.'

Noni wanted to put her hand on his shoulder. His distress made her ache in sympathy, not to mention cringe for her previous assumptions. Thankfully, he wasn't looking at her. She had badly misjudged him. But how was she supposed to know?

He still hadn't finished; had probably bottled the whole emotional rollercoaster up inside and needed to vent. Noni had no problem with that. It was like an episode on TV except these were real people with real heartbreak. 'Jacinta's had no antenatal care,' Iain continued.

That wasn't good. 'We can help there.' She didn't think he heard her.

'Her baby's grown better than it could have under the conditions. I had her checked out the first day and the ultrasounds are all positive. But I worry that she even wants to eat well. It would have been very different if she'd come to me sooner. Like about seventeen years ago. I let her mother and her down for a very long time and I think she hates me for that. But even Jacinta knew the shady side of the Cross wasn't an option for a baby to grow up in, so that's given me a little leverage, for now.'

He sighed and rubbed the back of his neck. 'She's due in eight weeks and we've got a lot of cramming to do in the next month or two before her baby arrives. And then she'll have to learn to be a mother.' He laughed again mirthlessly. 'The crazy thing is I'm actually excited about my grandchild. Which is lucky. Someone needs to be.'

Iain shook his head. 'So that's the story. Unless it comes early, I've got eight weeks to learn to be a father before I become a grandfather.' He seemed to shake off the despondency of his memories and fixed a slightly teasing gaze on her. 'Greg Soams spoke highly of you both, so you and Win get to share some of this. From the little I've seen of you both already I know you will help.'

She really wanted to ask how he knew Dr Soams, only she didn't want to push, considering he'd been so open with sharing their story. It wasn't a 'need to know' right at this moment but it nagged at her.

'I'm sorry. I'm venting.' Iain looked at her. 'Surely enough about me. Now that you know I'm not a cradle snatcher, seducing girls young enough to be my daughter, what about you? What's your story?'

He smiled, and she felt the intensity of that smile all the way down to her toes. Shocked at the unexpected connection, she felt her world tilt. She consciously inhaled a slow breath and slid her feet down onto the floor to ground her. It must be the empathy she was feeling for his plight. His and Jacinta's. Or hunger. Or tiredness. Phew.

When she looked at him again, his eyes were trained on her face. A small smile played around his too-sexy mouth and she could feel her cheeks warm. He was looking at her like she was suddenly a woman and not just a means to an end and she tried hard not to respond to his magic – but apparently once he turned on the charm it could knock her sideways. For goodness sake, he was too old for her. 'Just how old are you?'

He laughed. 'I'm thirty-five. How old are you?'

Well, she could say it was none of his business. But it served her right. 'Twenty-five.'

She did some quick mental gymnastics. He must have been young when he'd fallen in love with Jacinta's mother. So, a wild, youthful passion – she knew about those. If Adele had been much older than him – he mentioned he'd lied about his age – then maybe that was the reason Adele hadn't told him she was pregnant. Noni tried to ignore the voice inside that suggested she go with the temptation of attraction instead of the usual back-pedalling. Six years of a taboo against men had become a habit.

But that tiny voice deep inside whispered to her. *Imagine if you gave him a chance to flirt with you? How would it feel? Two adults with chemistry, passing in the night . . . nothing long term – just a taste of what other women have, the ones who don't have a checkered past and a five-year-old illegitimate son. Then he'll go. Back to the city. And you'll at least know how it feels.*

But she'd never been into affairs and she wasn't sure she knew the rules – if there were rules. And anyway, she wouldn't do that under Win's roof – even though Win would laugh and say the choice was hers. She could feel her heart thumping. No way! Her life had boundaries.

She stood up. Escape looked good right now. 'Somehow, I don't think you're any sort of "old" man, and I think Jacinta will settle under Aunt Win's care. And mine. My aunt and I will help you in any way we can.' Her mouth felt dry and her heart *thump-thumped* like a train. Geez. 'This is a good place to run to when you're feeling challenged and Jacinta won't be micromanaged.' *Unless you try*, she added silently. She thought seriously about that for a moment because he definitely looked the type. Another reason she shouldn't be attracted to him.

'I know this is a good place because it's where I came,' she told him, sharing just a bit. 'We'll be here for Jacinta when she wants us.' She didn't say they'd be there for him because that might not be in Noni's best interests. The jury was out on that one. *Stay on track*, she reminded herself. 'Just let Jacinta settle in and what's meant to be will take its course.' Lordy, she sounded like her aunt. 'Right now, I need my beauty sleep.' Although she spoke calmly, she could still feel the vibration in her chest, like the rabbit that went past her earlier this evening. Scared of the intruder. Unsure of what the darkness held. Except hers was the deep, sleepy darkness in his eyes. 'Goodnight.'

She backed out of the room and then spoiled it by nearly running up the stairs. She, who didn't run away from anything! She kept her eyes on the steps ahead. To look back wasn't an option.

Chapter Seven

Jacinta

The next morning, Jacinta sat on the verandah and answered the questions Harley badgered her with. She'd never had much to do with little kids; had always thought they were shy and boring. But Harley amused her. He was like that black-and-white willy wagtail outside her window on the tree branch this morning. Jumping up and down and twittering insistently, *Wake up! Look at me!* Lucky she was a morning person.

'So where did you live before you came here?' Harley tilted his head as he asked and she could see all the freckles across his nose.

'In Kings Cross.'

'Is that in Sydney?' For a five-year-old, he had a fair grasp on the world. His eyes watched her as if she was going to say something really exciting. She wasn't.

'Yes, I'm surprised you know that.'

'Aunt Win said you came from Sydney.' He squirmed in his seat as if barely able to contain himself. 'I want to go there.'

'Why?' So did she, but he was a little kid. 'It's full of strangers.'

'People come and go here all the time.' Apparently, Harley didn't mind the idea. Strange kid. 'They're strangers until we get to know them.'

'Ah, but in the city, nobody cares about you.' *Unless some random father picks you up and transports you to a hick town in the country.* She preferred strangers who weren't going to watch you twenty-four seven.

Harley narrowed his gaze on her when she didn't say anything more, and shrugged his skinny shoulders. 'And the city's big. And the trains run all day. They only come once a day here. I could catch trains. I love trains. Do you love trains? Did you go on trains in Sydney?'

Trains weren't fun at night. 'Yes. And I can't say I loved them.' She'd better ask him something or he'd never stop asking questions. 'Have you lived here all your life? Is it always this quiet?'

He looked around. Looked around again as if searching for the quiet she was talking about. Another willy wagtail had settled on the lawn a few feet away from them and had begun to tweet belligerently. A truck started up down the street with a low rumble, and somewhere in the vicinity she could hear sheep bleating.

'It's noisy on Saturday mornings,' he told her.

Just then his mother called. 'Harley! Inside, please.'

He grinned cheekily at her. 'Cricket this morning. Gotta go. See ya.'

Jacinta couldn't help smiling. 'See ya.' She watched him run away and glanced down at her Sudoku. Sometimes, her brain felt like it ran on speed and maths helped to calm it down. She was about to tackle it again when she was distracted by the show that started through the kitchen window.

She'd missed family stuff this last year. Stuff she would probably never be a part of again, she thought, and she stamped down on the spark of self-pity. Her mum might have been sick, but they'd had fun, loved each other. They'd been a two-person family.

She watched Noni and her son laughing at something Win said, and she found herself wondering about the boy's father. Someone else had missing links, too. Though she'd bet Harley's dad hadn't been a loser like her baby's dad. Still, the kid looked happy enough.

Conversation drifted out the window. 'Come on, Harley. Can you put the cricket kit beside the ute? I'll lift it in when I find the thermos. There's three hours of sitting under a tree for me this morning and I'm going to need my caffeine.'

'I can't find my white shoes, Mummy.' The miniature version of Noni stood with his hands on his hips and looked at his mother.

'Do I wear them, mate?' His mother mimicked his stance. 'Where did you have them last?'

'Here they are.' Aunt Win came back into view with a pair of shoes in one hand and a thermos in the other.

Both combatants smiled at her and Win turned away to fill the container with coffee.

Jacinta's eyes rested on Win. She'd felt the warmth from the older lady from the first moment she'd met her. Noni had been lucky there. There was no such luck in Jacinta's world since her mum had died. She felt a wave of loss and guilt about whether she could have done more for her mother. That somehow, she could have prevented her dying. Her mum had loved her, and even though she'd been sick for so long, they'd been a team. Until her mum's boyfriend had come along. She chewed the quick of her fingernail, scowled, and looked back at the window. If she hadn't

45

got a boyfriend her mum wouldn't have fallen pregnant. If she hadn't been pregnant she wouldn't have died. That was why she hadn't stayed with him – couldn't stay with the man she blamed. Though she had a new person to blame now: the man who should have looked after her mother from the beginning.

Win's voice broke her maudlin thoughts. 'You losing shoes is hereditary, Harley. Your mother loses everything, and I still haven't figured out how she manages to get it all back. Some guardian angel's looking after her, so you better hope they look your way, too. Now, both of you get out of here and have a good morning.'

Harley ran out of view, probably to get the kit from the carport, his cricket hat shoved into his hand by his mother.

Win handed the thermos to Noni. 'Here's your coffee, and here's that rulebook you said to remember. But they're only under-sixes. Kanga cricket is designed for people who don't know the rules. Someone else will umpire.'

'They'd better.' Noni grimaced and kissed her aunt on the cheek. 'It'll be fun.' She said it staunchly, but Jacinta could see her chewing her lip as she came down the steps. Jacinta had no idea what Kanga cricket was.

'Good luck.'

Noni jumped at the voice as he came around the front of the house. Jacinta hadn't seen Iain appear either. He did that. Crept up on you. So annoying.

'Mr McCloud. I didn't see you there.'

'Iain, please. I feel like my father if you call me Mr McCloud.' He flashed one of those women-slaying smiles Jacinta had seen him use on waitresses and she rolled her eyes. The guy was up himself.

Noni glared at him instead of fainting and that was funny. Jacinta smiled. *Sucked in, Iain.*

Noni said, 'I wish I had time to swoon, Iain,' and emphasised his name deliberately, 'but I really can't spare it.' She gave him her own version of a brilliant smile. 'Ciao.'

Jacinta saw him wince and then she felt mean. Which only made her crabbier, so she crossed her arms and watched the scene play out. At least she wasn't under her father's microscope like she'd been the first day in the flat. Every time she'd turned around he'd been watching her. Then all those tests – though the ultrasound had been cool. She'd carried a little snap of her alien baby in her wallet since then so that had been a bonus.

She heard her father's drawn-in breath as the table-top truck reversed out past his car and missed the rear bumper of his Lexus by a couple of centimetres. Then Win came out and stood beside him.

Jacinta heard her say, 'She usually doesn't hit anything. But she comes awfully close.'

Iain turned his head and looked at her. Win dried her hands on her apron and smiled. 'I think she enjoys the challenge of taking it to the edge.'

Iain laughed and to Jacinta it sounded like it came from a place that creaked and groaned with disuse. Come to think of it, this was the first time she'd heard him laugh. He stopped, as if surprised at himself. Then he looked across and saw Jacinta. 'Morning, Jaz.'

She nodded her head at him. She wasn't sure if she liked the nickname, but she didn't hate it.

He stared at her for a moment and then turned back to Win. 'I've arranged an out-of-hours visit for Jacinta with Dr Soams this morning. She'll probably have to have more blood tests after that.'

Win gave him one of her pats on the shoulder. 'I may not be here when you come back, then. I spend Saturdays away with friends. They pick me up so Noni can have the car, and she runs the house when I have guests.'

Jacinta listened with dismay as Win went on. 'I usually come back home on Sunday afternoon, after lunch. We have Sunday night together then Noni goes to work Monday and I get Harley off to school now that he's started. It suits us both.'

Win went back into the house after that and Jacinta heard her father climbing the steps. She turned her head away, but she could hear the creak of the boards as he came closer. So, tonight there'd be just Noni and her father. And the kid. She preferred when Win was here.

'Does that all sound okay with you, Jaz?'

'Fine.' She turned her head back and spoke to the newspaper under his arm. The thought of Win not being there made her grip the side of the chair. Just because Win was the easiest person to talk to didn't mean she could be relied on to be here, she brutally reminded herself.

Jacinta was just a strange pregnant girl paying to stay here with her even stranger father. Why would Win stay around?

Chapter Eight

Noni

Harley bounced up and down in the rear of the twin cab utility in his new white cricket gear. Noni glanced at him in the mirror and smiled. 'Is your seatbelt tight enough?'

'Yes. How much loooonger,' he drew out the word agonisingly, 'until we get there?'

'Five minutes. You know that,' Noni said indulgently. 'You're really excited about this, aren't you?' Which was why she hadn't wanted the team to fold when the coach broke his leg. She just hoped nobody expected her to know much as the new coach.

Harley began to jiggle again. 'Can't wait. Can't wait.'

Well, she hoped Harley had more of an athletic gene than she did. She'd never been much good at team sports, unlike Aunt Win, who'd been a mean tennis player in her younger days. Lucky she'd put Harley's sunscreen on before she left, Noni thought, because she doubted she'd catch him once they pulled up. He was an adventurous little soul, so the idea of a new game, new mates, and a big green field delighted him.

'There it is, Harley.' She swung down the side street to the cricket fields on the edge of town and pulled up under the big fig tree that she hoped would keep the car cool for the ride home. She parked and undid her seat belt. In the back, Harley's seat belt clicked open and he was out of the car in a heartbeat.

Noni gave herself three seconds to relax. Brown paddocks stretched away to the soft hills in the distance and white dots of sheep grazed on what looked like scant foliage and fodder, but they appeared healthy enough. A couple of brown horses nosed around an outcrop of rocks, one of the many such stone piles that studded the hills, and in the distance a meandering line of green trees indicated the serpentine route of the creek that would be the lifeblood of this particular farming enterprise. Aunt Win and Noni's mother had grown up on a station like that out of town, but Noni's dad had been a mechanic so they'd lived in town all her life. Still, she did love the open spaces. Maybe one day she and Harley could get some acres out of town. She knew Win dreamed of it but the guesthouse gave them another wage.

She opened her door and climbed out to turn her gaze to the other open space. A cricket field with a dozen white mini-maniacs swarming like bees across the grass and a small crowd of parents waiting. For her.

Determinedly, she lifted her chin, plastered a smile on her face and began to walk towards them. Most of the parents here were a lot older than she was – years ahead of her, with Harley's teammates being their second or third child – and because she'd only become a fully fledged midwife last year, she hadn't been a midwife for them unless they'd had another baby recently. But she recognised their faces from the shops and businesses in town, or they were big brothers or sisters of her friends at school. There was the auctioneer from the sale yards . . . *Now why couldn't he have been the coach?* His voice would carry further than Noni's.

It was going to be a stinker of a day and with a sinking feeling she realised she'd left her hat on her bed at home.

Just after lunch Noni rubbed the pain between her eyes and hurriedly put her hand back on the steering wheel. She swung the ute into the carport, just missed Iain's car, and jerked to a halt. Harley vibrated with energy and catapulted out of the car and into the house before she could ask him to carry anything in.

She sighed and rested her arms on the steering wheel to lay her head down for a few moments. The moments stretched into a minute.

'Can I carry something for you?'

She opened her eyes and saw Iain's face peering in at her. Her head throbbed. She stared at him and even that hurt.

When she didn't answer he said, 'How was Kanga cricket?'

Now she'd have to talk. 'Not so good! I forgot my hat and had to umpire out in the sun for a couple of hours.' Her voice cracked and seemed to be coming from a long way away. 'I think I've got sunstroke.'

Iain frowned and reached across to feel her red forehead. 'You twit. You're burning up. Take yourself inside and lie down. I'll fix the gear.' He opened the door for her and helped her out of the car.

His hand felt cool against her arm and she leaned on him for a moment while her head swam. 'You're the guest. I'll be fine.' Her voice petered out and she swayed again.

He muttered something derogatory about the other parents and lifted her into his arms with ridiculous ease before she could protest.

That inside voice whispered to accept his help with grace. At least his arms were cool and safe, even though the ceiling swayed and dipped. She should complain, but instead she lay limp against his firm chest, battling a sudden upsurge of nausea.

In defence she squeezed her eyes closed. The red light behind her eyelids glowed and the nausea increased in firm, solid steps up her throat like the riot police advancing. She prayed she could hold out until she made it to her room, desperately concentrating on small, shallow breaths, trying to keep the queasiness under crowd control.

If she dared to look she could see his occasional glance to her face, and ridiculously she found herself wishing for long, fluttering eyelashes rather than thick, stumpy ones. She felt like a log in his arms and wondered if he could carry her forever. By the time he'd made it to her bedroom at the top of the stairs his breathing had changed, and she guessed he couldn't.

Despite everything, her mouth twitched. *Not as fit as you thought you were, old boy.* So much for being a knight in shining armour. That must have been why cavaliers saved damsels in distress on horseback.

But after checking he had the right room, this hero did lay her gently on the cover of her bed. Her head swam in a whoosh of vertigo and she moaned as the nausea rose. Horrible.

She heard a rattle of something being tipped out, and cracked open her eyes to see the big plastic dish she kept her hair clips and brushes in appear beside her on the bedside drawers. Through the slit of her eyes she could tell he watched her for a moment before heading for the door.

'I'll be back in a minute with some fluids.'

As soon as the door shut she bolted unsteadily for the en suite and let the riot police do their thing. Too unsteady to do more than rinse her mouth and splash water on her red face, she turned slowly and headed back to the bed. By the time her head hit the pillow she felt terrible, but at least the nausea had eased. She was far too sick to worry about being embarrassed.

A young female voice from the doorway said, 'What happened to you?'

Noni forced her eyes open and squinted up at Jacinta. 'Sunstroke,' she gasped, before shutting her eyes quickly as the nausea rose again.

She could hear Jacinta moving around the room and the rattle of the blinds being drawn. The darkness soothed and the sound of the running tap in her bathroom penetrated, but now she couldn't open her eyes. A cool, wet cloth landed none too gently on her brow and she jumped, but it still felt good.

'Sorry, I didn't mean to drop it.'

'S'okay,' Noni whispered. 'Feels great. I didn't pick you for a nurse.'

'Iain's coming up with a drink. My mum used to get migraines. I'll go and talk to Harley.'

'Thanks, Jacinta.' But the girl disappeared at the sound of her father's footsteps.

Noni pulled the cloth from her face as he entered and gingerly opened her eyes as far as they would allow her to. Iain seemed to fill the doorway as he came into her room, and she felt like putting the facecloth back over her face. Even when she was horribly sick, he made her uncomfortably aware of him.

Noni grimaced and sighed consciously to relax. He'd only brought her a drink. She forced herself up into a sitting position and took the glass he offered.

'Take your time. Little sips are often the answer. You should know that.'

Now he was talking to her like a three-year-old. 'How? I've never had sunstroke.'

'Well, what about Harley?'

As if. Too miserable to get angry, she said, 'I wouldn't let him get sunstroke. I make him wear a hat all the time.'

'Typical.'

She swivelled slowly towards him and saw him raise those damn eyebrows again before he murmured, 'Don't do as I do, do as I say.'

She fell back onto the pillows as the effort of being upright took its toll. 'Not true,' she managed to mutter, before she closed her eyes. 'If you're going to harass me, go away.'

He gave a soft chuckle and she felt her stomach clench for a different reason. *Go away,* she repeated silently. She'd rather be sick.

'You look better. One more sip and I'll leave you in peace.' He slid his arm under her shoulders and effortlessly flipped her pillow. She wished he hadn't touched her. When he took his arm away she could smell his aftershave. It was a wonder it didn't make her heave. Crazy.

Noni leaned back on the cool pillow he'd turned, trying to re-establish her personal space and avoid his eyes. 'Thank you, Iain,' she said, trying to raise her voice above a whisper.

'You sound like a polite little schoolgirl. You must be ill.' She saw him smile before giving her a wave as he strode out the door.

She peered at her watch, squinting to see the hands in the dim room. Twelve-thirty. She didn't even want to think about lunch. They'd manage. She'd have a sleep and get up at five to make the . . .

Her eyelids closed before the thought could be completed.

Night had fallen when Noni woke. For a moment she couldn't remember the day, and then did. Her tongue stuck to the roof of her mouth and she sat up slowly to sip from the full glass beside her bed. Thankfully, the lemony taste loosened everything up. Even her brain. 'Hell. The tea.'

She put down the glass and swung her legs over the side of the bed. *Whoa.* The room swung and she rocked back and forth perilously until it settled.

'Bright,' she muttered, and looked up at a sound at the door.

'Very bright.' Iain carried a tray and the smell of hot quiche floated across the room to her.

'Have you got sonic ears or something?'

'Something.' He carried the tray across and set it down at the side of the bed. 'How are you?'

'Better than this afternoon.' She looked at the tray. 'Sorry. I'm supposed to make the tea.'

'You can make the tea tomorrow night.'

'Yes, Doctor,' she joked, and to her surprise Iain jerked. 'What's wrong?'

'Nothing. I thought I heard Harley call.'

Noni sat up straight again. 'Harley. I have to get him his tea and make sure he has a bath.'

'Stay there!' Iain looked at her as if she were a halfwit. 'He knows you're not feeling well. The boy is five years old. Jacinta can look after him. Do you do everything for him?'

'Excuse me,' she bristled. 'I realise that with your vast experience of child-raising you know best.'

'Low blow,' he said quietly. 'I'll see you later.' He left her lying there, guilty and gutted. Being ill was no excuse.

'I'm sorry, Iain,' she called, but he'd gone. So now he was a victim. Well, he shouldn't have implied she spoiled Harley. No one had ever said anything critical about the way she raised her son. They wouldn't have wanted to because she may just be a tad touchy about that subject. That's what happened when you grew up as a young mum. Old ladies tutted. Old men looked down their noses at you. Everyone thought they knew better than you on the subject of how to bring up a child. Except Aunt Win. She'd never interfered.

Noni glared at the ceiling. She didn't want the meal he'd brought up, anyway. And she hated being in the wrong.

She lay there for a while and tried to sleep, the smell of the quiche drifting in tantalising tendrils that taunted her. *Damn him.* She sat up and caught a view of herself in the mirror of the dressing table. She looked like Jacinta. Frowning and glaring. It must be contagious. The silliness made her smile and realise how much of a goose she'd been. She'd get up and apologise as soon as she'd had a shower and eaten.

Thirty minutes later, she found Jacinta and Harley playing snakes and ladders in the library while Iain read his paper beside the screened open window. The warm night breeze stirred the curtains. They all looked up when Noni came into the room and, strangely, she felt like an outsider in her own home. Now, that was an unpleasant feeling.

'You okay, Mum?' Harley spoke from his seat on the carpet, and Noni quelled her disappointment that he didn't get up and cuddle her. She really needed a hug.

'Fine, thanks, darling.' She looked at Jacinta and smiled. 'Thanks for pulling the blinds and the cool facecloth, Jacinta. It made me feel better.' She forced herself to meet Iain's eyes. 'Thank you for looking after me, Iain.'

'You're welcome. Sit down before you fall down.'

She blinked at his tone, but he was looking at his daughter.

'Jaz, would you get Noni another glass of the lemon barley water, please?'

'I'll get it.' Harley jumped up as Jacinta stood.

'You can come too,' Jacinta said, and they both left the room.

Noni took a deep breath, but before she could say anything Iain forestalled her.

'Don't apologise. I shouldn't have said what I did.'

Why didn't she feel appeased? 'Who said I planned to apologise?' She raised her eyebrows at him but had to smile at the twinkle in his eyes. 'You rat. That's it. I'm going to apologise if it kills me. I'm very sorry for my comment, Iain. So there.'

He smiled. 'Very graciously offered. Now, calm down. I won't tease you. Did you enjoy your tea?'

She glared at him then burst out laughing. 'Yes, thank you,' she replied meekly, but the expression in her eyes warned him not to push her.

'So, tell me why you're the coach at junior cricket and nobody else could have relieved you from umpiring?'

Noni leaned back in the chair and closed her eyes. 'The usual coach broke his leg last week and is still in hospital. No other parent offered to take on his job so I said I would.'

'Have you ever played cricket?'

'No. I didn't want to, but nobody else put their hand up for the job.' She'd already said that. 'The season's just started and without a coach the team would have folded.' She shrugged. 'Harley's excited about playing.'

'So, Supermum takes on the world.'

She glared at him, ready to battle.

He held up his hands and laughed. 'I'm sorry. I couldn't resist it.' He felt his forehead and rubbed it.

She leaned forward. Did he have a headache as well? Maybe there was a virus going around and it hadn't been sunstroke. 'What's wrong?'

'Nothing. Just checking to see if you'd burned a hole through my head with that last look.'

Noni quelled the urge to throw a cushion at him, as if she'd known him forever. How could she feel like this after only one day?

Harley bounced into the room and Jacinta followed, carrying her drink. Noni took it, sipped and decided she'd avoid looking in Iain's direction. That way lay dragons.

The phone rang. 'I'll get it.' Harley rebounded off the floor and raced into the hallway. His polite greeting and enquiry on the phone made Noni smile. *Good boy.*

'It's for you, Mr McCloud. It's Miss Soams.' His schoolboy voice struggled over the words.

Noni watched Iain frown as he left the room. *Interesting.* He'd said Dr Soams had suggested they come here. So he knew the family and not just Greg? How well did he know Greg's daughter?

Noni rolled her eyes. Penelope, a girl she'd been to school with, had been the Burra Show Society Princess the year Noni had been pregnant with Harley – and hadn't she rubbed it in. Aunt Win, a life member of the Show Society, had not been happy, she'd even had words with Dr Soams over his daughter, but Noni was over it. She and Penelope would never be friends. The woman was a witch. Noni sat up straight.

As if sensing her disquiet, Harley climbed onto her lap and she cuddled him. Immediately, her equilibrium began to level. 'You had a big day today, too, mate.' They cuddled for a little while until Noni glanced at the clock and saw the time.

'How about you go to bed? I'll be up in a minute to see you. Say goodnight to Jacinta.'

Harley had never been a problem at night. 'G'night, Jacinta. G'night, Mummy.'

She heard him say, 'G'night, Mr McCloud,' as he passed through the hall. Her heart swelled. *Good boy, again.*

She looked across at Jacinta. 'How was your day? What did you do?'

'We went to see Dr Soams, and that Penelope woman took some blood.'

Jacinta scowled again and Noni hid a smile behind her glass as she took a sip. 'Did it hurt?'

'Nah. But Miss P is a pain.' She indicated the phone call with a twitch of her head. 'She was all over Iain, and it was gross.' She shrugged that away. 'Plus, I hate needles.' She looked thoughtful. 'Lucky, I s'pose. If I didn't I probably would have tried heroin.'

Noni choked on her drink. She started to cough and put the glass down hastily.

'You all right?' Jacinta jumped up, belly and all, and hovered near Noni's chair, ready to thump her on the back. Iain came through the door and stared at Noni as tears streamed down her face and she gasped for breath.

'What are you doing now?' He strode across the room and tapped her firmly between the shoulder blades until she drew a deeper breath. He handed her a handkerchief from his pocket to mop up her face.

'Drink down the wrong way,' Noni gasped, and took another sip to soothe her throat. It started another fit of coughing, but she managed to wheeze it under control.

Iain leaned towards her again. 'No. Don't help me any more,' she told him. 'The cure is worse than the disease.'

Jacinta looked from one to the other and shrugged. 'I'm going to bed, too. See ya tomorrow.' She cast one warning look at Noni and shook her head. *Don't tell my father*, it said.

'See "you" tomorrow, not "ya", thanks, Jacinta,' her father corrected.

'Spare me,' his daughter threw over her shoulder, in exactly the same tone as he'd used.

Noni tried not to laugh but couldn't help it. Of course it started the coughing again and she got up from the chair and backed away from Iain. She held up her hands as he advanced towards her.

'Spare me,' she spluttered.

He dropped his hands and stood looking at her for a moment with a penetrating gaze. 'What was that all about?'

'Girl talk.' Noni had her breath back now. She should tell him what had passed between them, but it might destroy any chance of gaining Jacinta's confidence. She'd find another way of getting the message across. Maybe via her aunt.

Iain raised one eyebrow. 'Fine,' he said, glancing at his watch. 'I have to go out now. I'll be a couple of hours. Are you well enough for me to leave you in charge of the house?'

'I do run this guesthouse every weekend,' she said sweetly.

'If you're sure.'

He'd probably go to see his friends Greg and Penelope Soams. *Ugh, Penelope.* He could have her. 'Perfectly fine. Don't let me cramp that style.' He didn't say anything. Just looked measuringly at her as he turned towards her before leaving.

'Goodnight, Noni.'

'Goodnight.' She watched him leave, then got up, climbed the stairs and tucked Harley in. She came back down and sat in the empty room for at least another hour before heading back to her bed. She still had a vague headache, and when she looked in the mirror her face glowed an unattractive red. She felt like crying at the inelegant ruddiness, but accepted the likelihood that her emotional turmoil was all a side effect from the sunstroke.

Chapter Nine

Win

Winsome Frost waved to the driver who dropped her off at the Rumblin' Tummy Restaurant. Time for her Sunday lunch with Greg Soames and, smiling, she tweaked her flowing caftan. His wife, Margarite Milson, who had so sweetly slid Greg out of Win's friendship and orbit in her twenties, had passed away two years ago and, apparently, Greg thought enough time had passed for grief.

The late Margarite had been fond of imparting to anyone who would listen that Winsome Frost was such a hippy. In contrast, Margarite herself was exactly what a doctor's wife should be.

In response, Win had leaned even more heavily towards Aquarius to widen the gap, rather than moving back towards conservative. But lately, she suspected she might be tiring as a child of the moon.

Win wasn't quite sure how this lunch meeting had evolved. It was Greg's idea initially, and the first time had been fun. Gradually their lunch dates had escalated to four times in as many weeks, and she had to admit she'd begun to look forward to them as a regular

Sunday highlight. Though it proved annoying Greg wouldn't let her pay.

She tried not to ruminate about the coldness his wife had always shown to everyone, including Greg. Perhaps that was why he said he loved Win's nurturing soul and had mentioned the need for a future with warmth.

Greg's brown eyes brightened and he rose when she entered the restaurant. He solicitously ushered her into her chair before the waiter could, then he stood there until sure her chair was exactly where she wanted it. When he sat back across from her with such a welcoming smile on his face, she looked at him quizzically.

'You look pleased with yourself.'

'I have you here, haven't I?' He leaned forward and patted her hand. 'How was your kayaking?' His eyes rested on her face as if she was the best thing he'd seen all day. It felt strange, awkward but pleasant, to be the centre of his attention. Though, she kept wanting to make sure she didn't have a spot on her nose.

They were so different. He so straight-laced and respected and she, well, she enjoyed life and to hell with what people thought. What did he want her to say? She felt the urge to shock him. Make him see their differences. 'Are you wondering if it was uncomfortable to sit in a boat with no clothes on?'

He shrugged just a little ruefully. 'I try not to.' A distinguished-looking man in his early sixties with a suspiciously humorous twinkle in his brown eyes, Greg was one of the kindest and gentlest men Win knew. She'd always liked him far too much and he'd always tried hard not to look askance at the mention of her hedonistic weekends.

Win laughed. 'If you want specifics, there were eight of us this weekend. On the water the breeze caresses your whole skin, and the sun feels divine at this time of year. We climbed up to the waterfall as well. And Johnny wrote a new song for the band. Plus, we jammed and recorded a long, rambling, relaxation instrumental for Noni that has definite potential for her antenatal classes.'

'That sounds very productive.' She could read his mind. All while they were naked. Greg did have a stumbling block with her recreational regime. Tough. Perhaps, it was time to confront the naked elephant in the room.

'Naturism is a lifestyle, Greg. I'm embracing nature, the environment, respect for others, healthy eating, non-smoking and drinking, and physical exercise as well as nudity. Only on the weekends. Does that sound terrible?'

'No. Of course not.' He grimaced. 'It sounds very healthful – of which I am an advocate. Of course.'

'Of course you are, Doctor. Do you want to talk about this some more?'

He looked at her and smiled a little sheepishly. 'No.'

'Anytime you do, let me know.' Win resisted the urge to ask him if he wanted to join them for the shock value. 'So, how was your weekend?' she asked, still having trouble suppressing the smile as she thought of Greg joining her weekend naturalist group.

'Quiet, except for one episode where I strong-armed your house guest into helping me with an emergency caesarean. Twins.'

Win's brows rose.

Greg nodded. 'True story. You should have seen the theatre sister's face when Iain had both babies out within ten minutes and the mother sewn up again well under the hour. She didn't quite applaud but she wanted to.'

He poured Win a glass of water and then sat back. 'It's such a shame we can't entice him to come here and practise. It would solve a lot of our problems.'

Win watched Greg's face, wishing she could help him but knowing she was unable to. 'No chance of that, I suppose. Noni would be thrilled, too. She's Bachelor of Midwifery so isn't a registered general nurse. She's worried the labour ward will shut. She'd have to work in Wagga if that happened.'

Greg sadly shook his head. 'I asked. He's a dyed-in-the-wool private hospital practitioner. Great guy in an emergency. Really skilled at caesareans. Though, with the particular private sector he attends, he's used to more caesareans than natural births and most of the vaginal births happen under epidurals. He wouldn't fit in here. The midwives would kill him.' Greg laughed in delight at the thought and Win enjoyed the sound, and sight of his face creased with mirth. He should do it more often.

Win tried for more humour. 'He could change.'

Greg laughed again. 'He's the hot-shot consultant at his Macquarie Street practice. His rooms have a view over the Harbour Bridge. Our boy moves in a different world. A world we can't offer him.'

Win didn't have time for possessions outweighing sense. 'Doesn't mean he's happy there. We have charm as well.' Then she frowned. She'd listened to enough hospital news over the years to know that such multiple-birth emergencies weren't normal. 'How did you end up with twins? Don't you usually refer them on to the bigger hospital?'

'You're right.' His eyes brightened and he leaned forward. He loved to talk about his work and she found it all fascinating as much as she enjoyed his enthusiasm. She wondered what he had in mind when he retired to keep his mind active. She suspected the thought of how he would fill his days had crossed his mind. Wasn't long now. *Travel? Gardening? Naturism?* She smiled wickedly.

Greg sat forward and lowered his voice. 'You know, we normally don't deliver twins here, especially if they're both breech like these little tykes. But mum arrived in established labour and we didn't have the forty minutes up our sleeve for the ambulance to take them to the base hospital.' He shook his head at the situation. 'Poor woman looked terrified and had never made the first antenatal appointment to book in. Lives with her partner up in the hills and they were going to have the baby at home. He got cold feet when she went into labour, thank God. Nearly had a heart attack when I told him there were two babies.'

Win shook her head. They were lucky Greg's skills were so versatile. It was common for country doctors to be able to turn their hands to anything, but times were changing, and when Greg left more skills would be lost. 'I didn't think that sort of thing happened any more. Undiagnosed twins are rare enough, but no antenatal care?' That made two un-looked-after pregnancies in a week with Jacinta, she thought.

'Social services will look into the reasons.' Greg thought for a moment with a worried frown and then he shrugged. 'You can't presume to understand people's choices. Would have been tricky with twins without a second surgeon. Iain walked into theatre, scrubbed like he owned the place, glanced around and wanted to know where the paediatricians were! Not used to having to deal with babies as well as mums.' Greg's eyes twinkled again. 'Precious lot, these consultants. You should have heard him. "Just the two of us?"' Greg grinned at the memory and Win thought he looked ten years younger when he did that. 'I said we were damn lucky he was here or it would be the midwives, the theatre sister and me. Not that we haven't done it before. But he was expecting a force of neonatal staff, I think.' He laughed and Win smiled along with him.

'Welcome to obstetrics in the country,' she said. 'I imagine he found it a bit different. We can just hope he'll fall in love with it. Did he mention the guesthouse?'

'Made me promise not to mention him being there to Noni.' His voice dropped to imitate Iain's precise vowels. 'If Noni Frost finds out I'm an obstetrician, my peace is gone.'

Win chuckled. 'They do seem to strike sparks off each other.'

'Apparently,' Greg dropped his voice again into that remarkably good imitation of Iain's measured tones, 'judging by the classes, she'd stand up for her women and let the doctor know if she doesn't agree with their management.' Greg smiled and said in his normal voice, 'I said I'd not mention it, of course.'

Win thought about that and stroked the thick plat of hair at her neck. 'So, he doesn't want Noni to know he's just what she's looking for?' Win sighed. 'That will cause an explosion when it gets out.'

Greg looked momentarily worried. 'Does that leave you in an awkward position because you're aware and Noni isn't?'

Did it? Win considered it momentarily and decided that none of it was her business. She'd always been careful with any information Greg shared. 'I think it's up to Dr McCloud to proclaim that news and deal with his own fall-out. Noni won't be happy that he kept it to himself.'

'He says he's going straight back to Sydney after Jacinta's baby is born, if not before.'

Win nodded. 'Noni is a stickler for honesty. We all are, but she's obsessive about it. She won't be sorry to see your doctor go, in that case. Which might be a blessing. Especially if he hasn't been truthful about himself.'

Chapter Ten

Noni

The birth brought back so many memories. Noni smiled mistily at two of her previous antenatal students as she stood beside the bed. There were many things she admired in these two young women as they met each new challenge their unplanned pregnancies threw at them.

Kylie rested wearily back on the beanbag and hugged her baby to her breast. Aimee, heavily pregnant, stared with awe at her friend.

Noni suspected that Aimee was uncomfortably aware her own labour was fast approaching. She made a mental note to take Aimee aside and answer any new concerns she might have now that she'd witnessed Kylie's labour. Maybe introduce her to Jacinta if there was time. A week had passed already since the lodgers had arrived and she had the feeling Jacinta could do with a young friend.

The new mother looked up, tired but triumphant. 'Thanks for staying, Noni. I did it. You said I would, but I can't believe it.'

Noni leaned over and brushed the damp tendrils of hair from the girl's forehead. 'You were incredible, Kylie. Congratulations. She's beautiful.'

She drew Aimee closer to the bed and hugged her briefly. 'You must be tired, too, Aimee, you're a great support person. Birth is pretty amazing, isn't it?'

Aimee nodded and ran her finger gently down the baby's foot. 'Look how tiny her toes are.' She brushed a tear away from her cheek. 'I can see it's all worth it, though.'

'Definitely.' Noni smiled and tucked the bunny rug around mother and daughter as they lay skin to skin. She stepped back to check the infant's airway was clear and she was feeding correctly, and saw baby Sarah's little jaw move up and down vigorously as she pushed into her mother's breast.

'I'll drop in over the weekend to see how you're getting on, Kylie, but I have to go now. Cricket practice.' *Oh joy.* 'You and baby have some time to get to know each other. Aimee will call the other midwife when you're ready to shower.'

While she'd been teaching their antenatal classes, Noni had realised that neither young woman had a peer-support person to be with her during labour. It was such a shame Jacinta couldn't have met these two before now. The connection she'd encouraged between Kylie and Aimee had worked beautifully so far. Which was lucky because she really had to go. She closed the door quietly, leaned back against it and rolled her shoulders.

Aunt Win's words to her five years ago at her own son's birth floated into her thoughts. 'When it gets tough, just remember you're designed to do it.' Those words had been recalled to other women many times in the years between.

Then, Noni had been twenty, single and blown away by the whole birth experience, too. It would have been nice to have had a friend like Aimee, someone in the same situation, to make her feel less like a social outcast. Although there had only been the one woman – Penelope – who had really rubbed in Harley's illegitimacy, but Noni wasn't going there.

She pushed herself off the door, smiling. She didn't regret a single moment with Harley.

'Hey, Noni,' Cathy called out to her from the nurses' desk. 'The supervisor wants to know if you're still here.'

Noni moved over to stare into a large box of chocolates an appreciative family had left for the staff. Cathy slapped her fingers as she meticulously divided the treats into bags for the staff. 'Tell her I'm just going and I'm not claiming overtime.' She clasped her hands as if in prayer. 'Please, may I have mine now?'

Cathy grinned from her superior height. 'Poor baby. No lunch again? Have two.' She smiled down at Noni. 'They might make you grow.'

Noni poked and carefully chose two soft-centre chocolates, then grinned up at the taller girl. 'Well, you'd better not have any, then.'

'Touché. You missed the ward meeting.' Cathy handed over a copy of the minutes. 'If we lose our jobs, you might wish you'd claimed overtime.'

The smile slipped from Noni's face. 'We are not shutting Burra's birthing unit. There has to be a locum somewhere. The Riverina is a haven to live in.'

'Obstetricians want cities, not towns, my friend. And their wives want bright lights and private schools for their kids.' Cathy shook her head. 'It's not over yet. Dr Soams said there's a chance of a temporary guy doing emergency calls for the next few weeks, but it didn't sound promising. There's another meeting with the board in a fortnight. Which reminds me, when are you going to let Harley come and have a sleepover? Nathan keeps asking. He'll be fine with us, you know.'

'I know. Soon.' As soon as she could bear to let him. She would. 'Honest.' Noni looked at her watch and grimaced. 'Damn. I've got antenatal classes tonight. Second night so better not be late, and Harley's Kanga cricket training starts in twenty minutes. Kylie will give you a buzz when she's ready for a shower. Catch you later, Cath.'

She grabbed her bag from her locker and took off out the door in a half-run. Harley wouldn't be happy with her if he was late.

Chapter Eleven

Jacinta

'Hello, everyone. Welcome to week two. Tonight, we're going to go through the anatomy and physiology of labour and later the dietician is going to come in and talk to you about any dietary concerns you may have.'

Jacinta eased her aching back and watched Noni move around the room, avoiding the way her father gazed and smiled at her. Jacinta wasn't sure if Noni hated him or found him attractive. Either way, it was weird to be in the middle of whatever strange dance they were doing.

'We'll also watch a YouTube video of a normal labour,' Noni went on, as if a great treat lay on offer and Jacinta stifled another sigh. 'This clip is set in the Netherlands and the woman has chosen to have a home birth with a midwife as her carer. If you decide to birth at home, under your own steam, there isn't the option of medicated pain relief, but water and positioning along with good support carries you through.'

Jacinta shifted in her seat, and when she looked around she decided a few other girls looked as horrified as she felt. She'd seen her mother die in a hospital having a baby. But at least she'd had people trying to save her.

'Home birth is accepted practice overseas. It's gaining momentum in Australia with the new government-funded homebirth initiatives now an option around the larger centres,' Noni carried on. 'Continuity of care with your chosen midwife has robust research for improving outcomes for mothers and babies. Maybe one day we'll have it here in Burra.'

Jacinta thought of the worst night of her life and shuddered as Noni passed the plastic pelvis around the room. Jacinta handed it quickly on, and with a sick fascination watched it make its way back to the front.

Noni showed the little doll. 'See the increased space in the pelvis for the baby to pass through if you stay upright instead of lying back on the bed?'

Jacinta didn't want to think about labour. She didn't actually put her fingers in her ears, but her mind chanted *lah, lah, lah, lah*, as she tried to drown out the words. Noni meticulously described the mechanics of labour, and Jacinta wished she'd missed this night.

'So, my advice is to stay off the bed, ladies.'

Her father's light tone jerked her out of her introspection. 'What's the bed for, then? You'll have people hanging off lightshades if you keep this up.'

Noni's gaze turned to him and her eyes opened wide. Jacinta had to smile at Noni's expression. It reminded her of Harley's face just as he went to hit the ball with his cricket bat. Iain was going to get it. Big time.

'The use of the bed? Why . . . mostly, for putting your suitcase on, of course.'

Iain inclined his head at the circle of laughing faces and Jacinta felt her own lips twitch. *Good answer, Noni.*

Of course Iain wasn't finished. He opened his hands as if saying, *I'm a reasonable man.* 'I can see how squatting could help, but what about the fact that these days, in our society, a large percentage of the population aren't practised in squatting? I'm not sure how long a woman could take that position.'

It was like watching ping-pong. Back and forth, back and forth. They made Jacinta's head swim, but at least they were distracting her from her memories and to her relief, the swirling images began to retreat.

Noni wasn't fazed. She could give as good as she got, and some of the other participants sat forward as they watched the match. 'That's why we have bathrooms. A toilet offers the perfect position for those of us without the benefit of iron calves to push in labour. Sling a towel across the bowl to allay any fears, mum is supported in a familiar position, and gravity is pointing in the right direction for the descent of the baby. Birthing balls to sit on are great, too.'

Noni shifted to the edge of her seat and mimed concentration in pushing, and Jacinta couldn't help admiring her lack of self-consciousness. No way would she do something like that in front of a room full of people.

But she couldn't help thinking that her father had a point. When do women having babies actually get onto the bed? Iain must have read her mind because he asked, 'Do you have many babies born on the toilet?'

Noni narrowed her eyes, but the silky voice stayed innocent. 'No, but we do have far fewer epidurals, less Syntocinon drips, our caesarean rate is low, and forceps deliveries are very rare.'

She pursed her lips and glanced innocently at the ceiling. 'Nope, and I can't remember the last episiotomy.'

Jacinta looked sideways. Iain's lips were pressed together as if holding back a smile, and Jacinta wondered about the strangeness of being here. They'd only been living at the guesthouse for a week and she felt as if she'd known Noni and Win for years. Which was a heck of a lot longer than she felt she'd known the man beside her doing his best to flirt with the instructor. Was he a player? Funny, she hadn't thought that before, even though she'd seen how women acted around him.

If this were Sydney, she wondered if he'd be pushing hard to score with Noni. But with a divorce and a daughter he hadn't known about, heck, Noni should stay right away from the disaster of her father's love-life. Jacinta hoped she would. She liked Noni too much to see her get hurt or be used by him.

Noni laughed at something he'd said that Jacinta had missed, and glanced at her dad. Now, she was doing it back. *Spare me*, Jacinta thought, and when he turned to her she glared at him and whispered, 'Stop flirting with Noni. You're embarrassing me.' He flinched. *That's right*, Jacinta thought. *You've already failed two women with the worst possible results. Do you need another casualty on your slate?*

During a lull in the classroom noise Noni said, 'Before we go any further, has anyone got any questions they'd like to ask?'

Jacinta surprised herself and put up her hand.

Chapter Twelve

Noni

Noni saw that Jacinta's movement had caught her father's attention and made him refocus on the room. He'd been scowling at the floor before this, and now she knew where his daughter had inherited her ferocious expression. Funny how she could pick when she'd lost his attention, and how she knew when it had returned.

She'd become far too intuitive about Mr Iain McCloud. Jacinta's voice broke into her thoughts and she vowed not to let Iain distract her again. 'Last week, you mentioned the bag of waters and that they sometimes break before you go into labour or during labour.'

Noni nodded.

'What happens if they don't break?' the girl asked cautiously.

Noni smiled. She wanted people to think. To consider what to look for and what could be different in their own labour. 'That's a great question, Jacinta. Sometimes, the bag of waters doesn't break at all. Or, earlier in labour, sometimes the doctor asks if you want him to break your waters to help the labour along.' Noni looked around the room. 'This is another example of informed choice.'

'Spare me.' The words were quietly spoken, but Noni heard them. She blinked and opened her eyes wide, but he appeared fascinated with the ceiling. 'You have a problem, Iain?'

'No.' His answer was short.

Then keep quiet, she ordered silently. Noni proceeded to ignore him.

'A midwifery tutor once told me, "The membranes are baby's best protection before birth." I believe intact membranes can offer fluid-filled protection, with the wedge of membrane against the cervix lessening the sharpness of bony head against the cervix with dilatation. It can also protect the cord from compression. So, think about that choice if someone suggests it would be quicker if your waters were broken. Do you need to be that fraction quicker at the expense of feeling more of baby's head hard against the cervix? Does the baby's cord need to lose its cushion of safety that might just be stopping that cord from being compressed against your pelvic bones? Should that bag be broken before nature decides the time is right?'

She noted Iain's frown, before carrying on. 'Sometimes, but rarely, the baby is born while the amniotic sac stays intact. Keeping in mind that a baby will not open its glottis – that is, breathe in – until the face is exposed to air pressure, then the mother or midwife would break the membrane to allow the baby to start life outside the womb. The clever glottis is why they don't breathe under water in waterbirth. The old wives' tale is that any baby born within the caul will never drown.' She loved this bit. 'The first midwives used to save and dry cauls and sell them to sailors to keep on their person while at sea.'

She was unsurprised when Iain rolled his eyes. 'And they wondered why people burned them as witches.'

The men in the class chuckled.

Noni let them have their laugh, secure in her own beliefs. She smiled at Jacinta. 'Another one of my hobbyhorses, I'm afraid, Jaz. But I'll move on.'

The class went well and Jacinta asked another two perceptive questions about labour.

Noni decided that Iain enjoyed being a pain, but she noted her own satisfaction and a certain excitement in keeping ahead of him. He obviously knew a bit about childbirth, even though, as far as she knew, he'd never been present at a birth. She wondered about that and assumed he'd read a lot or talked about it with friends. Either way, she could handle his basic knowledge.

Noni felt quite positive about the group as she closed the windows at the end.

'We'll wait to see you lock up before we leave.' Iain's voice made her jump and she turned around slowly to face him.

'Thanks, but I'm fine. I do it every week.'

'I'm sure you do. We'll wait nonetheless.' He turned and sauntered out into the foyer.

'Condescending.' She slammed down the next window and flicked the lock across, thinking, *What does he think I am? Some wimp afraid of the dark?*

The logical side of her brain disagreed: *What are you getting so uptight about? You know you hate it when the lights are out and you have to walk across the deserted parking area.*

She turned off the fan and had a last glance around the room.

They were waiting outside for her. 'Thank you.' *That didn't sound gracious*, she chided herself. Jacinta scowled at her and she scowled back.

Iain smiled. 'Well, that was fun. Goodnight.'

'Smart alec,' she muttered.

Then she heard his voice drift back across the parking area. 'I have sonic ears.'

Noni gunned the motor on the bike and decided to go for a ride. Blow away some of the unexpected irritation that had bubbled up at the end before she felt confined to the house for the night. She carried a torch if she needed it, and if she drove down to the river she could at least look at the moon and drink in the serenity.

The bank of the river lay deserted, crickets chirped, and now that she'd arrived, she really didn't want to get off the bike, but the moonlight called her.

Ha. He'd say it was a dumb thing to do, leaving her bike unattended to go down to the river. But she made her way to the water. When she leaned against the tree and looked at the moon she started to think of the snakes and spiders that could be collected in the piles of flotsam left from the last flood. Or in the branches above her head. All of which made the idea not so attractive.

Noni walked back to the bike. Why should it matter if Iain irritated her? She climbed onto her bike and to her horror it started to tip sideways in the uneven soil, beginning an inevitable slide. She strained and held it for a moment but recognised the losing battle. She had to smartly pull her leg out of the way before it was caught underneath. *Hell.*

Noni swore again and reached over to switch off the petrol. She sat down beside her bike on the edge of the grass, well aware from past experience that the bike was too heavy for her to lift once gravity had it.

She reached for her mobile phone. Aunt Win insisted she took it with her. Good old Aunt Win.

'Hi, it's me,' she said when her aunt picked up. 'I'm fine. Is Iain there?' She listened for a moment. 'Oh. Penelope is there? No. It's fine. Don't worry.' She heard the sound of other voices and then Iain came on.

'Where are you?'

She lay back on the grass beside the road with the phone against her ear. 'At the swimming hole down by the creek looking at the moon.' She moved the phone away from her ear as he raised his voice. When he stopped, she put it back to her ear.

'No, I'm alone. If you aren't too busy, could you come and help me lift up my bike?' She moved the phone away from her ear again as the volume increased. Her lips twitched.

'No, I haven't had an accident. I didn't put the stand up properly and it fell over. I'm not strong enough to lift it back up.' Her grin faded and she pulled the phone away from her ear and glared at it.

'Don't call me Superwoman, and don't bother coming. I'll ring someone else.' She jabbed the talk button to cut him off.

It took him four minutes to get there. With Machiavellian nastiness, he'd brought Penelope. Round one to him.

'Oh, dear, Noni,' Penelope said, immaculately groomed as usual, all saccharine and good sense. 'I always thought that bike too dangerous for a woman. You really should get a sensible vehicle.'

Iain said nothing and Noni gritted her teeth. He strode over to the bike and reached down. Both women watched the muscles in his arms hardening as if accustomed to the application of weights. Iain easily stood the bike up. Their eyes clashed.

'Noni's lucky she had you to call, Iain.'

'Mmm.' He looked at Noni and she ignored the amusement there.

She picked up her helmet, nodded, and smiled sweetly at Penelope's sympathy. 'Thank you for lifting my bike, Iain.' She put effort into being very polite. 'I'll see you at home, then.' She pulled on the helmet, switched the petrol back on, and started the bike. Then snarled bad words all the way back in the dark.

The rest of the week continued in the same vein. Petty irritations, a very busy time on the ward, and the uneasiness she seemed to feel whenever Iain McCloud entered her orbit. Noni intensely disliked not feeling her usual calm and competent self.

Avoidance did help and she tried to see as little of the lodgers between shifts as she could. Jacinta became less prickly and the first seeds of trust and friendship between the guests and their hosts began to flourish and spread rapidly. Jacinta was settling in nicely, and Noni was quite happy to proceed at the younger girl's pace.

To Iain, she remained very polite.

On Friday, after handing over to the new shift, Noni overheard Dr Soams speaking to the charge sister.

'I'm tired. We need another qualified obstetrician full time. I can't carry this load much longer. The hospital had better step up their advertisements or they'll have to shut the birthing.'

Noni listened with deepening despair. They had a wonderful unit, caring midwives and a caring doctor, and they provided a marvellous service to the community in the town the women wanted their babies born in. Planning a midwifery-led unit that could run low-risk births without medical support was a great idea, but it took time to set up and then establish. If the birthing stopped they'd be pushing uphill to get it open again. They needed at least a short-term solution, urgently.

Noni imagined all the women having to go away to the local base hospital to have their babies and sighed. It would cause tremendous distress, not to mention the financial hardship on relatives travelling the hundred kilometres each way. There had to be a way to keep Burra open for births.

She roared into the driveway after work and could see Iain out in the yard, bowling a cricket ball to Harley. That was good of him. She craned her neck to see the shot her son played just before she lost sight. She jammed the bike into its slot, glanced grimly at the time, but stopped anyway to lean against the side of the house to observe. She could see Harley's concentration, his little tongue poking out, as he watched the flight of the ball.

Whack! It went sailing over Iain's head and landed in the fishpond.

Harley whooped with pride and Iain went over and clapped him on the back. They had their heads together, and inexplicably Noni felt left out. Again. Maybe it didn't matter how hard she tried. Maybe Harley needed a dad to do boy things with. Secret men's business.

'It hurts when someone lets you down, you know.' Jacinta's voice spoke with a brittle edge behind her and Noni turned slowly around. She suspected the girl would be glowering. Yep.

'Don't trust him,' Jacinta continued. 'My mother trusted him. He let my mother and me down, and he'll let you and Harley

83

down. He wasn't there playing with me when I was five, like Harley.' She looked Noni in the eye. 'We'll be gone soon.'

Noni ached for the woman-child in front of her and ached for herself for what might have been. 'He didn't know you existed. How could he have come if he didn't know?'

'He walked away. Didn't try at all. My mother should have forced him to acknowledge me. Then she died and left me, too.' Jacinta's voice cracked and she moved hurriedly away.

Noni turned to follow her – pregnancy and grief didn't go together well – but just then Harley saw her and called out.

'Did you see that, Mummy? Did you see how far I hit it? Iain – I mean, Mr McCloud – has been showing me how to stand and the way to hold my bat.'

Noni sent one more glance after the distant figure of Jacinta and faced the two males coming towards her. The girl wouldn't thank her if she drew attention to her tears. 'Terrific shot, Harley.'

'Mr McCloud said he'd come and help coach the team if you wanted him to.'

Iain looked sheepish as he made his way towards her. And so he should! She may not have been first choice for coach, but at least she had stepped forward when no one else had. It shouldn't hurt that he thought he'd do a better job.

'That wasn't very diplomatic, Harley.' Iain gave her a searching look.

'What's dip-lo-mat-ic?' The boy looked from one adult to the other.

'What you're not. Now, skip inside while I talk nicely to your mother and tell her she really is a good coach.'

Harley, still confused, did as asked.

Iain tilted his head. 'I'm sorry. I didn't mean to imply you weren't a good coach.'

She sighed, suddenly exhausted. 'Drop it. I'm tired and I've got classes tonight. Tell them at cricket I couldn't make it and you came in my place. Controlling twelve five- and six-year-old boys is much harder than managing one. You'd be doing me a favour.'

It was only half a lie. He'd be a better coach than she was. She left him standing, staring after her, and trailed up the stairs more depressed than she could remember.

'Hello, everybody. Welcome to week three.' Noni looked at the circle of people smiling at her, their faces eager for snippets and suggestions she could add to their toolboxes for labour.

Three weeks into the sessions and the backdrop of light coming in the windows had changed as the days slowly grew shorter. The rapport between the participants had also grown. Noni hoped they'd all stay friends for many years to come. That was the beauty of antenatal classes in the country; the babies would be born and go to the same preschools and schools, the same sporting clubs, and the parents would meet time and again, with a history that came right back to Noni at the front of the class. She loved her job. So much so that it was sad when families moved away. Like Jacinta and Iain – when they left she'd never see them again.

She forced that thought away. 'Is it my imagination or are all the women in this room getting bigger?'

Everybody laughed and the girls patted their stomachs, even Jacinta.

'Tonight, the topic is "Power and Progress in Labour".' Most of the women quieted, but Noni pretended not to notice. She handed out some tip-sheets and then pointed to a poster of stylised female faces taped to the board. 'As you can see, this lady's smiley face is happy because she's started labour. You can tell by the contractions – the small, evenly spaced hills drawn underneath her. She's in early labour. She looks excited and giggly.

'The contractions are probably ten to twenty minutes apart. This is a really good time to stay home and keep busy. Lean on the kitchen sink when you have to.' She put her hands on her hips and rocked from side to side, before continuing. 'And potter around doing small tasks to keep yourself relaxed and mobile. Pop anything last minute into your bag for the hospital. Like the phone charger.' The men smiled.

She pointed to the diagram again. 'Now, this next lady is looking a little less amused and her contraction hills are closer together and a lot steeper – tightening more strongly and coming about three to five minutes apart. If you look at her face, she's really concentrating and her mouth is a straight line. She needs to be in the shower, with her man rubbing her back. Or she could try sitting on an exercise ball, concentrating on a spot on the wall. She doesn't want to talk about the shopping list or when the council rates are due.'

She rolled a big blue ball out from the side of the room, sat on it and began using it to roll gently from side to side as if she had a contraction.

A few of the women giggled. The men smirked. This was why she wore her scrubs and T-shirt to classes. Who knew what position she might end up in. She stood and pushed the ball to Jacinta to try.

Iain's eyebrows crinkled in disbelief. 'It doesn't look safe to me. What if she falls off?'

Noni wondered if he had any ideas for natural pain relief. Most things worried him and she began to suspect that he'd be the harder work in labour than Jacinta.

'She'll be fine, Iain. You can have a go in a minute and you'll see how secure it is.'

Jacinta straddled the ball and it glued itself to the floor as the base of the non-slip ball flattened. She sat, looking a little surprised at how comfortable she felt. Noni helped her to stand again.

Noni answered the unspoken question. 'It's called a birthing ball, so it's slightly sturdier than an exercise ball and you can use it in the shower, too. It's non-slip and encourages terrific positioning of your pelvis. Plus, it gives your legs a rest from standing up.' The ball rolled over to Iain.

He looked at it with distaste. 'No, thank you.'

'Wimp,' Noni said under her breath. He couldn't have heard her. After the ball had gone around the group and everyone else had tried it, she went back to her poster and tapped the board.

'Our third lady is looking decidedly unamused.' The room had stilled, their attention all hers. 'This lady's contractions are close together, very steep and sometimes they even double up. Coming two to three minutes apart. That's from the start of one contraction to the start of the next. She's not getting much rest between them. She's in strong labour and almost ready to snap at her partner if he says or does the wrong thing.'

The men laughed quietly. The women didn't. Noni smiled reassuringly.

'This is all normal. One of the objects of antenatal classes is to learn different techniques to help you stay relaxed and loose, to allow these contractions to do their job as efficiently as possible. To be aware of the changes and help you recognise where you are in your labour.'

She pointed to a poster with women walking, sitting, lying over a beanbag and even squatting.

'A lot of the time, medicated pain relief can actually make your labour slower and still not give you the type of relief you want, so try the alternatives first. Get off that bed and move. Relief will come when you have your baby in your arms and moving will help you find that moment more quickly.'

Chapter Thirteen

Jacinta

Iain stiffened beside her and Jacinta sank lower in her seat. She just knew he was going to say something embarrassing again. Seriously, couldn't he just shut up? She felt like putting her fingers in her ears. She so didn't want to talk about labour.

Iain's mouth opened and she sighed before he'd even started. *Here we go.*

'That's too airy-fairy for me.'

Whose labour is this going to be? Jacinta thought suddenly, and judging by Noni's face she agreed with her.

Iain said, 'If a woman's in pain, and you give her something to help her, isn't something like morphine going to make her more relaxed and speed her labour – not slow her down?'

This must be why he'd told her, 'Don't worry about labour, you won't feel a thing. They can take the pain away.' She'd let him say it because she wasn't talking to him about it. But now, apparently, he'd had enough of this 'natural, medication-free birth' stuff. It wasn't the pain she worried about, half the women you passed on the street had done it so she knew she could in theory, it was the thought of dying that terrified her.

The night she would never forget but tried constantly to wipe from her mind flashed in frames, and she heard the sounds in sequences as her mother's life had trickled away while they'd waited for the ambulance.

Iain went on like water torture. 'Spinal anaesthesia isn't new. I thought lots of women, especially first-time mothers, had epidurals. When everything is numb from the waist down they have no pain, can talk normally, even brush their hair while the labour progresses. I really can't see anything wrong with such a civilised progression.'

Jacinta wondered distantly why Noni didn't answer. Then she saw Noni's face. If Jacinta wasn't so terrified, she'd laugh. As it was, she was having a hard time breathing.

Noni's words washed over her as the images came faster. Her mother's pale face. Her weak voice telling Jacinta not to swear as they waited for the ambulance. The blood!

'Sometimes, an epidural anaesthetic can help, yes,' Noni spoke slowly. 'Sometimes, it's absolutely essential for a woman to have adequate pain relief in that form. But medication for pain relief isn't the only way to manage labour. You forget, women are designed to have babies, were born to do it, and at least eight out of ten women statistically are capable of having an active, normal labour.'

But every now and then one of them dies! Jacinta kept her eyes on her shaking fingers, squeezing them together in her lap until they hurt as she relived that night.

She barely heard Noni say, 'If somebody doesn't force an epidural down our throat or bomb us right out on a narcotic drug. You have to remember that while the option for pain relief is there, so are the risks that are associated with any intervention.'

Noni's voice tethered Jacinta like the string of a kite as the distant wind of the past tried to blow against her. If she kept hearing her she wouldn't be totally lost in the memories.

'You have to be careful that the reason you're having pain relief is because you *need* it, which is the perfect reason to have relief, not just because your partner or doctor would feel more comfortable if you'd stop groaning. That's why immersing in the bath during active labour helps so much. You're in your own space and nobody can get to you.'

From a long way away Jacinta heard Noni say, 'Gee, can you tell this is a favourite lecture of mine?'

A few people laughed, the sound at odds with the fear and grief and horror of the memories in Jacinta's mind.

'We'll discuss this again, and there's also a night when Dr Soams comes in and explains the pros and cons of medicated pain relief, which I'm sure you'll enjoy, Iain.'

Jacinta felt her father sit back in his chair beside her. It was over. *Thank God.*

She heard Noni say, 'We might just stop here and have the break now.' But the string snapped and it was too late for her. She couldn't escape the pictures in her mind.

In the distance, she could hear her classmates' conversations as they broke out and people shifted chairs and filed out of the room to make a cup of tea. Iain asked her a question, but she couldn't answer him. Couldn't make his words clear in her head. It was too full of the past. She didn't want to speak to him.

Noni approached. Jacinta could smell the lemony scent she always wore. She heard her voice distantly say, 'Can I have a go, please, Iain? Perhaps, you'd leave us for a couple of minutes while I talk to Jacinta?'

Out of the corner of her eye she saw Noni's hand wave him away.

When he'd gone, Noni slid off the seat and crouched down in front of her. 'There's something wrong here, isn't there, Jacinta? Something big you haven't told us.'

Noni waited. Didn't push. Thank God. Jacinta swallowed the tears in her throat. Tried to find the words. After a few more moments, she risked looking up through the blur in her eyes. Then she said it. Said the thing she'd been thinking since she found out she was pregnant. The reason it didn't matter if she lived in a squat or with a millionaire dad on her doorstep: 'I know I'm going to die when I have my baby. I don't want to die. I'm scared.'

Noni's face softened and her eyes made Jacinta's tears well back up in her throat. The last thing she needed was sympathy. Noni should know that.

'Oh, sweetie. You're not going to die. It hurts and labour takes what seems like a long time while you're having a baby. But then you have your beautiful little cherub and you know it's all worth it.' She squeezed Jacinta's hand again. 'I can see this is big. I think you should go home with your dad now, and I'll come and see you when I finish here. Okay?'

She wanted Noni to come back with them right this minute to stop Iain asking questions, but she couldn't ask that. 'Will you ride straight home?'

'As long as I don't drop my bike, I will.'

Noni always made her feel better. Jacinta felt her lips twitch. She saw her father hovering at the door. Noni gestured him in. 'I think you should take Jacinta home now, Iain.'

He looked at Noni and then at her and that must have been enough because he offered her his hand. 'Come on, Jaz. Let's go see Win.'

Chapter Fourteen

Win

Win heard Iain's car whoosh into the car park way before she expected them. They were early. She hoped nothing bad had happened.

She took one look at Jacinta's pale face and red eyes and knew something was very wrong.

'Jacinta?' She kept her voice low and gentle, as if talking to a frightened foal. 'Can I get you something?'

The girl looked tragically at Win, shook her head, then turned towards the stairs. Win frowned. Harley was tucked up in bed and maybe Jacinta just needed her bed, too.

'Why don't you have a nice shower, honey, and I'll bring you up a hot chocolate when you come out?'

The girl paused, turned back, and the desolation in her eyes made Win take a step towards her, intending to hug her. Then Iain came in, Jacinta stiffened, and the moment was lost.

Jacinta said, 'Thanks, Win. That would be good,' in a flat little voice that made Win frown, but she was gone before she could frame another question.

She glanced at Iain and he raised his shoulders as if he too were another lost soul. So, something had happened. But nobody was offering explanations.

They both watched Jacinta disappear up the stairs. Win gestured Iain through to the kitchen. 'I'll make the hot chocolate and there's fresh tea on the table for you. You can tell me what happened.'

Iain sighed, the depth of it bottomless, despairing and just a little frustrated. He ran his hands through his hair and, following her through to the kitchen, put his hands on the bench as if he needed to hold on to something. 'There's something she's not telling us. Noni and I were having a slightly heated discussion on natural forms of pain relief versus epidural when labour starts . . .'

Despite her concern about Jacinta, Win smiled. Noni's reaction to an 'epidural in early labour' would have been more than interesting. Those sparks would have been flying again.

'Noni noticed Jacinta had withdrawn,' Iain said. 'As in, wouldn't talk – couldn't talk – so of course she suggested we leave early. Jacinta still hasn't said anything. I brought her back here hoping she'd open up on the drive, but nothing.' He tapped the bench with insistent frustration. 'I wish I knew how to help her, Win.'

Poor man. And a little hopeless, too, Win thought dryly. He'd only just met the girl a few weeks ago. What did he expect? That she'd blurt out all her secrets just because he could claim paternity?

'You're doing fine.' She added milk to the saucepan on the stove to heat, then indicated the pot of tea on the table and began to lay him a cup and saucer. 'Your intentions are good and she'll work it out. I have great faith in that girl.' He didn't look reassured so she added, 'And you have us as backup.'

'Bringing her here might be the only thing I seem to have done right,' he agreed, but looked despondently back through the door towards the empty stairs. 'Nowhere else have I made progress.' He ran his hand through his hair again. 'Thank goodness we didn't stay in the apartment. I know she would have left, probably gone back to the drug dealers.'

He looked shocked he'd said that out loud and Win brushed that aside. 'Noni mentioned that. She told me that Jacinta confessed she hated needles or she might have tried heroin. So be glad she's needle-phobic and has a strong will.'

'She what?' His voice rose a little until he pulled himself back under control. She watched the struggle as he grappled with an even worse scenario. 'Heroin? And Noni didn't tell me?'

She watched his face harden and Win sighed out loud this time. *Seriously. Men.* 'No. She didn't run and tell you because Jacinta asked her not to. So, she told me.' She spoke to him in a similar tone she used for Harley. 'And I'm telling you. That way she hasn't broken her word to Jacinta. I'm surprised you missed the distinction.' Win gave him the look – until finally he nodded.

He held up his hands in surrender. 'I never said I was good at relationships. Never thought I'd have the workings of a female teenage mind on my list of needed skills.' He shrugged with a little despair. 'Obviously. With a failed marriage and divorce behind me, the experience wasn't available to learn from. But I now have an unknown daughter who hates me.' He grimaced.

'You're being dramatic. Jacinta doesn't hate you.' She patted his shoulder then turned back to lift the milk off the stove and pour it into the mug she'd prepared with drinking chocolate. 'You'll learn how to communicate with her.' Win smiled at him. 'At least you understand Harley.'

Iain's expression lightened and he gave Win a mocking bow, as if acknowledging her positive spin. 'That's true. I do have a fair idea how a five-year-old male's mind works and know to keep that demographic busy. If only the rest of the people in my life were as easily understood.'

Chapter Fifteen

Noni

Noni arrived home an hour later and found Iain waiting for her as she came through the door.

'She's asleep,' he said.

She looked at his strained face and felt a little sorry for him, but her focus of worry rested on Jacinta. 'Did Jacinta tell you she's scared of dying in labour?'

He seemed to look through her for a moment, shook his head, and then refocused. 'She said that?'

Noni nodded and saw him wince.

His hand lifted to run through his hair, which looked very much like he'd been doing that all night. 'Every time I think I'm getting to know her I realise how much I still have to find out. I'm running out of time before the baby is born.' He let out an exasperated huff. 'Adele should have told me about Jacinta when she first found out.'

For some reason, that made Noni want to strangle him. She kept her hands by her sides, but they tightened into two little fists. 'Great idea. Blame the poor woman who didn't want to ruin your young life.' Noni felt like stomping her foot. Instead, she said quietly, 'For all you know, she might have been trying to find you for years.'

She reigned in her frustration and fell back on her midwifery training. 'Important fears and significant events in Jacinta's life that we know nothing about are going to make a difference when she goes into labour.'

Iain took a turn around the room. 'So, how am I supposed to know which moments? I'm getting seventeen years of grey hairs in less than a month.'

'And very becoming it is, too.' She tried to lighten the mood because now she did feel sorry for him. Mainly because he genuinely was worried about Jacinta. His dilemmas weren't easy ones. And he was being good with Harley. The boy hung off his every word. At least she could do something about lightening that load. Noni tilted her head. 'Forget the cricket tomorrow. I'll take the kit and umpire.'

His laugh came low and harsh and a little startling. 'No, if you don't mind, I'd like to go. I'll need something to take my mind off all this and the boys are easy. Do you think Harley would mind if you stayed home with Jacinta? Maybe she'll tell you more.'

She closed her eyes for a couple of seconds. *What about if I mind?* But her instincts said it did need to happen. 'I think that's a great idea.' She rubbed her forehead. 'I have to go to bed. It's been a big week at work again. We haven't found a replacement obstetrician yet, and I may still lose my job. Everything seems to be going wrong at the moment.'

He looked at her as if he was going to say something and then changed his mind. Some silly childish part of her hoped he might return the favour and listen to her work problems like she'd listened to his concerns, but she couldn't understand why she'd thought he would. He was just a temporary lodger, after all. A slightly demanding one.

'See you tomorrow,' she said, and turned away, but before she reached the stairs she heard his voice.

'Thank you, Noni. I don't think I could have handled this without you.'

She sighed and whispered, so he wouldn't hear, 'Yes, you would have.'

She trod the stairs and his voice floated up. 'No, I wouldn't, and I've still got sonic ears. By the way, I'm not a wimp.'

Chapter Sixteen

Noni

Of course, Harley's team won for the first time at cricket, and Noni hadn't been there to see it. Harley came through the door as if he'd been fast-bowled towards her.

'You should have been there, Mummy! Iain is the best coach. We won and I hit a four!'

Noni looked at his little face, glowing with excitement – or was that sunburn? 'Did you have your hat on?' She touched the heat on his face.

'Mummy! I said I hit a four.' Her son frowned at her in the beginnings of disappointment.

Here she was, thinking about whether Iain had looked after her son well enough! 'I'm sorry, darling. That's wonderful news.' She plastered a smile on her face like a bandaid. 'I was just feeling sorry for myself because I didn't get to see you hit a four.' She hugged him, but he wriggled away like a fish to hop around the room in his delight.

She smiled indulgently at this tiny child of hers, all brown floppy hair and long-lashed eyes, dancing from foot to foot with unsuppressed exhilaration. 'So? Tell me all about it.'

'Harley!' Iain's voice cut in from the carport. 'Come on, mate. Carry your own gear from the car.'

'Gotta go.'

Noni frowned as he raced out the door to do as Iain bid like an obedient puppy. Selective deafness seemed to be the answer when she'd demanded that same request. There was that pain in her heart again. Was Harley missing out because she chose not to have a man in her life?

'How's Jacinta?' Iain's voice interrupted her pity party.

Noni looked up from the sink and glared at Iain. Took in the calm face, the strong jaw. The ability to umpire and maintain control over twelve five-year-olds when he couldn't possibly have had any experience at the task and still look as if he'd been sitting under a tree reading a paper. 'Your daughter is fine and my son is sunburnt.'

Iain studied her thoughtfully, not saying anything for a moment. Then slowly, his face twitching as if suppressing a smile, he said, 'Is that really the issue or are we working on another level here?'

Noni stared at him. She felt the weight of tension in her shoulders. The ache in her strained neck. How did he know that? *The rat.* She turned her back on him. 'Aunt Win's gone and Jacinta is in the lounge. It's good news the team won.' There was a monotone of misery as she mumbled the words.

He came up behind her and she felt the air vibrate as he closed the distance – though how she knew was another conundrum. He stopped, not quite touching but very near, and the hairs on the back of her arms lifted as her heart rate picked up. She stood straighter.

She didn't give a sign of her awareness of him, but understood on that same level that she should shift or he would close in. Why? Did she want that? Stubbornly, she didn't move. She hadn't known him that long that he could invade her space. So why let him now?

She was too slow and the point became moot. They touched and the fizz of awareness sizzled along her spine. His torso closed right up against her back, warm and solid, and her front jammed against the sink and she knew she should shimmy away, but instead she stayed rigid, her emotions hurting and confused, and dammit, she wanted comfort. Needed it on a subliminal level, despite the fact that it hadn't been there before. Why was it so enticing now?

She leaned the back of her head on his chest and strong arms came around her. It would be nice to have someone to lean on once in a while – as long as she remembered he was just a stranger being kind. Though look what had happened last time she'd accepted comfort from a stranger.

Slowly, he turned her and she buried her nose in his chest as he smoothed the flopping hair from her fringe back from her forehead. The scent of his warm body, the sun, and some woodsy cologne proved a heady mixture, and she closed her eyes to savour it. She breathed in slowly. Then another inhalation. *Mmmmm.*

'You needed a hug, didn't you?' His chest vibrated as he spoke, and strangely, she could feel the stimulation of her senses buzzing, as if she'd plugged herself into an energy source, charging away like her mobile phone in a power surge.

'Yes. I did,' she mumbled into his shirt, appreciating his arms firm around her. A minute ago she could hardly lift her feet and already she felt better. It might even be that her sense of humour could reset to normal. Or almost normal. Her brain whispered irreverently, *This guy knows how to embrace.*

'What are you doing?' Harley's voice intruded and Noni tried to pull away.

Iain held her firmly against him. 'Your mummy needed a hug, just like you need a hug sometimes. We'll have to make sure she gets more.' His chest rumbled under her cheek. 'All right, mate?'

'Oh. Okay.' It must have been an acceptable explanation because it garnered disinterest from Harley. 'Can I play on the PlayStation?'

'Yes,' Noni said against Iain's chest, then jammed her lips together to contain her giggles as she heard Harley's footsteps recede. 'Right, then.' She shifted her cheek. 'How long does this hug therapy last?'

'Bored already, young lady?' He slid his finger under her chin and tipped it up so she would look at him.

Noni frowned. 'Your face seems so far away up there in the air. You're too tall for me.'

He brought his face lower. 'Is this better?' His lips were only a few centimetres from hers.

'What are you doing?' Jacinta's voice interrupted them, and this time it was Iain who tried to pull away. Noni held onto him as hard as she could, and after the first resistance, he stayed where he was.

'Your father needed a hug. Just like you need a hug sometimes. We'll have to make sure he gets more. Okay, Jacinta?'

'Yeah, right. Spare me.' But she didn't say anything else. She wasn't quite as disinterested as Harley, but she left the room.

'Cheeky little thing, aren't you?' Iain pretended to glare at her.

Noni could admit to feeling mighty pleased with herself. She smirked. Which was probably why he retaliated.

His lips came down on hers like a quilt. Soft and light and deliciously warm. Nice. She found herself stretching up on tiptoe to try to get closer to him. His breath mingled with hers – coffee, mint, heat. If they did much more of this she could forget about the room, Harley and Jacinta, how organised and set her life was, Penelope . . . *Distraction. Excellent.* She pulled away. She'd almost forgotten.

'Penelope rang while you were out. She wants you to ring her back.' She watched him open and shut his eyes slowly.

'That good, eh? My technique is definitely slipping.' He glared at her. 'You are not supposed to remember phone messages when I'm kissing you!'

'I nearly forgot about the message.' She grinned up at him. 'I imagine the slight will do you good. You're too sure of yourself, anyway.' She stepped out of his arms, suddenly full of bubbling electric energy, and moved over to the fridge. She could have shifted the furniture in the house around, she felt so energised. 'I think I'll make something super for tea tonight.'

She heard him mutter as he left the room, 'That would be appropriate, for Superwoman.' She had to smile because suddenly, with her borrowed power surge, she had this.

Later that evening, Jacinta and Noni dragged out the old sewing machine. Both sat on the lounge staring at the inside of the machine. They'd planned on hemming some baby-print muslin sheeting they'd bought for bunny rugs, but couldn't get the machine to make the needle go up and down. Neither of them had ever had much to do with sewing machines.

Jacinta threw the instructions onto the carpet. 'Get Iain to have a look at it. Men are supposed to be able to do things like this.'

Noni frowned. Win would never have said that. 'I dislike that mentality. There's no reason why I haven't got as much chance of figuring this out as your father. Unless he's a sewing-machine mechanic, which I very much doubt.' She looked up from peering inside the machine and caught Jacinta's eye. 'What *does* he do?'

Jacinta shrugged, looking not the least bit interested. 'I don't think he does anything.' She shrugged again. 'He definitely hasn't been to work since I've known him. I never asked him.'

Noni's eyebrows drew together again. 'Do you ever ask him anything? Aren't you curious about him?'

Jacinta shook her head and a stubborn look closed her face. Noni tried again.

'Maybe try to look at it from his point of view. Finding you was a huge change in his life. I think he's adjusting pretty well.'

Jacinta scowled. 'You're just saying that because he hugged you. You're on his side. I don't want to make your stupid bunny rugs, anyway.' She climbed slowly to her feet and kicked the book across the carpet, before waddling out of the room.

'Good one, Noni.' She sighed.

'What's a good one?' Iain spoke from the doorway as he watched his daughter pull herself up the stairs. Then he came into the room.

'Nothing, Big Ears. Are you a sewing-machine mechanic?'

He blinked. 'No, but men are supposed to be able to figure these things out.' He glanced at the machine and the twisted instruction booklet on the floor. 'Hand me the book.'

'Great, it's hereditary. Your daughter said that, too.' She kneeled on the floor next to the machine and scooped it up. Then chucked him the book. Hard.

He caught it easily. Noni watched his bent head as he tried to follow the diagrams compared to the real thing. He really did have a very nicely shaped head.

'So, what do you do, Iain?' she asked to distract her eyes.

Iain looked up warily. Why wary? Her mind spun. All sorts of crazy occupations sprang into her thoughts. Something he was ashamed of? Illegal? Was he a hit man? A gigolo? She smiled to herself, but he didn't see it.

He kept his eyes on the book and squatted near the machine. 'What do you mean what do I do?'

'It's a pretty clear question.' *Curiouser and curiouser.* 'Your job, profession.'

'Oh.' His gaze fell on the newspaper on the chair. 'I'm a stock-broker.'

Noni frowned and then slowly nodded. 'Okay. So, you just left work when you found Jacinta and nobody minded?'

He frowned. Glanced at her and then away. 'Plenty of people minded, but it was something I had to do. You probably guessed that money isn't a real problem.' He gazed around the room. 'Actually, I'm enjoying the first holiday, if that's what you can call it, I've had in many years.' Slowly, his face took on a look of disbelief. 'I took two months' leave and I've had three weeks, now. I'll be a grandfather in five weeks if the baby comes on time.' He rubbed his hand over his eyes and looked across at Noni, his face a mixture of trepidation and horror.

Noni's mouth twitched before she began to crack up. To be fair, she did try to stop the noises coming from behind the hand over her mouth.

Iain winced. 'It's not funny. I'm thirty-five years old, and I'll be a grandfather.'

'Would you like me to get you some hot milk?'

Iain glared at her and then huffed in disgust when she fell over on her back with the giggles.

He advanced towards her on all fours and planted his hands on the carpet on either side of her head. 'Stop your unseemly mirth, young lady.'

She looked up and saw the dark-blue ring around his corneas. His eyes really were quite beautiful. Framed in long lashes she wouldn't have minded having for herself.

Noni stared back at him. He was so close she could feel the heat of him. He looked a little like a predatory cat that wanted to eat her, and suddenly, her breath began to come a little faster. Warmth began to pool in her belly and her limbs turned soft and languid.

If she wasn't mistaken it looked a whole lot like he wanted to kiss her. She had to keep it light. Kiss him and roll away. It couldn't possibly feel as good as the kiss in the kitchen, because she'd been sad then and it had been purely medicinal.

'Your grandchild will be gorgeous. And you don't look too bad for your age.' She reached up and put her arms around his neck and pulled his face lower until they almost touched. 'Come down here a bit closer – you're always towering over me,' she said.

He stared into her eyes. 'I think you have the sexiest eyelashes I have ever seen.'

Noni could feel the smile expand in her. 'Idiot. I have short, stumpy eyelashes. Sexy lashes are long and sweeping, like Jessica Rabbit's.' *Like Penelope.*

'No. Seriously.'

'Right. Seriously. Sure, this is serious, just kiss me.' She could feel her newfound bravado draining away like suds down the drain hole. She tried to hold onto it. This was a bad idea anyway and she didn't know why she'd even considered teasing.

'No. This is important. Your eyelashes are like you.'

He really was only playing with her. He probably didn't find her attractive at all. Noni rolled away. 'Great. I'm short and stumpy. Thank you!' She glared at him. 'How to ruin a mood in three easy steps.'

'Ho-ho.' He glared back. 'Who remembered a phone message during our first memorable kiss?'

She tilted her head. 'How is the delectable, long-lashed Penelope?'

'Jealous, are you?' He smirked.

'Drop dead. You . . . stockbroker.' She got to her feet. 'I'm out of here.' She pointed to the machine. 'Fix the sewing machine for your daughter. Men can do that. Remember?'

Chapter Seventeen

Jacinta

Jacinta lay on her bed and stared at the ceiling. Five weeks to go until she stopped feeling like a whale. The whale calf/baby inside her rolled and dug something, obviously not a fin, into her ribcage. She rubbed the spot and shifted a fraction onto her side. The kid hated it when she lay flat on her back. 'Sorry,' she said out loud. She kept forgetting.

But she couldn't forget she'd have to go through labour. Obviously, lots of women laboured and didn't die. She wasn't stupid. The teachers at school had bemoaned the fact that she was too smart. Of course, she'd be pretty unlucky if it killed her.

Tears stung. Her mum had been unlucky. And her dad hadn't been there when he should have been.

She tried to block those memories, but it was as though a door had been opened, one she'd thought safely locked, and the recollection of that horrible day circled like a feathered scavenger and kept coming back to settle with black wings around her. Suffocating her.

She jerked her thoughts away, tried to settle on a distraction, and suddenly she could see the scene in the kitchen. She felt anger push away the ghosts and she latched onto the feeling with grim determination. Noni shouldn't have let him hug her. Now, she'd be let down too.

She couldn't believe her stupid father had managed to cuddle up to Noni. Not that she cared, but surely Noni had better taste. He was just using her, like he'd used her mother, and then he'd go blithely on his way without looking back. And the whole scenario could start again. Another woman missing him while struggling to make ends meet and he lived it up in his fancy apartment.

Why would Noni trust him? He wasn't trustworthy. Maybe she should tell Win.

After lunch on Sunday, Jacinta stood in the kitchen drinking a glass of water at the sink. Noni and Iain and Harley were out in the yard throwing the ball around. A car pulled up and Win climbed out and waved.

Jacinta felt relieved as she watched Win come in through the front door with her little backpack. It was stupid how glad Jacinta felt at seeing the older woman. *Get a grip*. She needed to remember she was nobody to these people.

'Hey, beautiful,' Win said as she put down her bag and opened her arms. Jacinta hesitated and Win just stepped across and closed the gap between them and hugged her, then let her go. The contact warmed her like a dose of sunshine. 'You look better every time I see you. How are you and your baby on this fine day?'

Jacinta could feel her cheeks heat at the compliment. Nobody called her beautiful, but you knew Win wouldn't say it if she didn't mean it. Maybe she did look okay as a whale. To hide her embarrassment, she put her head down and said, 'Bored.'

Win laughed and bustled to put the kettle on.

When she looked up Win winked at her. 'I've read about people being bored.' She shook her head. 'Never managed it myself. On a day like this, a glorious sunny Sunday, my mother sent us out to play in the mornings and told us we had to be back by the time the sun set.'

Good theory, Jacinta thought, *but I wasn't able to leave my mother alone.* She didn't say that. That wouldn't have been fair. Jacinta thought of all the times her mother had been almost too weak to walk and Jacinta stayed home with her. That was when she had downloaded the free books, using the internet at the library, and read them on her ebook reader in the corner of her mother's room. Sometimes out loud, sometimes not. Book after book, all the books her mother remembered from her childhood, and then the classics, and then as she grew older, whatever was on the book charts or recommended somewhere. She read anything and everything free she could get her hands on. But since Iain, she hadn't picked up a single book. Maybe she should.

Win had assembled the makings of tea and a plate of biscuits while Jacinta had been lost in thought.

Jacinta asked, 'What did you do on your Sundays, when you were a kid?'

Win waved her hand. 'We weren't in town. We were ten miles out of town on a sheep station, with no mobile phones or computers. We wandered all over. Never rang a friend to see if they were home, just walked there or rode my pushbike – without a helmet – and knocked on their door.' Her eyes twinkled. 'It didn't matter how far it was to ride, just on the chance they'd be home. I did a lot of stuff that would be thought way too dangerous these days. But never did I say I was bored.'

Despite herself, Jacinta smiled. Win was like a mother polar bear. Slow-moving, big and cuddly. Everybody's dream aunt. But she was old. Probably over fifty. Dangerous to Win was probably walking on the railway track. Jacinta had jumped trains, stolen food, learned things her mother would have hated, just to survive. 'I can't imagine you doing risky things, Win.'

Win smiled and there was a definite glint of mischief in her eyes. 'I did some stuff. If I chose to do something hair-raising it would be my fault if I got hurt. If I did something wrong then I had to pay for it. My mother agreed with people if they wanted to chastise me. It's different nowadays.' She filled the ancient gold-striped teapot with steaming water and settled the matching lid on it. 'Tell me about your weekend.'

'Iain's flirting with Noni and she's not complaining.' The words tumbled out before she could catch them. She sounded like a baby. Her cheeks grew hot, but Win just looked out the window with a smile on her face, before she turned to gaze at Jacinta.

'How does that make you feel?' she asked gently.

'Why should I care?' Except it was awkward, like she felt now. 'It's none of my business.'

Win tilted her head as if thinking. 'He's your father. And I think both of them are trying not to be attracted to each other. We'll just have to sit back and see what happens. They come from two very different worlds.' She shrugged and let it go, and somehow it did make Jacinta less anxious. 'How did Harley go at cricket?'

'They won. I've never seen anyone so excited. Noni didn't get to see the game, because my father asked her to stay home with me.'

Win poured a cup of tea for both of them. 'It's good to have a space without the men. There'll be plenty more cricket games in the future.'

'What did you do?'

'We went kayaking again. And wrote another song. That was good, too.'

It was nice talking to Win. So easy. As if she'd known her forever. Jacinta could feel the tension easing from her shoulders. 'We went to see Aimee and Kylie this morning. They're both seventeen and don't have boyfriends. They did Noni's antenatal class a couple of months ago. Wish they'd been in mine.'

'Noni's spoken of them. I know their mothers. They're nice girls, though both are a little estranged from their families at the moment. It's good for you to talk to someone your age.'

Talk? She couldn't seem to stop talking since Win walked through the door. And it felt good. 'Kylie's baby is a week old. She's gorgeous. And Aimee's due any day now. Kylie's going to be with her when she goes into labour and they said I could go to help with looking after Kylie's baby and be a support person, too.'

Win smiled at her. 'You may have to get up in the middle of the night.'

She shrugged. 'I don't sleep much, anyway.'

Chapter Eighteen

Noni

Aimee went into labour early on Thursday morning. Iain wasn't happy that Jacinta wanted to go, but he'd agreed to take her to the hospital if she was needed during the night.

When Noni entered the birthing suite at seven am, Aimee lay sprawled across a beanbag while Jacinta rolled the wheeled massager rhythmically over her back. The contraction finished and Jacinta reminded her to sigh after the pain.

Noni thoroughly washed her hands. 'You ladies look great. The night sister said you started labour at midnight and came in three hours later, Aimee. You did well to stay at home that long on your own.'

Noni crouched down beside Aimee and rested her hand on the young woman's shoulder. 'How's it going now?'

Aimee sighed heavily. 'I'm okay. I knew you'd be here soon. I rang Kylie and she rang Jacinta. They've just changed places so Kylie can breastfeed.'

Noni glanced at Kylie on the recliner rocker, feeding her baby. A pram stood beside the door. 'Pretty good team happening in here.'

She grabbed a footstool and placed it next to the beanbag, then settled herself onto it. 'Can I listen to your baby, please, Aimee?' she asked, lifting her foetal doppler out of her pocket. She squirted some clear jelly on the end of the plastic bell, and Aimee pulled up her T-shirt and shifted to allow Noni to rest the small, torch-shaped foetal ultrasound against her stomach. The steady *clop, clop, clop* of the baby's heartbeat brought a smile to Aimee's face as it floated into the air. 'Baby's happy. How're you feeling, Aimee?'

'Was excited,' Aimee said breathlessly, then grimaced. A look of resignation appeared on her face as a contraction began to build quickly. 'Gettin' stronger.'

She breathed, Jacinta rubbed and Noni soothed.

At eleven am Dr Soams dropped in before he headed off to Wagga for his monthly meeting. Aimee's labour had progressed as it should. 'I expect you won't wait for me, but if you do, I'll be back around five.

By three o'clock in the afternoon Aimee's contractions, despite being regular and strong, seemed to be taking too long to progress her labour to the next stage. The baby's head wasn't moving down into Aimee's pelvis as Noni would have liked.

'How much longer?' Aimee's voice had that exhausted, agitated tone that said she didn't have much energy left. Noni sponged her face with a cool, damp cloth.

'It's okay, sweetheart. You're doing beautifully. Do you want to go back in the shower?'

'We've tried everywhere, Noni. Nothing seems to be working now. I'm so tired.'

'You're certainly giving everything you've got, Aimee.' Noni frowned and some deep instinct rattled alarm bells of premonition. She reached for the blood-pressure cuff.

'Your blood pressure is climbing a little, too, Aimee.' She packed that away and pulled the foetal doppler from her pocket. They all listened to the baby's heart rate and even Aimee managed a weak grin.

'I'll just dash out to the desk and give Dr Soams a ring to keep him up to date with your progress.'

'I thought I wasn't making any progress.' Aimee's mouth curved in a tired smile.

Noni leaned over and brushed the damp hair back from Aimee's eyes and smiled back. 'Things are always changing. No contraction is wasted.'

As she walked up the corridor Noni couldn't keep the worry from her face. 'Not happy, Noni?' Cathy looked up from the report she'd been writing before going home.

'The head's stopped descending into the pelvis. She's dilated about seven centimetres and I've got goosebumps.'

Cathy straightened in alarm. 'I hate it when you do that.'

Noni grimaced. 'Yeah, so do I. I'll phone Aunt Win to say I don't know when I'll be home. Can you let Dr Soams know?'

'I'll leave a message on his phone. He's still at the base hospital for the meeting,' Cathy said.

Noni considered her options. She didn't like being away from the girls. 'Can you let me know if he gets back to you? I'll go back in.'

As soon as she opened the door she knew something was wrong.

'Noni! My waters broke and what's that?' Aimee's wail coincided with Jacinta's horrified squeak.

A thick purple coil of shiny umbilical cord pulsated between Aimee's legs, and Noni felt her stomach drop. *Cord prolapse!*

'Jacinta, hit the red buzzer on the wall a couple of times, please, and the other midwife will come in.'

She threw a thin pillow onto the bed. 'Kylie, help me get Aimee up on the bed, thanks. Things are going to happen really fast for the next ten minutes so I'll explain as we go along.'

Cathy skidded to a halt as she came in.

'Cord prolapse.' Noni didn't need to elaborate. She nodded at the medication cupboard and Cathy grabbed a vial of the medication to slow the contractions. She drew it up and handed it to Noni. Then she listened to the heart rate and everyone held their breath as the slow beats gradually sped up again and then sagged a little with relief as the regular beats filled the air.

'I'll phone the supervisor and theatres.' Cathy left the room at a brisk pace.

The three left in the room worked together to get Aimee positioned. 'We have to get gravity to keep your baby's head from leaning on the cord so that means on your hands and knees with your bottom in the air, my love. Almost bury your face in the pillow.'

It was easier said than done, but Aimee didn't complain. 'Cord prolapse means that instead of the head coming first, a loop of cord has flopped in front when your waters broke. That's probably why the baby's head wasn't coming down as we wanted, despite your good contractions. In your case, the cord has come right out and every time you have a contraction the cord can be compressed by baby's head coming down and leaning on it.'

Aimee mumbled that she understood. Noni went on. 'So, raising your bottom keeps that pressure off. Babies can have their oxygen reduced by pressure on the cord and need to be born as soon as possible. Unless a baby is ready to be born normally and Mum's already pushing, which you're not, this means a caesarean.'

The three girls gasped.

Noni nodded sympathetically. 'And hopefully, in the next twenty minutes. So, Aimee and I are going to get real close for the next little while as I get her ready for theatre.'

'Will my baby be all right?' Aimee's voice sounded muffled by the pillow and Noni saw Kylie squeeze her shoulder.

'Baby's heart rate is good. We want to keep it that way. The sooner we get you to the operating theatre the better.'

Cathy appeared at the door looking unhappy. 'The other surgeon is in theatre in the middle of a case. He'll be another hour.'

'An hour's no good for us,' Noni said, keeping her tone even. 'Ring the supervisor again and tell her we don't have time to do the hunt. She has to find someone now and we'll prep Aimee for theatre.' She didn't wait to see Cathy's reaction before she got on with what she needed to do.

Three minutes later, she was taping the catheter to Aimee's leg. 'Very tricky, this,' Noni mumbled in apology. 'How're you holding up, sweetheart?' At least she didn't have to manually hold the baby's head off the cord like they used to do. Filling Aimee's bladder with fluid had achieved a cushion to prevent the baby's head entering the pelvis, and the medication they'd given her had stopped the contractions for the moment.

'I'm scared.' Aimee had been shaved, changed, prepped for caesarean section and shifted onto the emergency trolley for transport to theatre – all of which was done upside down with Aimee in the knees-to-chest position. Past the first deep slowing of the baby's heart rate after the initial breaking of the waters, the heart rate had climbed back almost to normal and stayed stable. This was a good sign but could change at any second.

The orderly arrived, and with Noni on the other end of the trolley they whooshed through the corridors until they came to the operating theatre doors.

The theatre sister checked her identification list as quickly as she could safely do. 'Can you tell me your name? Show me your armband. Which operation are you having?'

Aimee mumbled the answers and Noni hurriedly completed the notes as the trolley burst through the second set of doors.

'I'm changing to theatre clothes. I'll be back in a minute, Aimee.' Noni turned and sped into the change room to don her theatre scrubs and mask.

When she made her way to Theatre One, Aimee had been shifted to the table and onto her back to allow the anaesthetist to pre-oxygenate her lungs before the general anaesthetic. So they'd found a surgeon. Positive thinking had won again.

Noni slipped her hand into Aimee's and squeezed. 'I'm right here and will be with you when you wake up.'

'I'm so scared for my baby, Noni.'

'I know, sweetheart. Think lots of strong, positive vibes as you go to sleep and your baby will know.' She watched the girl's eyelids flutter and the cold hand in hers loosened as Aimee fell unconscious.

Chapter Nineteen

Jacinta

Jacinta and Kylie watched Aimee being wheeled away and looked back at each other. Jacinta wasn't the only one totally freaked out by the drama. They both stood and stared at the empty doorway. Jacinta's hand crept down to her stomach and Kylie hugged her baby more firmly against her chest.

'Noni will look after her,' Jacinta said, trying not to let her voice shake.

Kylie nodded. 'I know.' She paused and took a breath. 'But crap. That could've been me.' She squeezed her baby tighter until the baby stirred and she eased the pressure. 'I can't imagine how I'd be if anything happened to Sarah.'

It still could be me, Jacinta thought, but no way was she saying that. *Please don't be me*. 'Do you want to wait here or look for somewhere we can get a drink?' she said instead.

Kylie looked around as if remembering where she stood. 'Let's stay here.' She smiled shyly at Jacinta. 'I'm glad I'm not standing here on my own.'

So was Jacinta. And those few words helped. A connection of a shared experience neither of them quite understood and still promised the possibility of horror. Jacinta tried to smile back.

'Thanks. Me too.' She walked over and picked up her floppy bag, which held her phone and purse. As she straightened, she looked at the disordered room, at the tilted bed with the sheets flung back, and wondered if she should try to tidy it. Getting Aimee to theatre had been a whirlwind of frenetic activity and focused speed. Noni had stayed calm, though.

Jacinta took a steadying breath. Held it. Let that thought settle into her mind. Then she let her breath out. 'Noni will look after her,' she said again, more to herself.

Cathy, the other midwife, popped her head around the doorframe. 'Hello, you two. What a day. You must be shell-shocked.'

'Hi, Cath.' Kylie lifted one hand off her baby and waved. 'Cath was here when I had Sarah,' she said to Jacinta. 'Will Aimee be okay? Will her baby be okay? Will she come back here?'

'They'll do the caesarean as fast as they can and she was over there pretty darn quickly. I have to go over in a minute to get the baby as soon as afternoon staff arrive. So, fingers crossed baby won't even have noticed something was wrong. And yes, she'll come back here, but not until she wakes up. They'll do a general anaesthetic because it's quicker than a spinal for her. Do you guys want to wait or go home and come back?'

Jacinta looked at her watch. 'How long do you think it'll take if we wait?'

'At least three hours.'

'I'll take Sarah home,' Kylie said. 'Do you want a lift, Jacinta?'

Tiredness swamped her. 'Yes, please.' At least she wouldn't

have to phone her father. And Win would be there. 'Will you tell Noni I've gone home, please, Cath.'

'Of course. We'll have you up here next. Now, don't you worry about this happening to you. It's very rare, you know.'

No, she didn't know. That was good to hear. 'Thanks.' She looked around and picked up Kylie's nappy bag and water bottle. Kylie settled Sarah into the pram and the two girls paused to look around the dishevelled room and then they left.

Jacinta felt like a part of a sad procession as they headed for the car park.

Win was there when she walked in the front door of the guest-house. She tilted her head at the expression on Jacinta's face and opened her arms. Jacinta didn't hesitate. She stepped straight into them and Win's arms closed around her.

Chapter Twenty

Noni

In the operating theatre, Noni's head snapped around as the scrub-room door burst open and the unknown surgeon strode, scrubbed, into the room. His gloved hands were clasped in front of him. There was something familiar about the set of the shoulders and the carriage of his head before Noni noticed his eyes.

When she'd said 'get someone', never in a million years would she have imagined that person to be Iain McCloud!

Iain nodded grimly at her. 'Yes, I'm a surgeon. They couldn't find an assistant, so you'd better get scrubbed, Sister. They're calling in another midwife and anaesthetist to resuscitate the baby if needed.'

Then he ignored her as he and the theatre sister began the skin prep and draping procedure.

Noni shook her head once as if to make the reality of Iain being a doctor soak into her numbed mind. It was too hard. So, she pushed that conundrum aside and concentrated on getting to the scrub sink and back as efficiently as she could before donning a sterile gown and gloves. Every second counted for Aimee's baby. Her head shook as she scrubbed her fingers and nails and she couldn't help but mutter as she washed. He'd said he was a stockbroker! Why would he say that if he wasn't? A pathetic little person in her head whispered, *Unless he's both.*

When she stepped up opposite him, Noni could barely keep track of the speed of his dissection through the abdominal layers. Any lingering doubt that Iain was a skilled surgeon left in that instant, banished for good.

She took over holding the retractor and received a grateful glance from the scrub sister, who'd been doing two jobs and only just keeping up. 'You don't need an assistant. You and Sister are almost at the uterus already.'

'Hold the sucker,' Iain muttered. 'I'm ready to pierce the membranes. There's not much movement here from baby but there might be enough.' The second anaesthetist and Cathy arrived at the same time and stood by the resuscitation equipment outside the sterile circle.

At the sudden gush of green-tinged fluid, the raucous sound of the large-wound suction filled the theatre. Noni had expected that the amniotic fluid would show signs of foetal distress and hoped that none of the soiled fluid would cause problems in the baby's lungs.

Noni held her breath for the last few seconds as Iain slipped his hand inside the uterus. He dexterously slid the baby's head out through the narrow opening, unravelled another loop of cord, then quickly drew out the limp, blue body of a baby girl.

Noni slipped the tiny suction tube into the baby's mouth in case she took her first breath with a mouth full of the green fluid. Iain clamped and cut the pale cord, and the limp baby was passed swiftly over to Cathy standing beside the table with a sterile drape over her arms so she didn't unsterilise the surgeon during the handover.

Noni turned to watch Cathy hurry over to the resuscitation trolley with her precious cargo, the extra anaesthetist close behind. There seemed to be minutes of silence, but must have only been seconds, before a weak cry could be heard above the sound of the oxygen.

'Breathe, Noni.' Iain's voice penetrated the slight fogginess of her brain and she sucked in a sudden breath before letting it out.

'Thank you.' She blinked and concentrated on a few slow breaths and loosening her shoulders until the terrible tension began to ease. Her brain cleared and she looked down at the wound Iain had begun to methodically tidy, and saw he'd already removed the placenta.

'How does the baby look?' Iain called across to the anaesthetist.

'Remarkably well and alert. No signs of cerebral irritation. They'll keep an eye on her over in maternity, but I reckon she got off scot-free.'

Noni and Iain looked at each other and both smiled in relief. Then Noni remembered.

'So. You're a surgeon!' Her voice came out carefully expressionless. She glanced at the now lustily crying baby. 'And a highly skilled one, at that.'

He didn't look at her, and appeared to speak to the wound. 'So it seems. Let's finish here first, shall we?'

'By all means, Doctor.' She saw his eyes narrow as she stressed his title. A sudden chill ran down her spine as she realised where they would have been if Iain hadn't been around as a spare surgeon. But that didn't excuse his underhandedness – and his lies. 'I'll admit you did an incredible job to get that baby out so fast.' Her look promised more discussion at a different time.

He shrugged as if to say, *I'll deal with it later.* 'What time did the cord prolapse?'

Noni glanced at the theatre clock. 'Seventeen minutes ago.'

'Your very fast work getting her here will have made all the difference. Well done, yourself.'

The important person who needed to feel the relief was asleep. 'It must have been terrifying for Aimee,' she said, feeling almost weak now that the situation was under control.

It took fifty-five minutes to repair what had taken six minutes to open. But still, the wound was of textbook neatness and the theatre sister caught Noni's eye as she handed her back an instrument.

She whispered, 'He did it in half the time it normally takes. Impressive, eh?'

'I'll say,' Noni hissed back.

'Okay, you two. Stop swelling my head.'

'But he's got really big ears,' Noni spoke in her normal voice and handed him the dressing to lay over the wound. Iain raised his eyebrows and Noni gazed blandly back.

He gently placed the dressing over the wound and pressed the adhesive onto the skin and then stepped back. Noni watched him roll his powerful shoulders as if the great man had found some tension of his own.

'I'll see you at Win's before class, then.'

'Will you do cricket tonight?' Noni stared at him hard. He nodded. 'Thank you. Then I'll stay until Aimee wakes up and sees her baby.'

The theatre sister watched them both with avid interest and Noni tried not to notice.

Chapter Twenty-one

Jacinta

Jacinta was sitting outside on the swing seat when Harley came out to stand beside her. She patted the seat in invitation.

He squeezed his little warm body into the small space next to her and she felt the comfort until he pushed the swing so they were rocking. Typical. He wouldn't be able to stay still. 'Win said your friend got sick and you needed company.'

Jacinta looked at the little boy. He always seemed to make her smile, and even now she felt her tension ease. *Thanks, Win*, she thought gratefully.

'They rang to say her baby is fine, so I'm feeling better,' she told him, a genuine smile on her face. 'My friend will get better, too.'

'My mum's with her.' This he said as if Jacinta should have known her friend would be all right.

Jacinta looked down at the small head. 'Yeah. She's a good midwife.'

'She's the best.' Harley said it as a matter of fact. 'But your dad's better as a cricket coach. I hope he gets home soon. I don't want to be late.'

Half an hour later her father arrived home. Harley was happy, and her dad gave her a wave as he reversed the car back out again.

Win came out to sit with her on the adjacent chair. 'Busy afternoon.'

'Very. I'm guessing Noni is still at work. She stays late a lot, doesn't she? Don't you mind?'

'Why should I mind? I know she does an important job. Harley gets a little cross sometimes, but he understands. She'll stay late for you, too.'

'I was thinking that.' She caught Win's glance and smiled. 'Thanks for being here, Win. And I'm pretty lucky we came to a house with a midwife, too.'

'Funny how things work out,' Win said. 'Like you being there so Kylie wasn't on her own today when things went silly. I believe chance like that is serendipitous. I trust in the future.' She stood up. 'Why don't you come in and help me set the table? Then we might just have a cup of tea while we wait for the cricketers and Noni to come home.'

Chapter Twenty-two

Noni

During the rushed meal before classes, both Iain and Noni avoided the conversation that had to come. Trying to address how confused she felt while rushing between places spelled disaster for Noni. Iain seemed content to let it lie. She wondered about that, too.

No doubt they'd all suffer indigestion with the tension that hung over the table as they finished gobbling before class. Even Win had been quiet. Iain stood to take the plates into the kitchen and motioned for Win to stay seated. It was one of the little things that Noni liked about him. She felt too mentally exhausted to catalogue the things she didn't like.

Jacinta didn't smile as she placed her plate on top of her father's and stood up to go change for the class. She'd been very quiet since she'd found out Iain had withheld his medical training from them all. Even her.

'Just forget I'm a doctor and treat me like a normal antenatal student tonight.' The extent of his explanation didn't begin to address it.

Noni raised her eyebrows. 'Even when you're obviously not normal?'

'Ha-ha.' Iain tilted his head. 'Don't you have to get ready to facilitate?

Noni considered his comment. She'd called herself a facilitator at their first night. Had he remembered?

Noni considered the surgeon status in the big picture. It was a shame he wasn't the desperately needed O&G guy who could save her job. 'So why did you choose surgery?'

'I really don't want to talk about it, okay?' Iain huffed a little and avoided her eyes, then headed off to the kitchen with the plates.

Noni frowned, looked at her aunt and shrugged. 'What's not to talk about? What was wrong with me being interested?' She hoped later she'd be able to talk about some of her work concerns now that she knew he'd understand. But then again, she was probably kidding herself. A sensible shop talk with Iain didn't look promising.

Chapter Twenty-three

Win

Win watched the byplay and marvelled at the unexpected foolishness of the tall man who'd just left the room. She'd seen the tight-jawed disappointment on Noni's face and suppressed her sigh. Boy was he going to be in trouble when he came clean. This had been the perfect opportunity to stop lying.

That was the problem with lies. The exit point needed guts. She hadn't thought Iain lacked intestinal fortitude, but there you go. Or maybe he was just realising what he might lose.

She stood up from the table just as the burnished mahogany grandmother clock in the corner began to chime the sixth hour. The melodious chimes made her pause and listen, and almost instantly her mood lifted.

She saw Noni glance at the golden face of the clock as the lyrical chimes settled over them. Her niece's shoulders drooped as the tension slipped from her and Win suspected she didn't even know why she felt better. Win had always been a strong believer in beautiful sounds lifting a person's frequency and mood. 'You scoot. I'll clear the rest of this.'

Noni lifted her head. 'Yes. I'd better get a move on. Thanks, Aunt Win.' She stood up. 'I'm so lucky to have you.' She hugged Win, who squeezed her for a second. Then Noni walked out of the dining room and Win heard her run up the stairs to her room.

Times were certainly interesting. She loved Noni like a daughter; had savoured the growth of the young pregnant woman into a strong and determined woman with a good heart. And that man, Iain McCloud, had better lift his game or Noni would shoot him down to size.

She wished she could have a good mull over all this with Greg, but he'd only be getting home now from his day of meetings and she wouldn't disturb him.

It was strange how the more time she shared with her old friend the more she wanted to spend. It had been a long time since she'd considered sharing her world as much with a man. She had spent most of her life being one of the group, with male and female friends in numbers, not putting herself out there for disappointment.

Too many years as a spinster. Too many years as the show volunteer who everyone knew. Too many years feeling that she didn't need a man to make her life with, and aware that short-term relationships in a country town didn't work.

Of course she'd had lovers; fun flings in far off places, always away from Burra. She liked things simple; uncomplicated. An affair in town would cause waves in the calm waters she enjoyed. But Greg made her question her rules.

Maybe she'd look foolish. Win wasn't so sure she really wanted to catch and hold her man, anyway.

She thought back to all those years ago when Greg Soams had come to town. Her first sight of him at Sunday tennis; a tanned athletic man in his early thirties, with a delightful sense of humour and a demeanour unlike any doctor she'd ever known. He'd been a breath of fresh air amidst the frisky station boys and pompous medicos, and he and Win had laughed together as they'd teamed up in the mixed doubles competition. Laughed a lot.

He'd been the one approaching her, and too many times he'd made her belly hurt with mirth. Naturally, she'd been halfway to being in lust with him when Margarite Milson had swooped in and whisked him out of reach.

As much as she'd disliked the homilies, the atrocious woman had been right. It hadn't been Win's forte to be proper, like a doctor's wife should, and Win had known that. She'd been more the quirky one, the one who played the guitar and wore long skirts and beads off the courts. The one who had travelled to India to live in an ashram for a few months.

Win had watched Margarite toss her gossamer hair around him, until he'd been trussed tighter than a moth caught in a web. The tragedy being poor Greg had almost suffocated under all that properness. Shame that.

Win had had a fun life and she wasn't finished yet.

The phone rang and she crossed the room to answer. 'Riverina Guesthouse.'

'Ha. Not the person I need to talk to, but just the person I was hoping to.'

Win felt the smile twitch her lips. 'Greg. And I was thinking about you, funnily enough,' she said calmly. 'Do you need to talk to Iain?'

'I do. It seems you've been having excitement there.' His words were filled with warmth. 'And when they all go off to their ante-natal class I wondered if I could drop by and share a pot of tea with you.' His tone held a hint of question. 'At my meeting today I came up with the brilliant idea of us catching up tonight.'

She couldn't keep the smile from her voice. And why should she? 'The meeting was that good?'

His voice teased. 'There was a moment there when I enjoyed it.'

'I'll get Iain for you,' Win said. 'And I'll put the kettle on when they're gone.'

Twenty minutes later Greg's knock sounded, within seconds of the departure of her guests. She suspected he may have been parked around the corner. The idea made her chuckle.

Win put the round tin filled with fresh Anzac biscuits on the table, the same ancient tin her mother and grandmother had used for their biscuits out on the farm all those years ago, and went to the door.

Greg stood there, the streetlight shining on his thinning hair, his smile playful, his lovely brown eyes alight with humour. 'You're a sight for sore eyes.'

'Come in, flatterer, I have the kettle on.'

She stood back, but as he passed he stopped, leaned in, and kissed her lips. His mouth was firm and cool against hers and a little frisson of delight ran through her. Then he pulled back and his eyes danced with mischief and something unexpectedly sexier.

She raised her eyebrows at him. 'What was that for?'

135

'Because I wanted to.' He stared directly into her face, with a slight challenge.

She patted his cheek. 'Live dangerously. That's my motto.' Then she shooed him through into the kitchen, pretending it hadn't affected her at all.

Greg sat at her table, his shoulders relaxed, his hand under his chin, as he watched her with a slight smile on his face.

'Stop watching me.'

'You give me pleasure.'

'What? Making a pot of tea?' She shrugged. 'You always were a cheap shout. Are you sure you don't want something stronger?'

Greg laughed and stretched back in his chair as if he were settling in for the night. 'One-doctor towns don't really allow for us drinking alcohol, but that doesn't stop us from admiring the finer things in life.'

Win put the pot on the table where she'd set two cups in the few seconds she'd had before he knocked. 'Are you calling me one of the finer things in life, Greg Soames? First time that label's been applied.'

'A crying oversight, then. You are my finer thing in life.'

Win raised her brows. 'Have a biscuit,' she said as she lifted the lid and slid it under the tin.

Greg inhaled, and even Win could smell the syrupy scent of the fresh Anzacs rising like mist. 'Don't mind if I do. You always were an amazing cook.'

'Really?' He had compliments aplenty tonight. But then, she was good at anything she enjoyed.

Greg nodded as he took his first bite with a reverence even Win felt impressed with. He pretended to chew thoughtfully and then rolled his eyes. 'Truly the best. Are you still judging for the Show Society?'

She sat down and reached for his cup to pour the tea. 'Thirty years with the cooking section. And still winning with my flower arrangements every year. In between, there's my debauchery. You know that.'

He finished chewing. 'I thought so.' He winked at her. 'Didn't know about the debauchery, though.' He leaned forward with interest and rubbed his hands.

Win calmly poured her own tea, but her mouth twitched.

Greg reached across and touched her wrist. 'I missed your life membership presentation. I read about it in the local paper. I'm sorry. I would have gone to cheer.'

'Noni missed it, too.' She shrugged. Something like that was not important compared to their medical work. 'You both had an emergency caesarean. But Harley came! He applauded enthusiastically.' She smiled fondly at the memory. Harley had nearly clapped his arms off.

He sat back but didn't shift his gaze. 'It's a big deal. I only know of three other people out of the entire town who are life members. That's a lot of volunteer hours you've given.'

Win could feel her cheeks heat. Real compliments were harder to deal with than vague flattery. 'Tell me about your meeting.'

His hand rested back under his chin and he was, well, she'd have to say, admiring her. She wished he'd stop. 'No. It's boring. You tell me how you're going with your lodgers this week. Are they causing you trouble? Has Iain told Noni, yet? Can I help in any way?'

Win looked at him. Apart from Noni, he really was the only one she could talk to. And Greg personified attentive. Sincerely.

He was such a nice man. 'We have had moments of unusual interest. I think Iain and Noni are falling for each other and that worries me for Noni's sake. And Jacinta's unsettled by it, too. And no, she found out he's a surgeon, but the stupid man didn't come clean about his obstetrics. I think he has a death wish.'

Greg laughed. 'You haven't warned him? Or is that because he can look after himself? Would you like me to have a word about his mortality?'

Win thought about that. 'He's a big boy. And it may help Noni to be more philosophical when they go. But thank you for the offer.'

'Something else worrying you?'

She frowned at him. 'What is this? Bolster-poor-Win week?'

Greg didn't bite. Which was kind of him when it hadn't been a friendly thing to say. But he kept hitting the nail on the head, which was most disconcerting. 'I suspect Jacinta has some dark secrets.' She sighed and shrugged a little helplessly – and helpless wasn't usually in her vocabulary.

She leaned forward. 'That girl worries me. And I'd say it's only through her strength of will that she wasn't using drugs, but she's had it pretty rough since her mother died. She reminds me of Noni when she was young – she has her singlemindedness – and if she wants to stay here when her father goes back, I'd have her.'

If she wasn't mistaken Greg looked disturbed by that, but he only said, 'Of course you would. Though, that won't make Iain happy.'

And there was the difference. Iain needed to learn a few lessons from this man.

Greg leaned forward. 'Come to dinner with me next week. Pick a night when you don't have to rush home.'

'Not rush home? Where are you leading with this?' she teased him. 'Good grief. Not a sleepover?'

Greg twinkled at her. 'You are welcome to sleep over at my house any time.'

Win had to smile. 'Penelope would adore that.'

'My daughter has her own life,' Greg said mildly. 'And I have mine.'

Win stifled a smile. 'Why the change? Is Sunday lunch not suiting you?'

'I said I was thinking today.' He stroked her hand and Win felt the gooseflesh rise on her arms. He was deliberately flirting with her. 'I had hoped our lunch dates would continue, but I'd like to up the ante. After all, I'm not getting any younger and if I'm to woo you I need to get a scurry on.'

She studied him, a little shocked he'd put that out there, but chose to smile as if he were teasing. 'To woo sounds a little serious for us. And I'm too old to scurry.'

'You're not too old to kayak and climb mountains so I think you'll be fine,' he quipped.

She guessed he had a point.

Then he said, with his face completely serious, 'I was going to leave this until next week, but I believe you may need time to get used to the idea.' He reached and took her hand. Looked down at it and then lifted her palm to his lips and kissed it before capturing her gaze.

'I want to spend the rest of my life with you, Winsome Frost, and I want to start as soon as possible. So be prepared for a proper proposal.'

Win's breath hitched like crochet hook in her chest. He did *not* just say that. She forced the breath back and sagged in the chair. Didn't he know how unsuitable she was?

Then she straightened. She would just have to remind him how unsuitable she was for him. She sat back with a bright smile on her face. 'Do you fancy Naturism as a lifestyle, Greg? Going to come with me next weekend and embrace nature?'

She expected him to look away but his gaze was wicked and her natural confidence faulted. Could she have got it wrong?

'I said I'm an advocate of a healthy lifestyle. If you'd like me to, of course I'll come. I guess I won't have to pack much. What time?'

Chapter Twenty-four

Noni

Noni stood at the doors of the maternity ward, instead of the ante-natal classroom, because they were doing the labour-ward tour tonight. She watched the first of the cars pull up with the class members. The staff on duty had been discussing the threat of closure.

When the couples had assembled, she took the group through to the ward, trying not to sound depressed when she pointed out the lovely home-like surroundings that soon could be used for storing hospital supplies and old beds. Then they went through to the garden and all sat down outside in the gazebo, where she passed around the birthing room goody bag – a knapsack filled with comfort items for their hospital stay. Everyone had to take a lucky dip and try to explain how the item could be used during labour.

One young father-to-be pulled out a pair of men's swimming briefs and the class roared with laughter. 'I don't know what these are for!'

It was good to laugh for a change. Noni straightened her face and explained, 'Now, Paul, you may have to rub Suzie's back in labour while she's in the shower, and you're going to get wet if you do the job properly.'

'I wouldn't wear these.' He screwed up his face. 'They're budgie smugglers.'

'That's fine,' Noni said kindly. 'The midwives in there with you won't mind if you don't want to wear anything.'

The class roared again. Noni smiled serenely at Iain. 'Your turn.' His hand dipped into the bag and he pulled out a plastic toy camera.

'To take photos of the baby,' he said in his confident tone. He then glanced at Jacinta and added hastily, 'Not during the birth, of course.'

'No chance, buddy.' Jacinta lifted her hand in the shape of a gun she'd use if he tried and the class laughed again.

The circle continued until the bag was empty. Then Noni ushered them into the birthing suite she'd prepared. The lights had been dimmed, the aroma of lavender lingered faintly and rainforest relaxation music played softly in the corner. She'd filled up the bath with warm water and set out the mat and beanbag on the floor.

'All the little extras in here you could bring yourself if you had to.' She pointed to the boomerang pillow and the speaker for the MP3 player. 'A scent you like, music, your own pillow. If you set up your room like this you can help yourself to stay as relaxed as possible while listening to what your body wants you to do. Remember what I've said. The contractions are powerful – the stronger they are, the better they're doing their job. Don't fight with them, that's a waste of energy and will slow you down. Work with them. Call them strong, not painful. Full of power, not fear.'

She looked around at the faces, eager to understand how their bodies worked and what they could do to help it along. Jacinta looked thoughtful and Noni hoped her exposure to the drama of Aimee's birth hadn't undermined her new faith in her body. Iain hadn't been pleased that his daughter had been a part of the crisis, but things happened. That was nature. It was unfortunate but real.

'Stay relaxed so these good contractions can push baby's head against the cervix and help it open. Then sigh afterwards to release any extra tension.' She looked at the nearest male. 'That's your job. Gently touch her shoulder. Make sure she's let go of the last contraction and is resting before the next one.'

Before they finished for the night, Noni took them in to see a birthing unit that had just been cleaned, so none of the bareness or hard edges had been hidden with quilts or dim lighting. 'If you were travelling somewhere and you had to have your baby in another hospital, it might look like this.'

The room lay sterile, with steel furniture exposed, and white sheets and bright lights glaring. There was no music and it smelled like a hospital. 'I want you to envisage turning this room into the room next door.'

Most of the class nodded their heads, seeing her point. Then she saw Jacinta's face. It had that look on it again. Noni could see her starting to shake and she tried to catch Iain's eye, but he was laughing with one of the fathers.

'Well, that's all, folks.' She pointed to the door. 'I'll see you next week back at our usual room.'

She moved swiftly to Jacinta's side and steered her out of the cold room and into the one next door.

'Jacinta! What is it?' She crouched down in front of the girl.

'Are you upset about Aimee?' Noni glanced up as Iain appeared at her shoulder. 'She's upset again.'

'Probably Aimee and the stark reality of being back in that room. Was that really necessary?'

'Fine. Let's pretend the labour wards don't usually look like that in the city,' Noni snapped. She wasn't responsible for Jacinta's state. She ignored him then and concentrated on the young woman. 'What is it, honey?' She rubbed her cold hands.

'Tell him to go away.' The whispered words carried to her father and he stepped back as if he'd been slapped. Noni wished she could have softened the statement, but Iain wasn't her first priority.

'Can you give us a couple of minutes, please, Iain?'

He walked to the door, turned in a circle, opened his mouth, didn't say anything and finally walked away.

Something had jolted Jacinta into this state. 'Tell me the real reason you're like this, Jacinta. I want to help you.'

The young girl looked up at her and Noni caught her breath. What she saw scared her. And Noni didn't scare easily. The blue eyes so like Iain's were filled with such pain she could hardly bear to witness it. Maybe she should call Iain back? But Jacinta started to talk.

'My mum died in a room like this. They cut the baby out right there.' Her voice caught. 'The nurses wouldn't let me in, the room looked like that one – I saw it when they opened the door to come and go, and I could hear them yelling. I couldn't save her.'

'Who was with you there, sweetheart?' Noni lifted the girl's small, cold hand and wrapped her own warm ones around it.

'Her boyfriend.' The tears ran down her cheeks. 'That's why

I moved into the flat with Nick. I couldn't go home and live with her boyfriend after she died. Until Nick threw me out.' She raised tortured eyes to Noni. 'Iain,' she spat the word. 'He's a doctor! A surgeon. If I'd called my father he could have come and maybe he could have helped. He could have saved her.'

Noni sighed with regret for the broken-hearted child in front of her. A child in a woman's body, carrying another child. She could feel the sting of tears at the back of her own eyes and blinked them away. She drew a breath and let it out slowly.

'Sometimes, people die having babies, Jacinta. Sometimes babies die. Sometimes, if a mother can't be resuscitated they may decide to do a caesarean as a last-ditch effort to try to save them both. When the baby is born that way, a surge of blood that was in the uterus can be shifted back into the mother's blood stream like a big transfusion and some mothers have been saved by this procedure. And some babies. But it's last-minute, which means the mother has had no pulse for at least four minutes before they do it. She's technically already dead so it can't make it worse.'

'It was horrible.'

'Absolutely.' Noni hugged her. 'The absolute worst thing anyone could see. Especially her daughter,' Noni whispered into her ear. 'Especially her pregnant daughter,' she said a little dryly and looked at Jacinta with raised brows.

Jacinta straightened and wiped her eyes. Drew a long, ragged breath, and straightened her shoulders as if the telling of it had somehow made it just a little less of a burden. 'You're telling me.'

'It's a tragic part of nature's truth that we as humans don't have a lot of control, not over all things and all circumstances. Even your father can't save everyone.'

'I'd like to say that's BS. But I know that. And I know tragedies happen. Like it almost happened today. But I'll never forget seeing my mum as she died. Never.'

Noni hugged her again. 'Sometimes, something could have been done better and we try very hard to learn from those occasions, but usually it's because of another medical reason as well as pregnancy and it's nobody's fault. Strong, healthy women without medical illnesses don't die without reason. I believe you're a strong, healthy young woman, Jacinta.' Noni met her eyes. 'We'll be there for you every step of the way. You're not going to die having your baby, not under my watch.' *Please, God.*

Jacinta just looked at her.

Noni tried the last thing she could think of. 'Your father will be there and he will make sure everything is right for you. So will I. Come on. Let your dad take you home. He's worried sick about you. And I'll be home soon, too.'

Half an hour later, Noni walked into the library. Iain leaned with both hands on the mantelpiece. He looked up when he heard her and shook his head.

'She told me. This bloody fiasco gets worse and worse.' He pushed himself away from the mantelpiece and walked agitatedly around the room. 'How I wish she'd been able to ring me.'

His eyes were deep pits of despair. Noni felt powerless to ease his distress. She didn't know how to comfort him.

Then he said, 'I can't get over Adele having the key to seventeen years of my daughter's life. Information that could have changed Jacinta's childhood.' His expression was bitter and his voice matched.

All Adele's fault again. Noni sighed. Poor Adele. Adele, who had died as her daughter watched.

Iain returned to the mantelpiece and pushed his hands with force. Despite the fact that it was very sturdy, Noni looked worriedly at it. 'How could a woman not tell a man he had a child?' he asked.

Noni winced. This was definitely not the time to mention that Harley's father didn't know about his son.

'Look, Iain. The circumstances were unique to everyone. For the moment, Jacinta is the concern.' She tried to be the voice of reason because they needed a plan. 'We need to find a way to reassure Jacinta. Dwelling in the past isn't going to help her. She still thinks she's going to die in labour, like her mother did, and that's the worst way to prepare yourself for a birth.'

His head shot up. 'That's it. I'll find out which hospital it was and how Adele died. There had to be an underlying medical problem or someone stuffed up severely.' Suddenly, he was a man with a purpose. 'I'll find out the details and we'll be able to put in safeguards, make her see it's not going to happen to her.'

He paced the room as if he wanted to leave now. 'Damn it. I'll have to wait until Monday to leave. The sort of search I'll need will have to go through a medical-records department.'

Noni had a sinking feeling it wouldn't be easy to gain access to medical records in a strange hospital. Even if you were a surgeon. She didn't like to underestimate him, though. He looked very determined and it was difficult to imagine Iain not getting his way. Her head filled with the image of him gliding into the theatre during Aimee's caesarean and the masterful way he'd saved the baby, and she knew without a doubt that he would get his way. *If he tried hard enough he'd probably get his own way with me, too*, she thought.

She blinked and felt a shiver cross her skin. Why would she think that? Because, she admitted to herself, he'd started to intrude on her thoughts at odd moments. She noticed when he was there and she noticed when he was gone. Unfortunately, she felt more than a little alive when he was there, despite the fact that she wanted to slap him half the time.

Iain looked down at Noni. 'Will you and Win look after Jaz for me while I go back to the city for a few days? I know it's a lot to ask, but I need to find out the truth. Please.'

'Of course.' Her answer was absent, because suddenly, she had to wrestle with her own crisis. She had the horrible feeling that she was dangerously close to falling in love with him. But why? He wasn't that loveable.

She cleared her throat and her voice strengthened. 'You don't have to ask that.' She had to get out of here. 'I'm going up to bed. Try to get some sleep.'

There was no way she would sleep tonight. Noni couldn't believe she'd been so stupid. She'd made sure Harley knew Iain and Jacinta would leave a couple of days after the baby was born so it wasn't a shock for him. She should have reminded herself more often. She'd suspected they would leave a definite gap for all of them. How could she be falling for someone she'd only known such a short while?

She sighed as she climbed the stairs. The last man she'd been involved with had only been passing through, too.

Chapter Twenty-five

Noni

Jacinta remained quiet over the weekend and Noni didn't feel much more talkative. By Sunday afternoon the house lay positively morose, almost as if they all were waiting for Win to come home and make them feel better.

Noni worried about Jacinta and the added burden of the maternity ward's possible reduction of services. It was less than two weeks until Dr Soams's retirement, and if she lost her job there'd be a major lifestyle change for them all.

She'd have to travel to the base hospital and wouldn't get the day shifts through the week she had now. She'd see less of Harley and Aunt Win could lose her time away if Noni had to work weekends. And the money she budgeted to increase her savings would be hit severely with the cost of travel.

Then there was Iain. Okay, she realised she could be falling for the guy, but she'd never been in love before. How did she know if it was the real thing or just the proximity of a particularly attractive set of shoulders tricking her? He'd only been here a month.

All weekend Iain had been obsessed with his quest, phoning people, setting up appointments in the city, and Noni had seemed to become invisible. She'd tried to stay that way, too, wary in case he started on again about Jacinta's mother not informing him of her birth.

The only happy person was Harley. His cricket team had won again. He still practised every day with Iain. But even his wonderful, exciting, man-bubble burst when he found out Iain was going away on Monday. Noni had no idea how he'd missed that piece of information. She'd done nothing but think of it all weekend.

It happened as the sun slanted into the kitchen at lunchtime on Sunday. Noni began to peel potatoes for later that night. Harley sat munching an apple.

She glanced at her son. 'Ian will be away for a week. It's nice that Jacinta is staying with us even though her father will be away.'

His face fell and Noni's hand paused. Hadn't he known?

Then he instantly brightened again. 'Can I go with him, Mummy?'

She blinked. She tried to imagine Iain and Harley in the medical-records department of a large Sydney Hospital together and almost laughed. 'Don't be silly.'

For her impudence she got 'the look'. As if she'd just slithered from under a rock as a two-headed monster. Harley's glare was a bit too reminiscent of Iain for her liking. 'That wasn't very dip-lo-mat-ic, Mummy.'

Noni dropped the peeler and sat back. She played back what she'd said in her mind. *Oops.* 'You're right. I'm sorry, Harley. I'll explain what I meant.' She gave him her full attention. 'No, you can't go with Iain because he's travelling all the way to Sydney.

And we've only known him for a month. You haven't even stayed over at a friend's house. He'll see lots of people in big hospitals. He won't be able to spend time with you and you won't be able to be with him while he talks to people you don't know.' She was proud of the sense of all of those arguments.

Harley's face screwed up as he frowned fiercely. Then understanding slowly seeped into the sinking, sad little shoulders, until he lifted his head in thought – a tiny glimmer of hope still not extinguished. Finally he said, 'Can I ask him, anyway?'

Noni felt her heart squeeze. *Poor little man.* She hoped Iain would be kinder when he said no. And unkindly for Iain, she hoped she'd be there to see Iain's face when he did. Harley's imploring eyes were most impressive. 'If you want to. But he can't say yes. And if he does I'll still say no. But how about we think about you staying at your friends when he's away? Then you won't miss him. Nathan's mummy has asked.'

They were sitting around the table with sandwiches an hour later when it happened.

'Iain?' Harley had his I'm-an-angel look on his face.

Iain looked up from his plate where he'd been glaring into some distant past. Noni saw the moment when his strong jaw relaxed as his thoughts returned to the room. 'Yes, mate?'

'Can I come to Sydney with you, please?' Iain didn't say anything and Harley rushed on, 'I've never been to Sydney. I wouldn't be a nuisance and I know you have to talk to lots of people. I could sit in the car and make sure it didn't get stolen. Mummy said once that lots of cars get stolen in Sydney.'

Iain met Noni's eyes across the table. She looked blandly back. Never for a moment did she think he might say yes.

'If you agree to sit in chairs in buildings, and not mind my car, and it's okay with your mummy, you can come.'

She knew he saw her mouth drop open. It was a wonder the table didn't fall into it. She felt as though her stomach had dropped to land on her feet. She felt sick. *The rat.* Now she'd have to fix this mess with Harley. Her own stupid fault for not forbidding her son to ask. As if she'd let him take her baby away. He'd never spent a night away from her.

Harley whooped most indecorously, Iain continued with his sandwich as if it was no big deal, and Jacinta looked at Noni with her eyebrows raised as an interested bystander. Noni covered her mouth with her hand and looked in horror back at Jacinta.

Not surprisingly, Harley didn't notice his mother's expression. He was smiling too hard and obviously imagining the treat in technicolour detail. As a last-minute thought he said, 'I can go, can't I, Mummy? You said I could ask him.'

Her brain had seized. 'No. I'm sorry, Harley. Not this time.' He looked at her like she'd put a garden stake through Buzz Lightyear until his face crumpled and he jumped up and ran out of the room.

She sighed and caught Iain's eye on her. 'Great work,' she said bitterly. She pushed away her plate and got up. 'I'm going for a walk.' She couldn't stay sitting at this table with everyone looking at her. She had to get away and think about how badly she'd handled this. Maybe she could let Harley go to his friend's. She'd known the parents for years. Gone to school with Cath. But she'd never been without her son. She had only just become used to her baby going to school. Nobody had ever minded Harley except

Aunt Win and her. All this was Iain's fault because he'd said yes. Why couldn't he have said no?

As she stood, dimly she heard the scrape of another chair, and someone else stood up.

'I'll come too.' It was Iain's voice.

'So I'm stuck with the washing up. I thought I was the guest.' Jacinta's complaint followed.

Noni turned her head. 'Leave it. I'll do it when I come back.'

'I would appreciate if you could do it, Jacinta.' Her father's voice cut across, low and expressionless, and his daughter hauled herself out of the chair and started clearing the table.

Noni breathed deeply when she hit the night air on the verandah. She could just smell the tang of the river, which meant the breeze blew their way. She felt Iain come up behind her and take her elbow. She shook off his arm.

He didn't try again.

'I'm heading down towards the river.'

'Fine.' He fell into step with her, but a little too fast, and Noni found herself skipping every second step to keep up.

After a little while, she stopped, and planted her hands on her hips. 'Hey. This is my walk. Slow down or go on your own.'

He looked down at her shorter legs next to his. 'Just a simple "Could you slow down, please, Iain?" would have been sufficient.'

She narrowed her eyes. She was the wronged one here. He'd expected her to let him take her baby to Sydney; had opened up the whole can of worms of her possessiveness with Harley, then dumped the whole permission thing in her lap and now her son hated her. 'In your dreams. Keep your own pace and leave me alone.'

He didn't start again when she did and she went a few paces before she realised he'd fallen behind. She stopped.

His voice followed her. 'Did you want to have a fight, or just bicker a bit for the fun of it?'

'Whatever you want, Doctor.' She stood there belligerently. She felt small, but by God she felt fierce. Her feet were planted firmly on the ground and her fists were clenched.

He came up to her and admired her stance. 'Actually, I didn't mean fisticuffs. I could offer you sympathy.'

Despite herself she wanted that comfort. Wanted to rest her head on his broad chest and sob for the hurt she'd caused Harley. For the pain of the five-year-old boy she'd never had problems with. For the absolute devastation of hurt that Harley could consider leaving her for five days without a pang. It was probably the beginning of the end of peaceful mothering.

'So? Can I hug you?'

She didn't answer but Iain did it anyway. He gently pulled her towards him and into his arms. She stood there rigid, her spine unbending, refusing to soften. She heard his breath whistle as he half laughed, before he bent down to look into her face.

'So. Resistance.' His finger touched the tip of her nose, then he kissed her there. Light as a moth.

Who said anything about kissing? But at the first touch of his mouth on her skin she knew she was lost. Rigid – but lost.

Then he kissed her again, her brow and her cheek and the spot under her lips and the side of her mouth. Light touches, tiny flutters of warm lips and breath against her skin that made her want things she shouldn't want. Wanting him to catch her mouth with his and make the pain go away.

Then he leaned forward and kissed her neck and, finally, as light as a feather again, on her lips. It felt so right, but she couldn't allow herself to respond even though every part of her wanted to. He stepped back.

'Hmm.' He took her hand and pulled her gently along until she fell into step with his slower walk. 'How about I tell you a story?'

She didn't say anything and he took it as encouragement. *A story?* Not what she'd expected. But then he did that a lot.

Iain said musingly, 'Once upon a time, there was a ferocious, white-haired mother ferret.'

'Ferret. Great, I'm a short, stumpy, white-haired ferret.'

He shook his head. 'You're so vain! What makes you think I'm talking about you?'

She reached up and flicked him in the arm.

He went on. 'I think ferrets are cute. Where was I? Oh, yes, a ferocious mother ferret. There was no father ferret and she was very protective of her baby ferret. By the way, she named him after a motorbike.'

Noni saw his teeth flash again and she had to smile. 'Get on with the story.'

'One day one of the handsome senior ferrets, who quite fancied this mother ferret, offered to take the baby ferret for a field trip. The mother ferret said no. She was very frightened in case something happened to her baby while she wasn't there to watch over him.' He looked down at her. 'Are you following this?'

'Don't push your luck!'

He mournfully shook his head. 'But the mother ferret should have known that the handsome senior ferret would have taken care of the baby ferret as if he were his own. In fact, he intended to leave his own baby ferret with her to keep safe while he was away.'

'Is there a moral to this story?'

'How about, "You mind my ferret and I'll mind yours"?'

She laughed, but to her mortification the sound turned into half a sob. 'Your ferret is seventeen. Mine's five.'

Iain stopped and turned her to him. This time she softened as she leaned against him. 'It's okay, sweetheart. I understand he can't come with me. I agree now I've thought about it more, but the boy is getting older. There will come a time when you have to let him go. You've done such a great job as his mum that when you do, he'll be fine.'

'Yes. I know. It'll do him good to get away from his mother when it happens. I might even ask one of the mothers if he can stay with his friend for a night, or a few days if he doesn't miss me.' She glared at him. 'At least while you're away and he's heartbroken.'

He hugged her and kissed the top of her head. 'You are a wonderful, stupendous, fabulous mother, and he's a very lucky little boy.'

She barely heard him. 'How long are you gone for?'

He threw back his head and laughed. He squeezed her once and then let her go. 'Five days. The research into what happened to Adele might take a while. Harley probably won't stay at his friends that long.'

She did feel better. They turned around and started walking home, and, somehow, her hand became caught in his and stayed there. When they arrived outside the gate he stopped and pulled her gently into her arms. 'I'll be back on Friday before you get home from the antenatal class,' he said quietly.

He bent his head and she stretched up as high as she could until their lips met. When she drew away he smacked his lips. 'Mmm. I've never kissed a ferret before.'

She flicked him again and he chased her into the house.

Iain left before Noni went to work the next morning. He'd spoken to Harley and whatever he'd said had stiffened her son's upper lip and caused him to come to his mother and apologise. Then he'd asked to stay at his friend's house for the four nights. Noni silently hoped he'd get homesick before then, and agreed.

Iain gave Noni five hundred dollars for baby shopping with Jacinta if they got the chance. Harley watched without complaining and glanced at his packed bag on the floor beside the door.

For some reason Noni felt like crying as the rear of Iain's car disappeared down the street.

Aunt Win put her arm around her, but Noni knew she too was still in shock that Harley had asked to go on his first sleepover.

Chapter Twenty-six

Win

Win hugged Noni but couldn't help shaking her head. How the heck had that happened? She would have lost that bet if someone had challenged her to put a stake on Noni's permission for Harley to stay overnight anywhere for four nights. Even if she did know the parents.

When she'd left her niece on Saturday everything had seemed fairly normal, except for the fact that they'd found out about Jacinta's mother. Win had been more concerned by Noni's growing attraction to Iain than anything else.

She and Greg had had a hilarious weekend, with Greg's initiation into naturism being surprisingly smooth and lighthearted. That man had many hidden depths and made her wonder if it had been her own prejudices keeping her single. Unfortunately they'd missed their lunch because he'd been called in for a child with croup. And then a man with chest pain had put an end to any chance of a recovery. He'd sounded most frustrated when he'd called it off. Muttering that 'retirement couldn't come quickly enough'.

Win had almost felt relieved because she would have liked to talk with Noni about her relationship with Greg, but her niece had so much on her mind Win couldn't find a good time. She could also see Noni was struggling with her own attraction to a man. The jury was out on Iain's intentions, though Greg seemed to think Iain was an honourable man.

Win sighed. She might just have to miss the next few weekends with her friends until Jacinta had her baby and their lodgers left.

Noni turned away as the car disappeared from view. 'Harley won't miss Iain if he goes to Nathan's,' she said. 'He'll be fine.'

'Yes, he will. And if he gets homesick, we'll just pick him up.' Win put in as much cheeriness as she could. 'This is a big adventure for him.'

Noni's strangled laugh made Win smile. At least she'd had that much response. 'The best thing you can do is have some girl time with Jacinta, and make sure she has everything ready for the baby. We could go on a baby-shower trip into Wagga?'

'Sure,' Noni said. 'Maybe late-night shopping on Thursday night, after I finish work. It'll give us something to look forward to.'

'It won't hurt Harley to miss you. And you won't have a five-year-old demanding your every moment. Why not do some pampering this week? You never have time for that. Take Jacinta and you could both get your hair done late Wednesday, and your toenails late Tuesday. You loved that when you were pregnant, remember?'

Win saw the surprise on Noni's face. The puzzled impression of a bizarre suggestion that wasn't so bizarre. *That's right*, she thought. *Maybe it is a good thing your son is away for a few days.* And she waited for Noni to complete her thought processes.

Noni shook her head as she considered it. 'Is it five years since I walked into the nail bar and had something done?'

Win glanced sideways. 'I believe it is,' she said judiciously. 'And Jacinta lost her mother. She's been living hand to mouth. She might enjoy something new to take her mind off the coming weeks. Go get your hair done together. Have a few days of girlie stuff. I'll treat you. I'm rich.'

Noni laughed and hugged her. 'You are not rich. But you've taught me to save and I can afford a few pamper sessions. I don't do it enough by your standards.' Her mouth tilted into a smile as Win ushered her back inside.

'There's nothing wrong with a standing appointment to have your nails done every fortnight.' Win glanced down. Hers always shone with some new gel design her long-suffering nail artist had to copy from Win's phone. 'I found some lovely Pinterest pins with feathers. You might like that?'

There was absolutely nothing wrong with the little pleasures if you were sensible with other things, Win thought.

Chapter Twenty-seven

Jacinta

'Pedicures with shellac are bad.' Jacinta squinted at her pink exfoliated feet and shiny black toenail polish.

'Bad as in bad, or bad as in good?' Noni said as she climbed awkwardly out of her own pedicure chair and reached for her wallet.

Jacinta knew Noni wasn't sure about copying Jacinta's choice of colour, if black could be called a colour, but as far as she was concerned, both pairs of feet looked perfect.

Jacinta looked at the small woman who had become more of a friend than a landlady or midwife in the last few weeks, but especially in the last three days. She had no idea of street slang, which was a little sad, as if Noni had had to grow old too soon. Still, she was the one Jacinta had just shared her first pedicure with. And seeing as how her new dad was loaded with cash, maybe it wouldn't be her last trip to the beautician's. 'Bad as in good. GOAT. Greatest of all time,' she added to tease. Not that she used that expression herself.

Jacinta kicked the flat black Nike skate shoes – probably the most comfortable flat soles she'd ever worn, even though her dad had bought them – until they were lined up straight, and pushed her feet in without untying the laces. Her toenails would be fine. 'I can't even smudge the paint because it's solid dry already.'

'Aunt Win has new Shellac every two weeks.' Noni smiled, which was good – because when she forgot to, Jacinta could tell she was missing Harley. And worrying about her work. Noni had told her something of her concerns there. Everybody had their worries. And she could see that Noni loved her hospital ward very much, so she hoped it all worked out.

Jacinta wondered if she'd be like that when her baby was born. Stressed if her baby was out of her sight. Worried about her work because she had to support her own child. She couldn't imagine having a baby that was totally her responsibility, but watching Aimee and Kylie had helped the reality of it to seep in. Pretty intense.

As long as her father didn't try to take over.

Noni had been coaching her on that by example. Giving her scripts for keeping control when he tried to muscle in on things that were her decision. She needed to think about making her baby proud of her and teach her – she'd dreamed it was a girl – not to be pushed around by a man.

Jacinta could see the sense of that. Her hand slid down and cupped the taut mound of her stomach. She was running out of room in there. But still, it was hard to imagine her baby in her arms as a real, live mini-person.

They'd been buying baby clothes, she, Win and Noni, and it had been so much fun she'd felt like crying. She couldn't help wishing her mum was here, but somewhere in the back of her analytical mind, the part she didn't let out much, she knew just how lucky she was, considering where she could have been. How lucky her baby was to be safe and surrounded by good people.

'Thanks, Noni.'

Noni waved to the beautician and put her wallet in her shoulder bag, before turning to face her.

'You don't need to thank me.' She wrinkled her nose. 'I took yours from the money your father left.'

'That's not what I mean. Thanks for coming with. Doing all this after work all week when I know you're tired.'

Noni smiled and Jacinta didn't know how she did it, but she managed to make Jacinta feel like the most important person in the world. As if Noni wanted nothing more than to spend two hours after a hard day at work with her getting black polish on her toes.

Noni said, 'It's been good, Jaz. I've enjoyed your company. And it's helped me pass the time while Harley is away. I haven't spoiled myself for a while, so thank you, too – it's way more fun with two.'

Jacinta could believe that. Noni worked harder than anybody she'd ever known. She never stopped. And tomorrow, both Iain and Harley would come home and everything would change again.

But there was hope in that, too. Perhaps her dad would know more about how her mum had died, even though that was something she didn't want to think about. She looked down at her fingernails. She'd wanted electric blue, but Noni had wondered, out loud, if she wanted everyone to look at her baby in the photos or her bright-blue nails? So, she'd gone for clear beds and French tips like Noni. They were bad, too.

Chapter Twenty-eight

Noni

Noni watched Jacinta walk in front of her and noted the way she slid her hand down every few minutes to hold her stomach. Jacinta likely didn't even realise she was doing it. She was probably having some mild Braxton Hicks contractions that were practising for the big event – an event that drew very near.

Noni could breathe a little easier now after the last few days. She'd discovered, in pampering sessions of all places, that the Jacinta she thought she knew wasn't a quarter of the girl who was really there. Jacinta McCloud was no shrinking violet or even a streetwise urchin with a chip on her shoulder. That was all a front.

Jacinta McCloud was an old soul, with enormous strength of will, a razor-sharp intelligence, and a quirky, understated sense of humour, which was lucky because she definitely had a tightening uterus. She'd need all of those skills to smile her way through labour.

Noni just hoped Jacinta's labour held out until her father came home. They'd had a backup plan of Iain leaving Sydney and driving straight home if Jacinta started labour earlier than expected, before he'd returned, but that hadn't been necessary. And the week had flown – except for missing Harley like an amputated limb from her body. She'd found herself wondering what he was doing all the time. He phoned every night to talk to her and seemed to be his usual self. Going to school from Nathan's was an exciting change. She told him she loved him before he went to bed, but she usually said that twenty times a day when he was home. Win said that was why he could leave her. He knew one hundred per cent that his mother loved him no matter what.

At work, babies continued to arrive with unusual regularity so there were no quiet shifts. Even more worryingly, they'd held another crisis meeting at work about Dr Soams's retirement and the Director of Nursing admitted that she held grave hopes for the maternity unit being able to continue as a birthing place. Which possibly meant the end of Noni's job.

Plus, she hadn't seen Iain for four days and Noni missed him more than she liked to admit. There'd been plenty of times she'd wondered what Iain was doing, too.

When Iain rang he only spoke to Jacinta, who answered her father's questions in monosyllables. He'd never asked to speak to Noni. Not once. Just, 'Tell Noni I'll talk to her when I come back.'

She'd started to wonder if it was his way of letting her know that the kisses they'd exchanged were just flirting on his part and she shouldn't place any expectations on them. Each day made her believe that theory more.

Okay. She got it. She wasn't expecting anything to come of it. Really.

*

On Friday, Noni stopped at the post office on her way home, with just half an hour before Harley got off the bus. She had plans for a hug so big it made her hands itch with anticipation, before she had to scoop her prodigal son off to cricket practice. Noni almost collided with Penelope as she rushed out the post-office door.

Penelope's heavily made-up face carried a look of such disdain she appeared in pain. Noni almost felt sorry for her.

'I hear Iain's in Sydney and left his daughter with you,' she said, shaking her head as if she couldn't believe it.

Noni did not have the time to angst over Penelope. Miss P. Funny how Jacinta's name for her made Noni smile inside. 'Yep. Nothing's a secret in this town.'

'Iain told me, of course. I was speaking to him last night. It seems a bit strange to leave his daughter with people he barely knows.' She smiled sourly at Noni. 'But Iain always has been too trusting for his own good.'

Noni smiled back. Sweetly. 'Yes. I heard he'd taken you out a couple of times as well. Such a nice man. See you.'

Noni fumed all the way home. *What a witch!* But it was Iain she was angry with. How dare he talk to that woman and not to her?

She slammed the door behind her as she came into the house and stormed into the library, not sure why she was in there, except it was the place she usually found Iain when he was at home.

Jacinta looked up from the sewing machine her father had repaired. 'Noni? Can I talk to you?'

Her attention was caught by Jacinta's tone, and after only a small, furious struggle, she stuffed her anger back in its place just behind her heart, then pulled a chair over to the little table beside Jacinta. 'Sure. What's up?'

'Iain said you had Harley when you were about my age. Were you scared about the labour?'

Girl-talk time. Perhaps Jacinta had felt more consistent Braxton Hicks contractions today? 'I was twenty when I had Harley. But, yes, I was a little scared. You ask Aunt Win.' She smiled at the memory.

'Where was your mum?'

Noni sighed and pursed her lips as she ordered her thoughts. It was a time she didn't really like to think about. She settled herself comfortably as she considered how to begin.

'Mum was thirty-four when she had me. Ten years older than Win and Win's elder sister. My parents adored each other and I sometimes wondered if I cramped their style a bit when I arrived. They were very romantic. My mother always said to wait until I found someone who made me feel like a queen before I made love.'

She smiled sadly. 'When I turned eighteen and left home, they did too. They sold the house, bought a plush mobile home, and joined a motorbike club for people over fifty. I thought they were mad, but a lot of relatives on my dad's side are pretty different. They were so happy being rebels.'

Jacinta's eyes widened. 'That's very cool.'

Noni had learned to be philosophical. 'Yes. I suppose it was. I lived in uni housing, anyway, while I did my midwifery degree, so it didn't make much difference to me. One day they were at a bike rally, just before I was nineteen, celebrating Woodstock memories, and there was a big pile-up of motorbikes on the expressway. They were both killed.'

Jacinta turned shocked eyes towards her. 'How horrible.'

Noni winced at the memory. 'Yes, it was. I was pretty angry with both of them. I was actually wild with anger.' She swallowed at the thought of telling the next bit. 'So I went out and lost my virginity to a blues singer who was passing through town. He'd found me crying. He was very attractive and really nice, but . . . well, the idiocy of unprotected sex.' She looked at Jacinta. 'It was really for the comfort of someone holding me. I should have come straight home to Win. He told me before we did it that I'd never see him again. In case I wanted to change my mind. I guess I thought I was getting back at my parents, which was pretty dumb. Then I found out I was pregnant. Terrible bad luck, I thought at the time.'

'Did you ever tell him you were pregnant?'

'His band was gone the next day. I never tried to find him. He had a mischievous smile, which is what I remember most. We had nothing in common except that one night, and he was a lot older than I was. I put "Father Unknown" on Harley's birth certificate. That was the only negative thing about having Harley. Apart from that, I wouldn't change a thing.'

'Who looked after you when you got really big, like me now?'

'Aunt Win. Harley was born over the Christmas break for uni, so I kept studying until then, had Harley, and went back through the week to finish when he was six months old.'

'You didn't think of leaving?'

'I did. Until someone told me I'd never make anything of myself, and that kicked me into gear again.'

'What a jerk! Who'd say that to you?' Noni saw the sudden fury in Jacinta's face. She looked ready to jump up and give that person a swift kick. Penelope had always been Noni's nemesis, but she'd told herself the universe worked in mysterious ways.

'Just someone. Anyway, as I said before, I was terrified. I came home to Burra and Win was with me through labour, just like your dad and I will be with you. It's natural to be apprehensive about what you're about to go through, giving birth to a child. Just remember you're designed to do it.'

She drew a deep breath. 'I did an important thing before I had Harley. I went to my parents' graves and forgave them. And I asked them to forgive me for being so angry with them. Then I forgave myself for my mistakes. I finally realised it had been their choice to live their lives as they wanted. Imagine if, because of me, they were old and unhappy because they never realised their dreams. That's worse than dying.'

Jacinta nodded, taking it all in.

There was just the end of the story to tell. 'So, after Harley was born, I became a midwife. I was lucky enough to get graduate mid-wifery year here through Burra maternity. For me, there's no better job than being there and helping a woman realise what she's cap-able of when she has a baby.' She slipped her arm around Jacinta's shoulders and squeezed her gently. 'You'll see when your time comes.'

Jacinta didn't say anything for a few moments. Then she smiled and leaned over and kissed Noni's cheek. 'Thanks for that. I'll tell you a secret I never told anyone: I always wanted to be a doctor, but I never knew why. School was so easy it was boring. Maybe I inherited that from Iain. I'll do it, too. My baby will be secure.' She shrugged. 'I'm gonna go to my room for a while.'

Noni watched her lever herself out of the chair and head for the stairs. She felt drained and rested her head on her arms. She wouldn't change a thing about her life but was still glad she wasn't seventeen again!

Then the school bus tooted. 'Harley's home,' Jacinta called from the stairs, but Noni was already up and halfway to the door.

*

Week five of antenatal classes included the visit from the retiring Dr Soams, and a discussion on intervention in labour. It seemed strange without Iain's presence in her class. Noni couldn't stop thinking about how he would be back late that night, and it didn't help that everyone kept asking where he was.

Dr Soams explained the reasons a doctor would consider it necessary to intervene in the natural process, and while sometimes Noni disagreed on the timing, she held her tongue. She kept a wary eye on Jacinta's face.

It was a fact of life that a woman's labour sometimes didn't have the smooth outcome she hoped for, and that delays and mal-positions of babies could exhaust a mother or a baby. Noni knew that if people understood the reasons for certain outcomes it helped them come to terms with them in the rare cases they happened.

After Dr Soams left, Noni answered any questions and reiter-ated her favourite saying: 'Knowledge is power. So be aware of your choices and what's really necessary. Remember your birth is unique to you, and all you're doing is giving nature the best chance of doing the job on autopilot. But help is there if you need it.'

When the class broke up to go home, Jacinta came up to Noni.

'Why couldn't they save my mother?' she asked sadly.

Noni put her arm around Jacinta and hugged her. 'That's what your father has gone to find out.' Then she smiled.

'He should be home by the time we get there. You can ask him.' She grinned at the young girl beside her. 'I've enjoyed my girly week with you. Now the men are back, our peace will be gone.'

Chapter Twenty-nine

Noni

When Noni drove the ute into the carport at her usual pace she barely missed the Lexus. Both Noni and Jacinta giggled.

'One day you'll smash it,' Jacinta said.

'Only if he parks it in the wrong place. Then it'll be his fault.' They smiled at each other and got out.

'I heard that!' They both jumped and turned to Iain, who was leaning against the carport wall.

'He's got sonic ears, you know.' Noni winked at Jacinta. She looked around but couldn't see her son. 'Where's Harley?'

Iain tucked Jacinta and Noni under an arm each and walked them to the house. For once Jacinta didn't pull away. 'He was waiting in the library for you, but he's fallen asleep. I left him there because I didn't want to disturb his sleep.'

They settled in the library and Noni managed to slide herself under Harley so that he was sprawled in her lap. It felt good to hold him and she kissed his downy face.

She looked up at Iain. He leaned in a relaxed pose against the worn fireplace as if he, too, was glad to be back here. Despite his relaxed pose, she suspected he was nervous about what he had to say. She tried really hard not to be sidetracked into just staring at him.

Her eyes roamed his dark hair, the angled lines of his face, his strong neck and shoulders and across his broad chest. She remembered reading somewhere that a woman unconsciously picks out her mate by the confidence she has that he could protect her future family from predators. She'd certainly feel protected with Iain – though maybe a little too protected. Still, he was good enough to stare at as she sat there with her son cuddled close.

Stop that, she admonished herself. 'Jacinta and I both want to know what happened. Did you find out why they weren't able to save Adele?'

Iain's eyes touched briefly on Noni before they rested on his daughter. Then he moved to sit beside Jacinta on the lounge and turned sideways to face her.

'There wasn't time,' he said. 'Your mother had a heart condition she may not even have known about. She should never have become pregnant again. The strain of the delivery caused her heart to overload and stop. They couldn't start it beating again so they tried the peri-mortem caesarean to see if that would help. I spoke with the doctor who was in charge of her case.' He paused to let that sink in. Jacinta's face looked scarily like Iain's when he wasn't showing emotion.

After a few more seconds when Jacinta didn't say anything, Iain went on. 'I believe they did everything they could to save her. They tried to save the baby before he died too. But it wasn't possible.'

'I had a brother.' Jacinta's voice was flat. 'I never thought about that before.' Her face remained unreadable. Noni wanted to hug her.

Iain lifted his hand and stroked Jacinta's hair, and Noni felt the tears prick the back of her eyes and tried desperately not to let them drip down her face. This was their tragedy and had nothing to do with her. She couldn't be the first to break down.

Iain said quietly, 'I know it was horrific for you to be there, but I truly believe they couldn't have done anything differently. I couldn't have done anything differently if I'd been there, except be there for you. I'm very, very sorry I wasn't there for you, but I will be in the future.'

Jacinta nodded and finally her face crumpled. Iain reached forward and gathered her in his arms and Noni felt herself softening more towards him. *Yes. Hug her. Thank you. Finally. She so needs it.*

After a few minutes, and a mop up of Jacinta's tears, they sat back and Iain looked across at Noni. It had been an emotional time, but she could see he still had his game face on.

'We have an appointment with a cardiac specialist on Monday in Canberra, and Dr Soams will run a few tests in regards to a bleeding disorder they also found with Adele. It hasn't shown up in any of the other tests you've had, so that's unlikely as well,' he told Jacinta. 'Unless something shows up I believe what happened to your mother won't happen to you.'

There was silence in the room as his words died away. Jacinta stared into the empty fireplace and Noni's eyes traced the lines of strain on Iain's face. It hadn't been easy for him, either.

Jacinta slipped out from under father's arm and looked unflinchingly up at him. 'Thank you for finding out. I think I'll go to bed now. Goodnight.' She didn't look at either of them as she left the room and silence settled again.

Finally, Iain said, 'Would you like me to carry Harley up to his room?'

Noni hugged her son and smiled at the little snoring noises he'd started to make. 'Yes, thanks, he's out for the count.'

Iain lifted him and she wriggled the blood back into her legs before standing up. Her baby boy was getting quite heavy. It made her catch her breath to see her son lying in Iain's arms, and she had a brief flash of other times he and Harley had shared.

It was going to be hard on both Harley and her when Iain and Jacinta went back to Sydney. Very, very hard.

Noni had to hurry to beat Iain to her son's room and turn back the sheets. She tucked them around Harley's shoulders when Iain had laid him down. She stood back then straightened his head on the pillow. He grunted and rolled himself into a ball, anyway.

It was so good to have Harley home. She felt as if someone had stitched her limb back on. She reached over to kiss his cheek. 'Love you, baby.'

She heard Iain leave the room and she stayed where she was, brushing the hair from her son's forehead as she thought about the changes in their lives these last few weeks. She also thought about the changes to come.

The arrival of Jacinta's baby.

The sexual tension building between her and Iain.

The prospect of Iain and Jacinta leaving not long after that.

She rubbed her forehead. Iain was starting to occupy a huge part of her daily life, even just in the number of times she thought about him. Little memories of the way he laughed. How she was starting to hoard anecdotes of incidents she knew would amuse him.

The hard part was to try to keep things in perspective. Especially when all she wanted to do was lose herself in his arms.

She'd missed him this week. More than she would have believed possible a couple of weeks ago. But she had to be sure of both their feelings before she did something stupid like say she'd fallen in love. If she could stop herself.

She stood up. 'Sweet dreams, Harley.' She pulled the door half closed behind her so that she would hear him if he called out, and walked slowly back down the stairs to the library.

Iain was reading the newspaper in the chair, but Noni's lips twitched when she noticed it was upside down. It was nice to know she wasn't the only one who didn't know what to do about their mounting attraction.

'So, can stockbrokers read columns upside down?' she teased.

He turned the paper round the right way. 'Ah. That's much better, thanks.' He folded the paper and tucked it into the side of the chair and stood up.

He looked at her like she was the best thing he'd seen all day. Maybe he'd missed her, too. Noni felt her face heat with the intensity of his scrutiny. He shoved his hands into his pockets as if to stop himself reaching out for her as she stood there. Tilting his head, he spoke. 'I'm trying to guess what you're thinking.'

She wished. Most of the time she was an open book. 'What you see is what you get.'

'What you get is pretty special,' he said softly. 'Is there much chance of you coming over here?'

She shook her head and they stood there, staring at each other across the room.

'How about we meet, say, at the table?'

Noni pursed her lips and nodded, and they both moved forward until they were standing together, almost touching. The top of her head rested under his chin and her face was level with his second top button.

His deep voice drifted down to her. 'You know, I've put some thought to this positional problem we have. Would you like to hear it?'

'Uh-huh.' She nodded her head, but she was actually savouring the faint drifts of aftershave that teased her nose. She really wanted to open that button of his shirt and bury her nose in his chest.

'Better yet, I'll show you.' He took her hand and knelt down on the floor, pulling her down on her knees as well. 'I think it could get better,' he said.

Still holding her hand, they lay down on the carpet with elbows resting on the floor and their noses almost touching.

'That's better. Would you like to hear about my trip to Sydney?'

She wanted his arms around her. It was crazy and she felt like she was balancing on the edge of some dangerous cliff.

Noni frowned. 'I'm not really comfortable. Can we go up to my room and lie on my big bed and talk there?'

She watched him blink and try to keep his face expressionless, but she saw the flare of emotion in his eyes. Her own lips twitched.

Iain was on his feet and pulling her up after him before she knew what was happening. 'Hmm, that's a hard one. Okay.'

He dragged her behind him at a very fast walk and Noni started to giggle. They climbed up the stairs to the top, where they slowed to an exaggerated creep past Harley's door and into Noni's room.

Iain stopped inside the door and looked around.

'I really didn't take much notice that first day you had sun-stroke. I've been trying to remember what your room was like. It's like I've walked into an underwater cavern.'

She'd chosen solid colours, different shades of blue and green in the curtains and the bedcover, and all the furniture was painted dark blue.

'I've never seen anything like it,' he said. 'It's very restful.'

'What were you doing, imagining my room?'

He grinned at her. 'Purely from an interest in interior decoration, of course.'

'I thought you were a surgeon. Or was that a stockbroker?'

'Yes, we have to talk about that.'

Noni stared at him. There was more? 'Help me fix these pillows so we can sit up comfortably, then.'

She felt him watching her and thought again about how much she'd missed him. How would she feel if he went back to Sydney in a few weeks and she never saw him again? She sat up with her back against the wall and patted the bed beside her. She tried to keep her voice normal.

'Tell me about your week. I'm dying to know how you found all that information about Adele.'

Iain climbed up next to her and nudged her forward so he could slip his arm behind her shoulders. She snuggled against his chest and looked into his face. 'This is so much more comfortable.'

It wasn't really. It was hard to stay sane. What had possessed her to suggest coming up here? As if she didn't know. Then she remembered that he hadn't even spoken to her on the phone once while he'd been away. She needed to hold that thought.

He looked at her as though he liked what he saw, and then

leaned over to kiss her firmly on the lips before sitting back as if he'd been perfectly circumspect. 'Ready?'

'Before you begin, I have a bone to pick with you.'

He sighed. 'It must be my technique. I kiss you and your mind ricochets off and remembers some trivia.' A long suffering sigh, then, 'What is it?'

Noni had noticed the kiss, but . . . 'You rang that woman and yet you didn't ask to speak to me once while you were gone.' She sat back away from his chest and folded her arms.

She watched him bite his lip to stop smiling. *Smug*. She hated that.

He held up his hands, in an innocent plea. 'I didn't ring to talk to Penelope. I rang to ask her father about Jacinta's antenatal visit. But, yes, I spoke to her and not to you.'

Noni's elbows came up and then down again as she sat with her arms crossed. 'Why not?'

He pretended to frown. 'Do ferrets sulk?'

She sighed heavily. 'Don't start that again!'

Iain laughed out loud then. He pulled her resisting body back onto his chest and kissed the top of her head. 'Because I missed you like crazy and I wanted to talk to you in person, not over a stupid phone. I picked it up plenty of times to do it but I knew it would just make me miss you more. All right?'

He stared into her eyes and eventually, she had to let it lie, because she had the feeling it was the truth. *But really?*

'Okay.' She uncrossed her arms. 'You can start telling me about Sydney now.' She slid off his chest to scoot down a little beside him, then snuggled in as close as she could get. Unconsciously, her hand lifted to play with the button she'd wanted to undo on his shirt.

Noni felt his chest rise as he drew a deep breath and then his hand covered hers.

'If you keep doing that I'm not going to be talking at all. Maybe we should go back to being uncomfortable on the library floor.'

She lifted her hand. 'I'll be good.'

'Why doesn't that make me feel better?' He sighed again just to tease her. 'Fine. I arrived on Monday afternoon and my flat was musty and lonely on my own. Did I tell you it overlooks Luna Park, beside the harbour? Harley would love it.'

She shook her head. 'You haven't told me anything about your life in Sydney.' *Or your work. Or your family, if you have any.* But she thought she'd better save those gripes for later.

She tuned in again and had to concentrate to catch up.

'I connected with some people I know who have access to the particular hospital concerned, and arranged a visit for late that afternoon.'

She was sceptical it had been that easy, but she didn't say any-thing. The heat that was building between them made her fingers itch to roam his skin. On an impulse she reached over and kissed the little triangle of skin below the collar of his shirt.

He turned to face her. 'How about I just kiss that bit of skin on you?'

'I don't think so.' She waved at him. 'On with the story.' But she'd been well and truly derailed and was enjoying the vibration of his voice more than the information he was giving.

He tut-tutted. 'Very unsportsmanlike. Anyway, my housekeeper is a whiz on the internet and she tracked down Adele's old residen-tial address.'

'Hang on. Housekeeper? Should I be jealous?'

Iain rolled his eyes. 'She's a grandmother.'

'So? You'll be a grandfather and you're sexy.'

He wiggled his eyebrows suggestively a few times, then became serious. 'She's thirty years older than me. But thank you, kind lady. Now, let me finish this so we can move onto other things.'

Other things, eh? Noni snuggled back and rested her cheek on his shoulder, dreaming a little about other things, until she remembered she should be listening and all of this was very important to Jacinta.

'I've studied all of the notes and findings for Adele's case. Apparently, she'd had chest pain most of the day so it would have been pretty scary for Jacinta at home with her even before she'd started to have the hemorrhage.'

She squeezed his arm in sympathy.

'On Wednesday, we discovered the name of Adele's boyfriend and traced him to Redfern. He wasn't as bad as I'd worried he'd be. He's still upset over Adele's and the baby's death. And he seemed genuinely relieved I had Jacinta. He'd heard she was pregnant but said she hadn't spoken to him since her mother died. Said she blamed him, but he blamed himself, anyway. I'm pretty sure he didn't know about Adele's medical history or I think he would have taken her to hospital earlier. Hopefully, he can get on with his life now that he knows a bit more.'

She squeezed his arm again. 'You did well tracking everyone down. I also think Jacinta will be more settled now that she knows.'

'I hope so.' This time the toll of remorse showed clearly from his expression. 'I don't think her mother had much of a life – in fact, I think it was borderline poverty for most of Jacinta's childhood. I've got a lot of making up to do.' He seemed to shake himself to get rid of the guilt that plagued him.

'Friday afternoon, I could finally access the coroner's report, then dropped in at work, and began the drive home after lunch.'

He said 'home'. Noni heard it, no mistake. That had to mean something.

He slid his arm out from under her shoulders and clasped his hands behind his neck with an innocent expression on his face. 'So that's my story. What are we going to do now?'

'Why, talk about my week, of course.' She leaned across and kissed him on the lips.

His hands moved from behind his neck faster than she could shift away, and he captured her face and rolled her body onto him in one movement. She was resting on his chest, looking into his face, before she knew it. The muscular hardness of his body was firm under hers and she felt the fever he caused in her bubbling away below the surface. If she didn't move now she was going to spontaneously combust.

He seemed quite happy about it, though. 'Now, that's a comfortable position for us to talk,' he said.

She sat up, placing her legs on either side of his body, and tucked her knees up to sit upright on his chest, looking down. 'Ha! I'm looking down on you for a change.'

'I can cope with this.' He lifted his hips and she rose in the air. 'Ride me, cowgirl.'

Noni blushed. Not just a little, but a consuming, hot-cheeked, cherry-red crimson. She felt his hardness through the clothes they wore and the heat glowed in her belly in response. She needed some space between them. Now.

She fanned her face. 'Ah, I'd better get down from here. I think my horse is smarter than I am.' She slid off his chest and sat, with her feet tucked up under her bottom. Struggled to talk sensibly. 'Maybe we should leave this room. Go somewhere you can hear about my week?'

His expression became ever so slightly remote and she wasn't surprised when he said, 'Love to, but if we're moving, can we get something to eat first?'

He was slipping off his side of the bed as he spoke, and Noni narrowed her eyes as she watched him move towards the door.

She didn't say anything. He'd deliberately cut her off. Why? There had to be a reason because she really didn't believe he was that shallow. She hoped, anyway. But she couldn't help the disappointment that gnawed at her. She jumped off the bed and followed him.

Noni never did get to tell him about her week. By the time she'd made a late supper and Aunt Win had reappeared, after 'giving them time to catch up', it never made its way into the conversation. She wondered if her side of the story ever would.

When she lay in bed that night, she mulled over Iain's active disinterest in her work at the hospital. Did he have a reason or was he just incredibly self-centred? Did she have room in her life for someone who might be fairly demanding and yet give only a small piece of himself back?

Maybe she was better off keeping the status quo. But what would she do about the fact that she was starting to feel only half alive when he wasn't around?

Chapter Thirty

Noni

After an early finish at Saturday cricket, they arrived home in separate cars as Noni had refused Iain's offer of transport. She planned to try to avoid him as she grappled with her confused thoughts and feelings, which had become worse. She really didn't have any prior experience to draw on, and she hated not knowing what she was doing.

The few times that morning Iain had tried to engage her in conversation she'd been very unforthcoming. Now, as she came through the door he held open for her, she pulled her body noticeably out of the way, avoiding any possibility of brushing up against him.

Aunt Win looked at both of them and pulled her cardigan tighter across her shoulders. 'Brr,' she said. 'Chilly in here.'

Iain frowned and disappeared into the hallway.

Win stopped beside Noni and said quietly, 'Do you want me to stay home this weekend, honey?' They were in the kitchen and Win was about to leave. She tilted her head and searched Noni's face.

Noni almost said yes. But she was a big girl. 'No. We'll manage fine. You have your time out. If my work problems don't resolve themselves there might be too few of your weekends to come.'

The older woman hugged her. 'Don't worry, Noni. We'll manage, whatever happens.' She picked up her bag and keys. 'Don't let a man get you down. But don't be stubborn either.' With those cryptic comments she opened the door and sailed out.

'Yeah, right. That makes sense,' Noni grumbled at the closed door.

'What makes sense?' Iain had come back down the stairs as Win shut the door.

'You and your ears are getting right up my nose this weekend. I'll be glad when you're gone.' She knew it was a terrible thing to say – plus, it wasn't true – but she couldn't do anything about it now that it was out. She pushed past him and ran up the stairs to her bedroom.

Noni lay across her bed. This was so unlike her. She hated these see-saw emotions Iain brought out in her. She hated not being in control. For the last five years, with Aunt Win's help, she'd known where she stood and where she was going.

She'd really enjoyed Iain's company for the first few weeks; she'd enjoyed their verbal sparring. But she had to admit she was starting to think serious thoughts about him, like worrying about his relationship with Jacinta and trying to heal the breach between them. She ached for his guilt at not helping Adele and worried about how he was going to cope with Jacinta in labour – and after the baby was born. His voice gave her shivers and she loved the little gestures that amused her, like opening doors for her and wor-rying about her safety. But it had only been five weeks. And he'd been away for one of those, so she was being foolish to fall for a man she really didn't know.

What about the risk she exposed Harley to if Iain moved out of their lives like he was supposed to in a few weeks? Harley had become very attached to Iain. Last week's explosion had shown that. She couldn't believe she hadn't been more careful of that.

But after last night, she'd felt that Iain didn't take her seriously at all. He wasn't interested in her life, apart from what affected him. He never asked about her job, never talked about his. She didn't even know his ex-wife's name or how long they'd been married. She wanted to know about his childhood and his life in Sydney. And she needed him to want to know more about her. Their relationship, if that was what it was, was all on the surface. She knew he found her attractive, but surely there was more to life than sex.

She gave a half-laugh, half-sob. There was no doubt in Noni's mind that with Iain it would be pretty wonderful in the sex department. Just the thought of him had her nerves humming in anticipation. But was that all it would be? Sex?

Then what?

Maybe she should have asked Aunt Win to stay home. She punched the pillow, then got up. She had to go back downstairs and make tea but that would mean facing Iain.

For the moment, she couldn't have one without the other.

'What are you doing?' Noni stopped at the kitchen door, her hands on her hips.

Iain gave a mock bow. 'Making tea so that the mistress of the house will be happy tonight and grant me favours.'

She tilted her head. 'Well, that was honest.' She watched him breathe a sigh of relief and had to smile. She wandered over and leaned against him.

'I'm lost here. I don't know what to do or not do, Iain. Are we moving towards a relationship or just playing games? If it was only me it would be no big deal. But Harley is involved and he's getting very fond of you.' She pretended to frown. 'But he just spent four nights with his friend so you've shifted down a peg. Plus you were hard on him at cricket today. He may hate your guts at the moment.'

Iain wiped his hands on a towel and placed them around her waist. 'Going up.' He lifted her up until she was sitting on the kitchen bench and their eyes were level.

'That is two of the many things that blow me away about you. You're brave and you're honest.' He ran his finger down her cheek and kissed her nose. 'I will endeavour to be as honest. To answer your questions . . .' He ticked them off on his fingers. 'You run your life like your antenatal classes. Up front and with a passion. I'm a more introverted kind of guy. I'm not used to sharing my thoughts and motivations with the outside world, really not used to it, but I'm trying.'

Then he ticked off a second finger. 'One, we haven't got a relationship – yet! But I think we could move that way in the very near future if it's what we both want. Two, we *are* playing games and I thought you were enjoying them. The trouble is, it's becoming harder to keep my fantasies about you under control and we have two young people in this house.'

A third finger went up. 'Three, my poor marital history is the reason I hadn't intended on rushing into a relationship. I don't want to risk destroying anyone else's life. I'm wary of commitment after my last failure as a husband. You deserve better than that.

'Four, Harley does not hate my guts and I realise he shouldn't become too attached to me in case we decide this thing between us isn't going to work out.' He kissed her nose again. 'Any more questions, Miss Please-Spell-It-Out?' His body was hot against her as she perched there, pleasantly trapped.

Noni pursed her lips. 'No. That just about covers it. You can go back to your cooking now.'

'Gee, thanks. What about my favours?'

Her quick response had left the building. Noni brushed down the hairs on her arms, trying to settle the tingling awareness that frolicked on her skin – just from the look in his eyes. She could feel her brain turn to mush as her hormones pinged messages around her body that left her soft with longing, and she moistened her lips with her tongue. Unfortunately, right now, she seemed to have lost control of her vocal cords.

Finally she managed, 'I'll consider the type of reward after we've eaten.' It was lame, but at least she'd said something.

'Can I have a down payment?' He slid his hips in between her legs as they hung over the front of the bench and encouraged her to wrap her lower body around him while his hands smoothed over her buttocks. It felt as if she'd stepped into a hot bath that made her ache with heat. So, this was what she hadn't realised she was missing!

His head dipped lower as he whispered, 'I want to kiss you, Noni.'

She breathed him in and sighed. 'I'm afraid I want to kiss you, too.'

He stared into her eyes. She could see her own reflected back at her. She whispered, 'But if I do, I may not want to stop.'

His lips curved. 'I can live with that,' he said.

When his mouth came down on hers, she slid her arms around his neck and she didn't get a chance to think about anything else. He was there. Strong yet tender. Her own need for him took over as she kissed him back, his breath and hers in an endless, mindless melding of mouths. It felt so right, it was hard to stop.

By the time they broke apart, Noni's breath was coming in quick gasps and she could feel the heat spiralling up her belly from where he pressed against her. Great waves of longing, or need, or just plain old lust assailed her. She'd never lusted after a man before, or really ached to be possessed. She was trying to work out how to get him up to her room when he kissed her again.

She pressed against him, squirming to get closer, and she didn't hear herself moan with the force of her arousal.

Iain did. He softened the kiss and gently pulled away to look at her. He stepped back and brushed her fringe out of her eyes. Her face felt flushed and she knew her breasts were rising and falling with the air she was dragging into her lungs.

'You are the sexiest woman I have ever seen or kissed. And as much as I'd like to take you here on this bench, I really don't think this is the place to go any further.'

Noni blushed. 'Good grief! What happened?' She looked around the room and it was the same kitchen. But she was different. Blown away. Definitely not in control.

He lifted her down and hugged her swiftly. 'It's okay, sweetheart.' He patted her bottom and shooed her towards the door. 'But I'd really appreciate it if you could take that delectable body out of my sight while I try to calm my libido.'

She glanced down at the noticeable bulge in his trousers and blushed again. She didn't say anything, just turned and walked mindlessly out of the door. She bumped straight into Jacinta's shoulder, even though the girl tried to avoid a collision.

Noni blinked. 'I'm sorry. I didn't see you. Are you all right?'

Jacinta's brows drew together and she tilted her head. 'Are *you* all right? You look weird.'

Noni gave a half-hysterical laugh. 'I'm going up to my room.' She wandered off up the stairs and saw Jacinta shaking her head in bewilderment as she passed.

Chapter Thirty-one

Jacinta

Jacinta turned to watch Noni float up the stairs, the tips of her fingers trailing on the rail, and screwed up her nose. What had all that been about? Then her father appeared out of the kitchen, holding a tea towel in front of him. *Der.*

He saw her standing there. 'Hey, Jaz, how are you?'

How did he expect her to be? Twelve hours ago she'd been told her mother had a heart condition she hadn't known about that had killed her in labour, and she was waiting to see if she had the same problem.

'You are not your mother.' He must have read it in her face. *Good guess.* He did that. And while she appreciated the sentiment she didn't believe it. 'I can see you don't believe me.'

She zoned in on his face. He had her attention with his mind reading. *Spooky.* Jacinta looked properly at him. For a second she thought about the first time she'd seen him through the peephole of the door at the Cross. Tall, square-jawed and determined to talk to her. He must have wondered what she'd be like. Especially behind *that* door. She hadn't thought of

Pedro and his pals for a while now. It was funny how life moved on.

'Which is why,' her father had moved on, too, and she needed to skip with her thoughts if she wanted to follow what he was saying, 'we are going to see Dr Soams tomorrow and the specialist in Canberra on Monday.'

She remembered now – she was going to die. That really sucked. 'What if they find something?'

'Then we head back to Sydney and you have your baby there with all the bells and whistles of modern technology. I'm happy to make that decision today if that's what you want.' He looked at her. 'Very happy.'

He didn't look happy. Could it have something to do with Noni? *Sheesh.*

She remembered the place where her mother had died. That had all the bells and whistles, too, and it hadn't helped her. 'I'd rather stay here. Let's wait until we see the specialist,' she told him.

'Fine. But if he finds anything we'll head back to a higher level of care.'

Higher level of care? The technology might be more flash, but she suspected she'd get no higher care than the type Noni would give her during labour. She'd seen big-city hospitals and nurses rushing from patient to patient. She didn't want to do this labour thing without her own midwife or knowing that Win was there in the background to come home to. She didn't know why she mentally clung to Win and Noni like life rafts, but somehow, she did feel 'settled' with them.

Plus, she wouldn't be able to have Kylie and Aimee come and visit, and she was enjoying the social-media contact she now had with them. She wanted to see their babies grow while hers did, too.

If her heart was okay, she wondered if her dad would rent her a room here. She could stay and make her life in this town until she knew what she wanted to do. There was a whole world out there now that food and shelter weren't her number-one priority, and she and her baby were going to do great things. There was even a uni close by.

As long as she didn't have her mother's heart problems.

'If you're not tired, will you come and sit with me in the study, Jaz?' Her father's voice broke into her thoughts again.

She was scatterbrained, that was for sure. So, she followed him because she couldn't think of any reason not to.

He stood back at the entrance to the study and gestured her to precede him through the doorway. He was weird. He did it for Noni, too. And Win. And she'd seen him put a hand on Harley's shoulder to stop him going ahead so that he did the same now.

Old-fashioned stuff people should have been doing for her mother but hadn't. Ever. She flopped down onto the overstuffed chair, feeling her anger at her father return. That was the whole problem. He should have been there for her mother. She crossed her arms over her huge stomach and lifted her chin. 'What?'

He looked steadily at her and didn't comment on her belligerent stance. 'I'd like you to tell me everything you can remember about your mother's illness. When she first became sick. Anything you can remember that can help me identify how old she was when she began to have trouble with her health.'

Mum's health. Jacinta thought about that. She did have good memories of them laughing together. 'Maybe when I was ten?' She remembered coming home from school with an award for maths and her mother had been in her room, lying fully clothed. She could see her as plain as day in her mind.

'After school, she was in bed and her face looked weird. Pale as.' She glanced at him. 'I remember thinking, that's what the saying meant – *white as a sheet*. She said she'd done too much at work and her chest hurt. So she was staying in bed.' She shrugged. 'She never went back to work at the meat works.'

'Meat works?' He said it softly and a muscle jumped at the side of his face.

It hadn't been all bad, Jacinta thought. She sometimes brought home sausages. 'After that she took in sewing. And ironing. She'd stand for an hour at a time and then she'd lie down. I started missing school on the days she couldn't get up at breakfast. When the people came to pick up the ironing I'd say she just stepped out.' Her dad had that look on his face again, so she tried to cheer him up. 'I'm a pretty good ironer so it was all done and they paid us.'

'You would be. Thank you for looking after your mother so well, Jaz. I should have been there.'

'Yes. You should have.' She sighed. 'But maybe we both need to get over that.'

'Hello, everyone. Welcome to week six. Only two more weeks to go until the end of classes.'

Jacinta could feel the flutter of anxiety in her belly, along with the bigger feeling of the baby moving, as she laughed. Too freakin' close and not close enough.

Noni carried on. 'Later tonight we're going to talk about breastfeeding, but first we'll discuss the social differences that affect you when you have a baby. I really love to target this at the people who say their children aren't going to change their lives.' She rubbed her hands together like a short blonde wicked witch, and Jacinta saw her father smile. The besotted smile. *Here we go again.*

Jacinta was thinking about the baby a lot more now since going clothes shopping, when it had morphed into something real. She knew Iain wanted to take her back to Sydney and if she couldn't stay here she'd have to manage on her own while he worked. What she really wanted was to stay here with Win and Noni. Looking after a baby on her own twenty-four seven looked a tad more daunting the more she thought about it.

She didn't think her father had thought much about it either, but maybe she'd missed that. She'd heard him tell Win he savoured these antenatal classes as much for the good he could see they were doing her as for the enjoyment he gained from watching Noni in action. Apparently, Noni was the least boring woman he'd ever known.

'Are you with us, Iain?'

Jacinta realised her dad had zoned out and at least Noni had targeted him, and not her. Yep, Jacinta decided, he really hadn't given much thought to the time after the baby was born. There might be some major lifestyle changes coming up for him as well as herself if she ended up living with him.

Noni said, 'This is the class where I break you up into two groups, men and women, and ask each group to write down all the changes you can think of that might happen after your baby

is born.' She smiled at Jacinta. 'The men especially start to realise how much of a difference one little baby can make. You mums
have a fair idea already.'

Jacinta moved to join the mums and soon everyone settled into
their new group. After half an hour of suggestions the two sheets
were compared in case some of the impending lifestyle changes
were missed.

One of the fathers said, 'Why didn't we think about this
beforehand?'

Everyone laughed.

Jacinta scowled at her father. Seriously, her mum had had to
do this all by herself because Iain had been too selfish to follow
up. The bitterness welled up. 'It doesn't seem fair that some people
don't suffer at all. If you didn't know about your baby it wouldn't
change your life a bit.'

To her surprise, Iain turned in his seat and then he stood up,
glanced at the room and then back at her. 'Jacinta, in front of all
these people, I swear that I would give anything to have known
about your birth and to have been there when you learned to walk
and talk and twist people around your little finger. I feel just as
ripped off as you do, and as for what I would have had to have
given up . . .' He looked around the room at Noni, all the prospective parents and finally at his daughter. 'If I'd had to give up
everything on every list we could make so I could have those years
back – I would!'

Jacinta felt the tears prickle at the back of her eyes and the
silence in the room seemed to last forever, even though it was probably only a few seconds. It was nice of him to say, but she wished
he'd sit down.

The father who'd spoken up before clapped. 'I wouldn't change back to not wanting children, either.' He smiled at his wife, and all the love he had for her was there in his face. 'We can't wait.'

Everyone started to talk at once and Jacinta sagged with relief to have the attention away from them, and she looked at her father as he sat back down. She put her hand on his shoulder. 'Okay.' She couldn't say much more because her throat was shut, but a croaky okay was a start. 'Thank you. But let's not talk about that, any more.'

Iain nodded. For once he didn't say anything.

Noni said, 'Let's go for supper now.'

'This hour we're going to talk about breastfeeding. You've all heard the slogan, "Breast is Best". Just remember it's still a mother's choice.' She looked around at the nodding heads. 'With some support from those closest to you it can be a wonderful experience for mother and baby. Breastfeeding is cheap, designed especially for your baby and is always on tap at the right temperature.'

She held up her doll. 'This isn't the most effective way to learn, but I'll run through a few pointers and hopefully it will cut down on early problems with the first few feeds in hospital.'

Jacinta wasn't going to breastfeed. Why would she flip her boobs out for anyone to see? *Creepy.* But she wondered how Noni was going to handle this. Her father very subtly leaned forward in his chair and she rolled her eyes. Of course he was interested. *Seriously? Get a grip, buddy.*

Noni had asked everyone to bring in a large doll or stuffed animal, to get the feel of holding the baby. Jacinta couldn't see how that was going to help.

'Right, I'd like you all to snuggle up to your baby.' Jacinta sighed and jammed Harley's Buzz Lightyear under her arm. This was ridiculous. There were lots of chuckles and comments about ugly babies.

'Then slide one hand back to support baby's head and the other arm tucks the body in close to you. Your baby should be almost wrapped around you, chest to chest.' Buzz felt hard and unwieldy, but it had been him or the stupid Toy Story Jesse doll.

'Now, slide your hand down until you aren't holding the baby's head, but supporting baby's back, just under the neck. Look at baby's drinking position now.'

Jacinta looked down at the green helmet sitting at her breast and looked up just in time to see her father killing himself trying not to laugh. She gave him a grudging smile. It was pretty funny. He had the Jesse doll.

She looked back to where Noni moved around the circle of people, checking and realigning any positions until she was satisfied. She smiled at Jacinta.

'Buzz looks perfect.'

'Pretty good name for a boy, too,' she said straight-faced and watched Noni put on her bland midwife's face and agree that Buzz was a lovely name. But her eyes did twinkle. Jacinta grinned at her. It was very easy being around Noni.

Noni didn't go to her father. He put up his hand and Jacinta felt like lifting Buzz to cover her eyes so she couldn't see.

'My baby won't suck.' His voice held mock sadness.

Jacinta shook her head and sighed, but the other men in the class were egging him on with mock sympathy. 'Ask the midwife. She'll help.' Everyone smiled.

Noni got that look in her eyes. Iain was going to pay and Jacinta couldn't wait. Noni wouldn't shirk the challenge and Jacinta found herself smiling along with everyone else.

'Come here, Mother,' Noni said as she flipped open the top two buttons of Iain's shirt and slid her hand inside against his chest. Jacinta felt her father tense in the chair next to her. Noni said, 'You have to let baby get at you. Don't be shy. How's that?'

Iain's ears actually went red. Jacinta jammed her lips together, but her cheeks ached from holding back the grin. The class egged Noni on. 'His nipples are too small,' one of the fathers called out.

She saw her dad look up into Noni's face and wink. She was blushing too. *Serves them both right.*

Noni moved on smoothly. Jacinta slanted her glance sideways to her father and saw him looking mesmerised. *Spare me*, she thought. She suspected Iain wasn't listening, just watching, as Noni slowed and became absorbed in what she was saying.

Jacinta felt her own cheeks heat. Noni's hand pointed to her breast, circling it as she explained something, and even pushed the fabric of her shirt right in to demonstrate what an inverted nipple was.

A whistle hissed in beside her and she glanced at Iain. Was he actually holding his breath? Noni cupped her breast in one hand, rounding it up as if offering it to a baby. Iain shifted in his seat.

That was when Jacinta wondered if he might actually be smitten and not just playing with Noni. That would cause problems because Jacinta couldn't see Noni moving to that big chrome flat of his in Sydney.

'Iain?' Jacinta whispered. He didn't hear her. She tried again. 'Dad.' Jacinta said it one more time. A little louder.

'Sorry, did you say something?' Then his face changed. Looked stupidly happy. 'You called me Dad!' He grinned at her. 'It sounded good, too.' He leaned over and squeezed her hand. 'Did you want me for something?'

'I said, could you get me one of those microwave sterilisers for the bottles? I'm not going to breastfeed.'

He blinked and opened and shut his mouth. She saw the effort it took him. *What?* No way was she doing that. It wasn't him showing his boobs to the whole world.

'How about we talk about it when we get back to Noni's?' he whispered back.

Jacinta raised her eyebrows at his inability to answer the simple question. She'd buy her own steriliser as soon as she figured out how to get money.

At least he wasn't looking at Noni, any more. He was staring at the floor and she got the feeling he suddenly realised that at the end of the pregnancy there really would be a baby – a helpless being that had to have decisions made for it. Had to be looked after. Had to be fed. Well, they were her decisions to make – it was her baby, not his!

When they all arrived home he didn't get out of the car. All of them had travelled together this week as he'd finally said he preferred Noni not to be left on her own to lock up and for some reason, she'd agreed.

'Can you go ahead, please, Jacinta? I want to ask Noni something.'

She gave him a give-me-a-break look. 'Yeah, right. Does she need another hug?' But she still went.

Chapter Thirty-two

Noni

Noni sat in the car as Jacinta waddled away and wondered if Iain really did want to give her another hug. Trying that in the car would be awkward. But he didn't move. Or speak.

While she waited for him to tell her why he'd wanted to see her privately, she thought about all the things she needed to do. Eventually, she ran out of items on her list.

'Well? What did you want to ask me?' Noni nudged him in the darkness.

'Something. I just need a minute.' It was so dark in the car she could barely make him out. It really made her listen to the way he spoke. It was deep, melodic and incredibly sexy. And the tension that was stretching the space between them had nothing to do with his daughter. Noni's pulse rate sped and she could feel the dryness of her mouth. She wanted to lean her head against his big, broad chest – or just turn her whole body and crawl into his lap. Again, technically awkward. What the heck was happening to her and was this what he'd planned? Or was it just an accidental explosion of lust between them?

Suddenly, he leaned and captured her face with one hand to stare intensely at her. She heard him breathe in deeply as if breathing in the scent of her. Then, his voice low and gravelly, as if he were stretched tight with tension, he said, 'You were incredible tonight. I loved watching you move. Listening to your voice. That was why I couldn't talk to you on the phone from Sydney. Your voice drives me crazy. Hearing you makes me ache. And those soft, husky noises you made when we kissed in the kitchen, I can't get them out of my mind.'

Noni's belly came alive with spirals of sensation and her skin flushed. Heat flooded her limbs. *Whoa there.* She licked her lips and tried to sound flippant. Tried to be the sensible parent and not the randy teen in that car in the dark. 'You're saying I turn on my antenatal class?'

'Hmm?'

'Hello, Iain? Is anybody home except hormones, or was Jacinta right and you want to give me a hug?'

His hand slid down her cheek and he breathed out as he sat back. He breathed out again as if forcing the fog from his brain. 'Right. You're right. This isn't the place.' He sat up straighter and gripped the steering wheel as if grounding himself. 'Breastfeeding,' Iain said, and Noni blinked uncomprehendingly. 'Jacinta wants to bottle-feed,' he explained.

It was Noni's turn to sit back. So, he didn't want to give her a hug. Fine. She frowned and thought about his statement. 'So, she doesn't breastfeed. What's the problem?'

He actually gasped. 'A baby needs the best care and nutrition. That means breastfeeding – but Jacinta said she wasn't going to breastfeed. Tonight. She asked me for a sterilising set for bottle-feeding.'

Horrified is us, Noni thought dryly.

Iain warmed to his theme. 'This is my grandchild here – a child that should be breastfed. "Breast is Best" and all that. You're a midwife. How can you say any differently?'

'As a midwife, of course I advocate breastfeeding. As a mother, I breastfed Harley, but as a friend of Jacinta's I support her decision. She's the one that has to do it.' She peered at him again, trying to see the expression on his face.

'I don't believe this!'

Noni realised he'd lost the plot in a whole new way.

'Breastmilk helps babies' immune systems, has essential components to encourage brain development and prevents sensitivity to allergies. Why wouldn't I want that for my grandchild? I want you to talk her into breastfeeding.'

She could hear the lack of reason in his voice and it unsettled her. This was a side of him she hadn't seen.

'Excuse me? This child may be your grandchild, but it's Jacinta's baby. I'll listen to her reasons for choosing not to breastfeed and, as I've said, I'll support her in her decision.' She stated the fact. 'You're losing it here. I'm not going to talk her into anything she doesn't want to do.'

'I'm losing reality? As a doctor I encourage breastfeeding for health reasons, but this is my grandchild!' His voice vibrated with suppressed frustration. 'I ask you to do a simple little thing for me and you won't.' He opened the car door and climbed out. 'Forget it. I'll tell her myself.'

Noni sat in the car on her own and sighed. He would blow it! Jacinta had just started to call him Dad, too. She should get out and try to stop him. Explain her reasons and try to get him to see Jacinta's point of view.

She didn't. His arrogance was an eye-opener. She wouldn't have believed he was so narrow-minded and authoritarian. It was better to find out now, she supposed, but it made her sad. Or maybe he'd just gone temporarily insane. That was his best hope for survival.

She almost smiled at another thought: Jacinta had enough of her father in her to fight her own battles. Noni got out of the car and went in the back door through the kitchen to Aunt Win.

Her aunt's face lit up as Noni came in the door and her arms opened. Noni felt the tension drain away. *Thank you, Aunt Win.* She stretched up and kissed her aunt on the cheek. Her soft face felt warm and comforting against her own. Like burying her nose in a bouquet of rose petals.

'Hello, Noni, love.' After their embrace, she stepped back to look properly at her and pursed her lips. 'How was your class?'

'Class was fine. It's Iain who's being a pain.' She lifted the lid of the biscuit barrel and snaffled a still-warm, incredibly aromatic Anzac biscuit. Noni slowly savoured the syrupy oat-and-coconut taste as it saturated her mouth, discovered herself briefly in heaven then swallowed, before talking again. 'Jacinta wants to bottle-feed and Iain doesn't think that's good enough for his grandchild.'

Aunt Win didn't say anything as Noni finished her biscuit, and pretending her aunt couldn't see her, Noni reached for another one. Once, she'd eaten the whole jar of biscuits at one sitting after a bad day when she'd been pregnant – Win had just watched her then as well. She must have seen the need, like now. It was funny how she'd never wanted to eat that many again. That episode encapsulated Aunt Win's method of support.

Win shrugged. 'So, why doesn't Jacinta want to breastfeed?'

Noni shook her head. 'I don't know. I haven't had a chance to ask her. Iain doesn't seem to think she has a choice. That's offensive. We all know breastfeeding is the ideal food for babies, but the baby is Jacinta's, not his. She has to make her own choices. You never did that to me.'

Chapter Thirty-three

Win

'As if it would have done me any good.' Win looked at her diminutive niece and snorted. Elegant women didn't snort, which was fine, elegance was for people like Greg's departed wife. Overrated. It was a very satisfying noise, she'd always thought.

She could see Noni ponder. What had she said?

'No. If you didn't agree with something I'd chosen to do, you pointed out the options so I was informed, then respected the fact that it was my choice. I have never felt threatened that you wouldn't love me if I didn't do what you wanted or thought best.'

Win hoped that had been what she'd done. It was what she'd intended. Noni had been an extremely easy niece to love.

'You're pretty wonderful, you know,' Noni said as she rested her hand on Win's shoulder and Win lifted her hand to pat the cool fingers. She'd always felt blessed to have Noni as her niece.

Then Noni said, 'I hope I can remember all this when things get sticky between Harley and me.'

'You will.' Win felt her throat close a little. 'You're an amazing mum.'

'And you are an amazing aunt. Thank you for that. I think I'll give the others the slip and go to bed. Will you let them know if they ask, please?'

'Sure, love.' Win watched her go. Her usually bright, bouncy niece was a little bowed. Drooped with the doldrums. Noni shouldn't have worries. She worked too hard. Gave too much. She deserved to be appreciated.

She also suspected her niece felt confused by her mixed feelings about their male lodger and that was a whole new ball game for Noni. She'd put up a force field against men since Harley had been born and this was the first crack in that shield Win had seen in the last five years.

Still, who was she to talk about force fields? She'd flirted her way through the last twenty years in her sixties-child persona, but there'd been a wall around her, too. And now she had a man knocking on her barriers as well. She wasn't quite sure what she was going to do about that.

Her dinner date with Greg had been cancelled again and he was on call Saturday night so couldn't come to the group week-end. She suspected he was relieved. But now she had the feeling she wouldn't have as much fun if he wasn't there. After one week. Maybe she had grown out of being daring. Found something, or someone, she'd rather spend time with.

She suspected Sunday would be the day. They were doing dinner, not lunch. It should be an easy decision. The man whose company she enjoyed above all others wanted to marry her. Had said he wanted to spend the rest of his life with her. That was huge.

But it was the minor things that bothered her.

Where would they live? She had no desire to move into his

house and she couldn't imagine him here. This was Noni's home and she wasn't selling the guesthouse.

She'd been totally unsuitable for Greg years ago, and had felt she was not what a doctor's wife needed to be, but soon Greg wouldn't be a doctor any more. She hadn't thought much on that. Maybe she'd better.

Greg said he loved her nurturing nature, and he deserved some warmth after living in the cold for so long. And he wanted to marry her. Of course they deserved a future together.

But Noni needed her. She would be devastated when Iain McCloud went back to his kingdom in Sydney, and of course Noni couldn't manage the guesthouse on her own.

Yet the other side of the coin was she'd miss Greg if he went off on his travels, or fell for another Margarete. She'd be devastated actually.

So Sunday promised to be the day for decisions. She needed to find something to wear, something she loved that proclaimed who she was, so he knew what he was letting himself in for.

Chapter Thirty-four

Jacinta

Jacinta heard her father follow her up the stairs. She went to her door and raised her brows in question. He looked like he was on a mission. *Here we go.*

'Jaz. Can I talk to you?'

She looked at him: serious face, cajoling eyes. She was not one of those bimbo waitresses. *Spare me.* 'Is this about breast-feeding?'

She watched him wince at her tone. Oh yeah, he was so having himself on. She narrowed her eyes at him. 'I'm not changing my mind. I'm not flipping my boobs out for everyone to see. I hate the thought.'

He spread his hands. 'Can we talk about it?'

She shrugged. 'You can talk about it.'

'I think you should wait until your baby is born to make the decision to bottle-feed. It might not be what you want to do and then it will be too late once the baby has the bottle. I really think you should breastfeed your baby and see how it goes.'

Was this guy for real? 'Um, no. Drop dead. I don't have to explain my reasons and if you're so keen on 'breast is best', get yourself a pump and you feed the baby.'

She stepped through into her room and shut the door. *What a wanker.* She flopped onto the bed.

Chapter Thirty-five

Noni

Noni showered, changed into her satin pyjamas and lay on her bed, staring up at the ceiling in the semi-darkness. She could just see the luminous stars she'd stuck there in the form of Southern Hemisphere constellations. It had taken her hours, neck bent while standing on the ladder, to stick them up. Aunt Win had stood underneath, astronomy book in her hand, directing the positions. Whenever she had really weighty matters to think over, she found that staring up at those stars calmed her mind. So why wasn't she calm?

Iain was really getting to her. When he'd arrived she'd known he spelled trouble, with his big, broad shoulders and his ability to draw the attention of everyone in the room as if it were his right. She hadn't met a lot of people with that sort of authority so it had been outside her frame of reference. Funny, she'd never put his ability to command attention down to their age difference. She had the feeling Iain would be Iain even if he were her age. Exciting. Charismatic. He'd resided under her roof charming her aunt and her son, as well as her. Why hadn't she been more careful? She should have known he would turn out to be a huge egomaniac who would only complicate her life.

Yet, at times they seemed to be incredibly in sync – she refused to say they were soul mates – but their minds did often run parallel and their sense of humour matched bizarrely. And the kicker was, last weekend's passion in the kitchen had blown her away, and made her want more.

The arousal she'd experienced tonight in the middle of her antenatal class had shocked her, too. She'd touched men's chests before and felt their hearts beat under her hand. She certainly hadn't wanted to rip off their shirts and run her hands all over them like she'd wanted to tonight. In front of a room full of people.

She'd seen the challenge in his eyes . . . and run to it. She could remember very clearly saying, 'Come here, Mother.' Could remember the feel of flipping open the top two buttons of his shirt to slide her hand against his chest. His hot, solid, incredible expanse of chest. She'd even said, 'Don't be shy. How's that?'

Her ears burned as she thought about it. *Insanity.* And the class had been egging her on. *Soooo unprofessional.*

She imagined again the catch of his breath as she brushed his nipple, the sudden tautness of skin beneath her fingers and the infinitesimal shift of his butt on the chair for comfort. *Oh yeah.* She knew what had been going on and she'd pushed him right to the edge when he couldn't get back at her. *Dangerous stuff, Noni.* Now, she'd run to her room to hide because she knew she'd be at risk of retribution and she was a coward.

Then, *bam*, the conversation in the car: a roller-coaster dive back to reality. Iain's attitude towards Jacinta's decision to bottle-feed her baby was such a let-down. Maybe some women would have seen nothing wrong with his assumptions, but she'd been there. She'd been the young mum in the position where everyone assumed they knew more than she did. Breastfeeding worked brilliantly for her, but not having pressure or expectations from others while she made that decision made it worlds easier.

Thank goodness she'd had Aunt Win right beside her saying, 'You know best, he's your child.' No matter how hard she strained her brain, she couldn't imagine Iain saying that to Jacinta. No. A relationship with Iain McCloud wouldn't work – he would try to control them all. She couldn't let him. She was strong enough to withstand him.

As long as he didn't touch her or she didn't touch him.

That was the problem. Every day she woke up and wondered if this weekend was the time she was going to make love with Iain. She was mad. Mad with lust!

He really was shallow, though. He'd never asked how her day had been when she came home from work. Wasn't really interested in her at all, except for her body. She hadn't even considered that part of her as particularly attractive. Unfortunately, her body was interested in his, too. It was all so very confusing.

Her bedroom door opened and Iain's head appeared around the door. When she didn't throw anything, his body followed.

'Win said you were up here.' He spoke very quietly as he peered into the darkness towards the bed.

'Did she tell you I didn't want to see you tonight?' Her voice trembled a little as her traitorous senses refused to hate him. She *did not* want to see him.

She rolled over and turned her back to him. 'I'm tired. Goodnight.'

She listened for the sound of him leaving. He moved so quietly that she couldn't tell if he'd gone or not. It was killing her not to roll back and look. The door clicked shut and she sighed.

Iain's voice came out of the darkness beside her. 'Did you move to make room for me? Thanks.'

She felt the bed shift as he sat on the edge beside her. 'Please leave, Iain. I'm not in the mood for games tonight.'

'I will in a second. I'm not here for the fun of it, Noni. I hate apologising and actually, I haven't had much practice.' He put his hand on her shoulder and rolled her back to face him. His hand was warm and solid and it stayed resting gently against her skin. Heating it. 'You were right. It's Jacinta's prerogative to decide how to care for her child.'

He chuckled in the dark. 'She waited until I had my say, which was nice of her. Then she blasted me out of the water when I said she had to breastfeed. Said I could do it if I was so in favour of it. You would have loved it.'

Noni relaxed slightly. 'So why doesn't she want to breastfeed?'

'She said she's not flipping her breasts out for everyone to see. She hates the thought, and she just doesn't want to.'

'That's a valid reason and not uncommon with young women. Some older women find it very difficult as well. I can't think of much worse than a baby at his mother's breast getting the message that she doesn't like him being there. Despite the loss of some of the benefits, it's important to enjoy holding and feeding your baby more than anything.'

'I see that now.' His voice became more rueful. 'So I was

wondering, can we go back to the part in the car where I wanted to hug you?'

Noni could feel herself softening towards him. That was what happened. Just when she conceded that to get closer to him was a bad move, here she was, with him next to her on her bed in the dark. With the door shut.

'Harley is coming up to say goodnight to me in a minute.' She didn't say *thank goodness*, but it was in her voice.

'Win said to tell you she tucked him in and he's asleep already.' His voice held the smugness that infuriated her.

She reached back, lifted the nearest pillow, and smacked him in the head with it. *Thwack.* 'Well, ask her to tuck you in, too.'

She moved to sit up but couldn't because he was sitting on the duvet.

'Ferocious little ferret, aren't you?' His breath tickled her face as he dropped a kiss on her forehead and stood to release the quilt so she could move. He was going.

Except when she was sitting, he sat back down again. 'Please let me apologise and then I'll leave you alone.'

She stared at a star over his left shoulder and didn't say anything.

'Has to be that good, eh?' He stroked a strand of hair out of her eyes. His finger felt like velvet touching her skin. So gentle. Then he said, 'I'm sorry. You were right. I was a pig.'

Something told her that was a big concession for him. He stood up, the gap widening, the cool empty space rushing between them, and she missed him already. 'Arrogant pig!' she stated.

He stopped. Turned his head. 'Arrogant pig,' he conceded, holding up his hands in surrender. 'Can I lie down again?'

Her eyes, accustomed to the dark now, could see his lips tilt. Her body said, *Hmmmmm, yes, please.* And the rest of her agreed. 'For a minute.' Not that Win would mind if he stayed. Win would say everything was her choice. Well, darn it. She wanted to choose.

'Would you like a hug?' He slid down next to her and she snuggled into his side to lie facing him. She played with the button on his shirt.

He stroked her cheek. 'You know, I thought my trousers had shrunk tonight when you were demonstrating the way to latch a baby onto my nipple.'

She smiled. 'Can I just undo these two buttons again?' Her hand reached in as she had in the class and he groaned.

His skin felt firm and warm and Noni's fingers slid across the solid wall of his chest until she found one of his small sinewy nubs. To her delight, his nipple hardened instantly in response to her touch.

She looked up and the heat in his eyes woke the hunger in her that had been asleep for too long. *Too, too long.* That's what happened when you fought down urges indefinitely – lust jumped on you and swallowed you whole. Like she wanted to devour Iain.

A sudden wild and predatory need for power rolled over her. Like a cat, she pounced on his other buttons until she could push back the shirt, and the sight stopped the breath in her throat. His chest lay very broad and ripped, his sixpack remarkably impressive, and she felt like growling. Those few hairs drew her eyes as her hands slowed their rush. It took a moment to calm the thundering that had grown in her ears.

Finally, when her voice could work she asked with an attempt at innocence, 'Where does this road go?' But it came out husky as she traced the darker fine hair down his midriff.

Iain groaned. 'I think straight to trouble for both of us. Now, give me your hands.' He caught her marauding hands in one of his and held them, then dropped a swift, sweet kiss on her lips. He glanced once towards the corridor. 'Does your door lock?'

'No.'

'Then I'll leave because what I want to do requires privacy.'

She frowned as the words sank in through the fog. 'Well, I suppose it does, but I've never used it.'

She watched him slide across the bed and pad to the door. Her body thrummed, her heart thumped like a steam engine, and she could feel the heat in her cheeks. Thank goodness it was fairly dim in here.

The lock clicked and her heart thumped again. He'd think she was an idiot for starting this then being nervous. Then Iain came back and discarded his flapping shirt on the bedside table, before climbing back onto the bed. Then he was beside her and his arms were around her and it didn't matter about her nerves any more. His hands ran up her body and he proved he was much quicker at removing clothes than she was. Before she knew it, there was only her skin against his and together they felt like silk on silk. Then he slowed again. Slid against her.

His lips met hers and it was as if they had both been shipwrecked for days without water and Noni felt as if she'd fallen into an ocean of sensations.

He whispered, 'There are a hundred places I've wanted to kiss for weeks.' And broke away to kiss the hollow of her throat, the skin beneath her ears and the valley between her breasts. Each place seemed to glow after his lips had been there, and she didn't know how much more of this she would be able to stand.

She heard his murmured endearments, and even some tiny moans of her own, and then she pulled his lips back to hers and was lost again.

The aching need grew in her belly and she rubbed herself against him more urgently. In the eye of the storm he reached over to remove something from his shirt pocket. Noni lay back and smiled. There were times when having a control freak in charge did help.

Then he pulled her to him and she forgot the mundane matters of safety and protection and discovered the ethereal world of losing herself in a man. The power and sensuality in both of them met and exploded into something dazzlingly magical. All she could do was hold onto the lifeboat that was Iain and exult in the storm.

Afterwards, he cradled her against him and she could hear the pounding of his heart matching her own. They dozed for a while under the quilt Iain had pulled over them both.

She turned her face and kissed the side of his chest. She loved him. He smiled down at her.

'I can't regret making love with you. It was beautiful,' she told him candidly.

He kissed the top of her head. 'You are beautiful and I love your honesty.'

'Well, if we're being honest, it's getting late and I don't like the door locked against Harley.'

'I'll unlock it, but first I want to say something.'

Noni felt her heart trip and drew a breath to steady it. 'What?'

'I love being with you, Noni. These last few weeks could have been hell, but they haven't been. I've felt more at peace and at home than I can remember for a long time. Jacinta and I really appreciate your input.'

'I thought you were the one with the input,' she retorted naughtily.

'Behave yourself, woman.' His finger tipped up her chin to look at him. 'You know our being together doesn't have to end when I move back to Sydney.'

Her hand clenched. For one crazy second there she thought he was going to ask her to marry him. *Goose!* Of course he wasn't, what did she expect after six weeks?

Chapter Thirty-six

Noni

So naive. Of course he wasn't going to ask her to spend her life with him just because she'd slept with him once. Cold water couldn't have done a better job of snapping her out of her fantasy. 'I think you'd better clarify that!'

'I'm asking you to come and live with me when we go back to Sydney.'

Not marriage. But he did actually ask her to go with him. To leave Burra. Leave Aunt Win. 'What about Harley?' she asked.

'Well, obviously Harley has to come too. I'm very fond of him. There's a very good school – I know, I went there. When he's in high school there's another quite close and he could come home for weekends.'

He really was looking long term. Then his words sank in and she stiffened. 'You mean a boarding school? You're planning my son's life and he's only five!'

Iain wasn't listening. She hated it when he did that. He lifted his arm out from under her and his hands moved to clasp each other under the back of his head while he contemplated the ceiling.

'Your motorbike really isn't suitable there, though, seriously it's far too dangerous in the city, but you wouldn't need it as you wouldn't have to work. I make more than enough money to support all of us. Jacinta and the baby could live with us, unless she wants her own flat – but you could see to all that.'

'How useful of me.' She saw him frown at her tone of voice and she moved away to sit on the edge of the bed with her back to him. She reached down and pulled on her pyjama bottoms and then her unbuttoned top over her head.

'What a pretty little picture you've painted, Iain,' she said, not hiding the sarcasm in her voice. But she did hide the pain. 'I've got another picture.' She switched on the bedside lamp and turned to face him. He blinked like an owl in the sudden light.

'How about you stay here and sell your car because I can get anything you need from the shops on my bike for you?' Her words came out in a hard little voice she didn't know she had. 'Jacinta can go into an unmarried mother's home and visit on the weekends, and when I get home from work we can have sex when I feel like it because I'll be paying the bills.' She raised her eyebrows. 'Are you feeling flattered?' She got up and opened the bedroom door. 'Goodnight, Iain.'

'That's not what I meant. I've said it badly. We should talk about this.'

Yes. But it involved raised voices and she wasn't doing that. She shook her head, not trusting herself to talk.

'Can I get dressed first?'

She gestured towards his clothes and he stood up. He held her eyes as he pulled on his trousers and slung his shirt around his shoulders.

He walked out the door without saying another word and she shut it. Firmly.

She went for a turn around the room. Then another. Yes, it hurt. He had as much as admitted to her that she was great fun and welcome in his bed as his lover. Sort of a compliment. She didn't need to work and he would pay for Harley's private schooling. But he would organise her life to suit him. He obviously wasn't ready for an equal relationship. Or a legal commitment. He'd told her that.

What about her commitment to the place she grew up in, all the people she knew, her job – though her job might go anyway. And what about her five years of being a single, independent mother? Should she just go off to be a kept woman in Sydney and lose all the respect she'd gained? And her self-respect as well?

She already had one child who didn't know his father. What if she had another child and their relationship didn't work out? Iain could dictate to her and not take her seriously for the rest of her life. More importantly, she would be cheating herself.

She didn't want to regret the time she'd spent in Iain's arms. It had been amazing; heartbreakingly beautiful, and promised so much more. Which left her with two options: say goodbye and try to forget him, or fight for what she hoped were good foundations to build an equal relationship with a real future.

Did he see what she was risking? Could he possibly love her like she suspected she loved him? Or was he just not thinking, and hadn't stopped to look from her point of view? He didn't have a great track record for that but he had listened and accepted when Jacinta had told him to take a hike over breastfeeding.

Noni had never backed away from a challenge and this could be the most important challenge yet. She would try to make Iain see his idea of their future short-changed them all, and she would give it until Jacinta had her baby.

Then the decision would be made. Either way.

With a dose of realism left over from the last hour and a sinking suspicion that she'd already lost round one, Noni set her chin.

The next day was Saturday and it started off well. Harley made eighteen runs before being bowled out. Noni turned to Iain and inclined her head in acknowledgement. 'He's definitely improving his cricket skills.'

Iain smiled and dropped an arm around her shoulders while they waited for Harley to reach them. Her son was looking and grinning at Iain, not Noni, but she didn't mind. The intricacies of the male sporting mind would probably always escape her. Her son looked happier, that was all that mattered.

'Well done, mate. Your mummy and I are proud of you. Your batting's getting better every week.'

Grinning, Harley looked at his mother.

'Congratulations, darling.' He even suffered a hug before wriggling free and running over to join the rest of the team.

After the game they packed up and went home. Aunt Win disappeared off to her usual haunts and Noni and Iain watched her leave from the front verandah.

Iain's brow furrowed as the car that had collected her drove away. 'Where does she go? You know, that's the first time I've wondered.' He looked at Noni and she tried to keep the mischief out of her face.

'Have I said something funny?'

Was it funny? Not usually, but telling Iain had a certain amusing slant. 'She's part of a naturist group. It's what used to be called a nudist colony. They have a retreat up in the foothills.'

Iain blinked and she could see he was trying to block out the picture that was forming in his mind of Aunt Win free to air. She saw him shake his head, blink again, and decide to forget about Win and look at her, instead.

Noni had turned to go inside. She stopped with her hand on the door, and spoke over her shoulder. *Game time.* 'What were you planning on doing this afternoon?'

'Are you sending out come-hither vibes?' From behind her she heard his low, amused voice. 'How about a video for the offspring and we could do some more talking in your bedroom?'

Okay, so round two had begun. Good. 'That sounds interesting. But not in the bedroom. I'm glad you want to talk. What should we talk about, Iain?'

'No idea.' His expression belied that.

Noni nodded her head. 'I have a few topics. I know very little about you, Iain. I'd like to hear about your life away from here. Somehow, I don't think I'd get to hear any of that if we "talked" in the bedroom.' She opened the door and paused for his response.

He gave an exaggerated sigh. 'I'm not so sure I'm ready for this, but I guess it had to come.'

Chapter Thirty-seven

Jacinta

Jacinta answered the phone. Noni and Iain were still outside waving goodbye to Win, so she picked it up. It was Cathy asking for Noni. They needed her. Now.

With Win not home, Noni couldn't have gone if Iain and Jacinta hadn't been there to mind Harley, and Jacinta's lips quirked at the idea of her father being dumped with babysitting.

Judging by the strange look on his face as he watched Noni zoom out of hostess and into midwife mode, he was finding it a strange experience to be relegated to background noise. Noni quickly reappeared in her uniform and gave Iain the run-down on the meal before she left.

As her motorbike zoomed away, her father frowned and Jacinta hid a grin. She put her chin on her hand and studied Iain's drawn brows. 'I wonder if your ex-wife felt like this when you were called out in Sydney?'

He gave her a look she couldn't read. He wasn't happy, that was all she could recognise.

'I was just wondering the same thing,' he said after a few

seconds. At least he'd answered. They were in the kitchen together staring at the casserole Win had left to put on at a certain time.

An hour later, Harley asked Iain to practise cricket with him and Jacinta watched them go outside. Four hours later, Noni still hadn't returned, so they pulled out the casserole and ate it. Two hours after that, Harley wanted to go to bed so Iain took him upstairs and tucked him in.

When Iain came back downstairs again they both looked at the clock. It was almost eight. Iain said, 'I wonder if Noni needs some help.'

Jacinta scratched at her cuticles, feeling unsettled. 'I wonder if the woman giving birth could be someone from the antenatal classes?'

'Could be,' Iain said. 'The odds are shortened that you would know the person in a small community. I think I'm actually coming to like that concept more, but before I came here I would've sworn I appreciated the anonymity of a big hospital.'

That was the first time her father had offered a comment that dealt with his life before she'd known him. 'Do you miss your work?'

'It's hard to imagine, but I find that's true.' He laughed, only there wasn't much humour in it. 'I might even be a more holistic doctor at the private hospital after Noni's classes.' The corner of his mouth lifted as he caught her eyes. 'My colleagues will be horrified.'

'The nurses will be happy.' They smiled at each other.

Jacinta went to bed at nine, but she woke at midnight when Noni came in. She heard her father's voice and then not long after all the sounds stopped.

Chapter Thirty-eight

Noni

In the early hours of Sunday morning, someone knocked on Noni's bedroom door.

'Noni, it's me, Jacinta. Can I come in?' she whispered through the door.

Noni pushed back the covers and slid out of bed, padding silently across the carpet to open the door. Jacinta stood there with enormous eyes and a towel between her legs.

Noni's first crazy thought was, *She can't! Two weeks early and she hasn't finished her antenatal classes!* Then she laughed at herself for behaving like a nervous mother.

'Come in, honey. So, tonight's the night.' Noni clasped Jacinta's cold hand and squeezed it. 'You'll be fine. Look, I have my little trumpet for listening to baby's heartbeat. Stand still for a moment and we'll see what he or she thinks of someone pulling the plug out of the bath.'

'It's a she,' Jacinta said firmly and Noni smiled to herself. She'd seen people paint rooms the wrong colour on their mistaken instincts. Noni bent her head to listen to Jacinta's belly through her instrument. She could hear the *clop, clopping* of a very happy baby. 'The heartbeat sounds fine. Trotting along without a care in the world.'

She stood up. 'Come through and have a shower in my bathroom. I'll get your things together and wake your father. Have you had any contractions, yet?'

Jacinta had her lip caught between her teeth. She shook her head wordlessly at Noni, her eyes still round with shock, as she looked down at the damp towel.

'Well you've had all those Braxton Hicks contractions. The tightenings will probably start soon.'

Jacinta jammed the towel harder. 'When do the waters stop dripping?'

Noni tried to keep the smile away from her lips. 'When you have the baby. You can't stop it. Just do like the cricketers do, and pad up.'

Jacinta pulled a face. 'That's disgusting, Noni.'

Noni watched her shake her head, but Jacinta couldn't help smiling, and Noni shooed her into the bathroom, well pleased with her state of mind.

She trod quietly up the hallway to Iain's room and pushed open the door. 'Iain?'

'Noni?' His voice sounded calm, as if he always had people stealing into his room in the early hours of the morning. 'Couldn't leave me alone?'

'Jacinta's waters have broken. She's in the shower in my room. I'll get her things.'

'Have you checked for cord prolapse?'

Noni frowned. There was something different in his voice. 'Just because Aimee had one doesn't mean Jacinta will.'

Iain's voice held a hint of steel. 'Don't patronise me. If it was a big gush, cord prolapse is a possibility.'

She raised her eyebrows. 'Don't be paranoid. The head was well down. Trust me when I say she's fine. I'm the midwife.'

'I want you to check.'

'You're a surgeon. Since when were you an obstetrician?'

'Oh, hell, Noni. For the last five years I've been an obstetrician. Now, please, examine her.'

Noni shook her head twice as if once wouldn't clear it. 'Let me get this clear. You lied to me *twice*? You're actually an obstetrician?' Noni felt as if someone had squeezed the air out of her. She wiped any expression from her face and spoke to his left shoulder. 'No. I won't examine her,' she said, her voice grim. 'You do it – though I'm not sure that's ethical.' She shook her head at the bizarreness of the situation. 'She's draining copious amounts of clear liquid and the foetal heart is reassuring. If she'd had a cord prolapse the foetal heart would show that.'

As his further lies finally settled into her psyche, she felt overwhelmed. She narrowed her eyes at him. 'I'll be there for Jacinta if she needs me until she has the baby, but I don't want to speak to you ever again. You creep!' She spun on her heel and went along to Jacinta's room to throw the last few things into the girl's bag before returning to her own room.

Iain was there when she went in and she dropped the bag in front of him.

'Noni?'

She ignored him, turned and walked out again. Then she stopped, came back and knocked on the ensuite door.

'Jacinta? How're you going in there?' As she listened at the door, the shower stopped. 'Here are some things to put on. Your dad is going to take you to the hospital and I'll stay here with Harley until the morning. Remember, you mightn't start having contractions until later in the day. If you need me sooner, I'll wake Harley and bring him with me. Okay?'

'Okay. I'm fine. Still no contractions. Tell Dad I'll be out in a minute.'

Noni looked at Iain. 'He's right here. I'm going to check on Harley.' She had to get out of there. She was going to throw something at Iain any minute now if she didn't.

She sidestepped to avoid getting close to him as she went past, and breathed a sigh of relief as she hit the corridor. Until he grabbed her arm.

'Get your hands off me,' she hissed. Her voice rose barely above a whisper, but the coldness in it would have frozen a volcano, and the fury in it bubbled dangerously, just below the surface of her control. She was such a fool. 'See to your daughter, Mr Obstetrician.' She looked down at his large hand against her paler skin and brushed it away as if it were a spider.

His black brows drew together. 'Look, I know I'm in big trouble, but we don't have time for this. I've been incredibly stupid, not explaining it all to you before now, but I didn't want to get involved in hospital politics.'

'Tell someone who cares.'

He followed her down the stairs to the kitchen and she could feel how close he was behind her. Noni thought there might actually be steam coming out of her ears. She hoped he got a vapour burn.

'Talk to me,' he said.

Noni threw up her hands, swivelling angrily to face him. 'I can't believe it. An obstetrician! No wonder you never asked about my work. You didn't want to give yourself away. What further proof do I need that you're untrustworthy? That you will lie to me every single day I know you? That's a pretty big blot on your copybook. And you asked me to trust you with our lives in Sydney?' She shook her head. 'All those discussions in the classes – you knew it all! You must have been laughing your head off.'

Iain winced. 'It seemed like a good idea at the time.'

She turned on the light in the kitchen and plugged in the kettle viciously. 'It seemed like a good idea at the time,' she mimicked. 'So that's how you know Dr Soams, too.'

'I met Greg when I was teaching an obstetric refresher course he attended. Penelope was there at the dinner afterwards, and we all got on like a house on fire. They stayed with us a couple of times in Sydney.'

Too little too late. Noni gritted her teeth and squeezed all the aggressive thoughts into a tiny cubicle of her brain and mentally forced the door shut on them. It was quite a battle, but she was strong. Stronger than he'd ever know. Then she drew in a deep breath and consciously relaxed her shoulders. *Forget about him,* she told herself. *Jacinta is the important one now.*

She felt Iain's hand on her shoulder and again she peeled it away from her skin. She felt her anger bubble up once more and slammed the lid shut. 'Please, keep away from me as much as you can in the circumstances.' Her words were very clearly enunciated in a dangerously quiet voice. 'Perhaps, you could put Jacinta's bag in the car. I really don't want her to have to cope with friction between the two of us.'

'Look, Noni, it's a long story and I'm sorry I misled you.'

She looked up at him and steeled herself. She refused to soften. He didn't deserve her giving him an inch after this. 'When all this is over, for me to even talk to you, you'd better have a bloody good explanation.'

The jug switched off and she made two mugs of tea and walked past him out of the kitchen door. She would have liked to have stomped, except she'd have spilt the tea.

It was the little things in life that were so frustrating.

Within half an hour Iain and Jacinta had left for the hospital. Noni would have kept Jacinta home, but Iain wanted her baby electronically monitored for any heart irregularities. It was four-thirty am.

Noni tidied Jacinta's room and smoothed her hand across the book of baby names lying on the dresser. She refused to think about Iain and his deception, or the fact that the man she suspected she loved had lied to her for weeks. Twice. Why would he do that? What else would he lie about?

She shook her head and straightened her shoulders. Jacinta was the important one here.

Chapter Thirty-nine

Noni

When Noni arrived at the hospital in her uniform she was glad to see the ward had quietened down.

'Hi, Noni.' Cathy was on again and sat at the nurses' station, waiting for the handover report. She grinned at her. 'I see the lodgers are in. I gather you'd like to be the extra in the birthing suite?'

'Thanks, Cath. Do you know how she's going?'

'Night staff are still with her. If you want to relieve them so they can come out, I'll fill you in later.'

'Sounds good.' Noni tucked her bag into her locker and headed down the hallway. She knocked gently and pushed open the door.

She found Jacinta sitting on the bed with the baby monitor strapped to her stomach. She looked incredibly miserable. She smiled wanly at Noni, who frowned at the long coils of paper hanging out of the machine. Judging by the length of it, she'd been strapped up since her arrival hours ago.

The night sister tilted her head towards Iain and raised her eyebrows as if to say, *It's not my fault.*

Noni crossed the room without looking at Iain and took Jacinta's hand. 'Hi, Jacinta. How're you going?'

The girl's big eyes looked tragic and almost hopeless. 'It hurts.'

'I know, sweetie. You'll feel better when you get up. When did the contractions start?'

'About an hour ago, and they're getting stronger and closer together.' Jacinta drew in a breath and closed her eyes. 'Here comes another one.'

They all watched as Jacinta breathed slowly in and out through the contraction with her eyes shut tight and her body rigid on the bed.

Noni frowned and shook her head. What were they doing, confining her to the bed with the monitoring? The night sister wasn't a strong advocate for excessive monitoring so it had to be Iain's idea.

'Big sigh as the pain finishes, Jacinta, and then let your muscles go really floppy.' She tilted her head and watched as Jacinta struggled to relax. 'Drop your shoulders. Good. Let's get you off this bed.'

Iain stepped forward, but Noni didn't give him a chance to speak. She picked up the strip of paper and it unfolded like a concertina in her hand all the way down to the floor. 'What a lovely tracing of baby's heartbeat. Look at all these contraction hills we've recorded.' She looked at him from beneath her brows. 'I can see the baseline rate is normal, there are two accelerations in almost every ten-minute period, plus the beat-to-beat variability is above five, as it should be for a healthy baby. You're happy with this, aren't you, Iain? I'm sure Jacinta would like a nice hot shower to help her relax.'

He tightened his lips but nodded. 'As you say, a healthy trace.'

'So we could take that off, now that we can see how happy baby is in there.' The night sister made a strangled noise and squeezed her lips together. Neither Noni nor Iain looked at her. They were too intent on their own private battle.

The night sister finally said, 'Jacinta started contracting at five-thirty and Dr McCloud was concerned. I'll leave you to carry on here, Noni, and give my report to Cathy. Good luck, Jacinta. Bye, everybody.'

'Thanks, Broni.' Jacinta smiled wanly as the other midwife left the room. Iain leaned against the wall and watched Noni with his eyes narrowed.

Noni ignored him. 'Okay, sweetie, let's get these belts off your tummy and get you into the shower.' Iain's rigid spine hinted at mutiny but he didn't protest. Noni's shoulders relaxed a little.

They shuffled their way into the chair in the bathroom and Jacinta leaned her head against the wall as Noni directed the hot water over her back. They'd kept on the pink crop-top bra and a tiny pair of bikini pants for her modesty.

Her groan of relief was clearly audible even to her father. 'That feels wonderful.'

'I know.' Noni resisted the urge to roll her eyes at Iain. 'Keep the nozzle of the hand shower over the part where the tightness is during contractions and the heat will help.' Noni showed her how to change the direction of the spray, then she draped a towel around Jacinta's damp shoulders to prevent a chill. 'I'm just ducking out here for a moment to talk to your father.'

Jacinta had her eyes closed. 'So much better. Thank goodness,' she said as she sagged into the chair. 'I might even sit on the ball, instead.'

Noni leaned forward and brushed the hair out of the girl's eyes. 'Good thought. Change spots until you're comfortable. You'll be fine. You're doing beautifully. Sometimes, a minute with just you and baby is what you need as well.'

'And you're designed to do it,' Jacinta chorused the last line with Noni and they smiled at each other.

'I'll be back soon.' Noni shut the bathroom door behind her and moved over to where Iain was still leaning tensely against the wall.

'We're both glad to see you, although I won't allow you to steamroll me all the time.' His level voice came across quietly but very firm. He was used to everyone doing what he said, no doubt.

Noni shrugged. 'I never thought you would. Jacinta needs you to stop thinking like an obstetrician . . .' One she'd needed for the last six weeks. She tried not to put an accusing inflection on the word, even though it tasted like dirt in her mouth. She couldn't believe he'd been here the whole time.

She forced herself to calm down. 'Think more like her support person. You aren't dealing with the usual high-risk pregnancy you'd be called in for. She's put on weight, and all her cardiac tests came back normal and we agreed to assume she's a perfectly healthy young woman with a healthy baby.' She looked up at him and refused to drop her eyes. 'Excessive monitoring of normal labour can cause stress for the mother. It can slow her labour by decreasing access to movement, and encourage early intervention with arte- facts in the trace that don't mean anything. You know that.'

Iain flexed his shoulders and straightened. 'Okay.' He ran his hand through his hair. 'Okay. I may have overreacted. It's early in the labour and, as you say, the trace is good.' He put his fingers on the bridge of his nose and inhaled slowly. 'I'll go home and shower and be back in an hour. Phone me if you need me earlier.'

She watched him go, still angry with him for his previous deception, but she could acknowledge his fear of something going wrong for Jacinta. But for crying out loud! Expecting trouble only drew it closer. Negative people shouldn't be in the birthing suite, and she strongly believed everything would progress as it should. That was her job. She wasn't going to look at Jacinta as if she were a bomb about to go off like her father did.

The bathroom held a fine fog of steam as Noni carried a small paper cup of ice chips over to the ball Jacinta sat on. 'How's it going, Jacinta?'

'It's so much easier here than on the bed.'

No kidding. 'Suck on these ice chips between contractions and I'll put a cold washcloth on the rail in case you feel faint from the heat.'

'They're getting really strong, Noni.' Noni could hear the first uncertainty in Jacinta's voice.

'Good. It's more tiring if they take too long to get that way. A quick build-up means you'll have more strength to draw on. Strong is good. When you feel the contraction tightening, try to imagine your baby's head leaning against the cervix, opening bit by bit.' Her voice slowed, became even more gentle. 'You want to be as loose as you can be to let the muscles do their work. Every contraction brings you closer to meeting your baby.'

Her fingers stroked Jacinta's neck and were rewarded by the sudden dropping of tension in the shoulders as Jacinta relaxed. 'Sometimes, letting the tension out with a sound helps. A little moan of release during the height of the contraction can help it be directed downwards, instead of pulling yourself upwards into tension,' Noni continued in her quiet voice. 'After a while, when the shower isn't helping any more, what should you do?'

Jacinta answered in the same slowing voice, 'Change positions and do something else.'

Half an hour later, Jacinta's voice began to slur as she rested her head on her arms against the rail. She moaned freely but hardly tensed her muscles now as the contractions rolled over her. As if she let any discomfort out with the noise and she was just left with the benefits.

Noni stayed careful not to disturb her concentration during each contraction, marvelling again at how women could fall into a state of almost dozing between the waves as the body's natural endorphins kicked in.

The door opened just as Jacinta growled another exhalation that rose in a crescendo of moans before falling away again. Iain was back.

Chapter Forty

Noni

Iain's face blanched. His accusing glare shot across the room to Noni as he hissed, 'What the hell? She's in pain. Suffering!'

Noni saw his almost wild glance at his daughter and prepared for the fight. Jacinta couldn't fight for her choices without using the concentration she already needed for the contractions. 'It's okay, Iain. Stop for a minute.'

'No. Listen to her groaning. What's she been going through since I've been gone? I thought I could trust you!'

Noni glimpsed the hint of panic in his eyes and she put her fingers to her lips and frowned at him. 'I'm just going outside to reassure your dad, Jacinta.' She stood and backed him out of the tiny space, and shut the door between them and the labouring young woman. Jacinta's next moan began behind the barrier.

Iain paced in a circle. 'For God's sake, give her some pain relief. What about an epidural?'

'Stop it.' Good grief. She had no doubt he'd be rock solid in an emergency, but the obstetrician had freaked because it was his own daughter. If Jacinta needed proof that her father loved her, then

238

here it was. But it wasn't helpful right at this moment. This was not about Iain. 'I know this is your daughter, but you're panicking. She hasn't asked me for any pain relief. She knows she can. You sat beside her when we talked about this in class. It's not our job to force pain relief on a natural process unless we are asked to by the woman.'

'I'm pretty sure she's asking when she groans.'

Noni rolled her eyes. 'Think about it. Is the epidural for you or for her?' Noni rested her hand on his arm. 'She's coping. She's in strong labour. If she can't stand it she'll ask for something, but I believe she's progressing very quickly.'

He shook his head. 'Have you checked her progress?'

Back to that again. 'And interrupt the whole flow of hormones that she's just got going? You want me to move her back to the bed when she's found her stride? Jolt her out of the focus she's found to put a number on her progress, just to relieve your anxiety? She's been contracting for an hour. Do you think she sounds like she's about to have a baby? Is she ready to push?'

He ground his teeth. 'It's unlikely.'

Noni sighed. 'So why? If she doesn't ask for pain relief then nothing will change in her care except we won't have to wonder how far she is.'

She stared up into his face and said very slowly and clearly, 'It's not about us. Not about you. Her baby is fine when I check every fifteen minutes. So, please decide if the information we may gain, and that's not guaranteed every examination, is more important than her staying undisturbed in the shower to get on with it.'

Iain paced away and then came back. 'In my hospital every woman is offered an epidural as soon as the contractions start.'

'I totally disagree.' She couldn't believe his lack of knowledge about normal labours. The glimmer of hope that he'd understand disappeared. She hadn't taught him anything. 'Something will happen that indicates progress. For goodness sake, at least wait for a sign. She'll ask for pain relief, and get it, or she'll head into transition and then want to push.'

He stood, glaring, shaking his head as if struggling to control himself, so Noni spoke even more clearly and slowly to get through to him. 'Baby's heart rate is perfect,' she repeated. 'I listen to it every fifteen minutes for a minute. The contractions are regular, coming every two to three minutes and lasting seventy seconds. She moans through them and still relaxes between them.' She looked into his face. 'Let her be, Iain. She's got this.'

He wiped his forehead. Visibly forced his shoulders down. 'She'd better not have that baby in the bathroom.'

Noni's eyebrows rose. 'Tell me, Doctor, where is the correct place to have a baby? On a bed so the doctor or midwife can see properly? I thought women could birth wherever they want to.'

He sighed. 'You're joking, right?'

She could see that really rattled him. Well, bully for him and his fancy hospital. She got that it could be needed for a higher-risk birth. Labour could require an epidural, a catheter, a drip and continuous foetal monitoring.

But they were low-risk in Burra. As far as Noni was concerned, they were damn lucky they had Dr Soams to share their belief that normal-risk women were capable of having babies without intervention if that was what they wanted.

But that was Iain's frame of reference and she needed to respect that. She tried for a smile of sympathy. 'Have faith. Just observe. Come back into the bathroom and sit with us.'

He sighed and eventually, reluctantly, he nodded.

They reopened the door and walked in. Noni rested her hand on the girl's shoulder. 'Jacinta, your father's back.'

'Hi, Dad.' Her voice drifted in the mist of steam, disembodied and vague. It seemed to come from far away.

Iain cleared his throat. 'Hi, Jaz. How're you going?'

She groaned without replying as another contraction rolled over her. When it had run its course, Noni watched Iain loosen his clenched hands with determination.

'I'm okay.' The sleepy voice startled him as Jacinta finished the conversation as if she'd never stopped it to groan.

Noni grinned and stepped back from where she'd been soothing Jacinta's back. 'Why don't you rub for a while and I'll get some more ice?' She gestured for him to change positions with her. 'You've probably never participated in this side of labour before. Not here to save the day. Try to remember the concepts from the antenatal classes, not the emergency situations you're used to.'

She watched him rub firmly when Jacinta groaned, and gently when she relaxed between them. Noni smiled at Iain's expensive shoes slowly becoming discoloured by the splashes of water. She'd told him in class to bring wet-weather gear. She shrugged and left them to it.

By twelve-thirty, they'd been in and out of the shower three times. Noni had bowed to Iain's pressure, assessed Jacinta, and found she'd been six centimetres dilated, so more than halfway there.

Noni had lost count of the times Iain had had to walk away to hide his agitation. His face had settled into a mask now and his glances at the clock had settled into a tic-like rhythm. He looked exhausted already, unlikely to take much more of this in a calm way. *This should be interesting.*

She could see for him this was nothing like being the consultant who came and went a couple of times during his patient's painless labour, but she had to give him kudos for trying hard to go with it.

Now, Jacinta had returned to sit on the birthing ball, leaning back against the shower-recess wall. The hand-held shower nozzle sprayed Iain's shoes when Jacinta's contractions were at their height. The waves of powerful cramps hit her hard and fast.

Iain's face had assumed a fierce mantle that was growing grimmer by the minute. Noni waited for the explosion, knowing it floated like a black cloud over all their heads. She'd been hoping they'd all be saved by Jacinta hitting transition and then the urge to push.

Finally, Jacinta gave a strange, strangled scream and Iain jumped. His hand slapped the wall so that Noni jumped in turn. Obviously, he couldn't stand it any more. 'Outside,' he mouthed, and she stood and walked through the bathroom door, glad he'd get out of the room because his stress had started to affect Jacinta.

'That's it.' His hands crossed in a cutting motion. 'I'm not putting her through any more of this. Get her an epidural.'

Noni raised her eyebrows. 'If that's what she wants, of course I can arrange that. But my instincts tell me she's going through transition. She's almost in second stage. Are you sure it's Jacinta who can't stand it?'

'Get it!'

Noni turned her back on him. 'Not unless she asks me for it.' She went back through the door to the bathroom. 'Jacinta? How are you going?'

'I want to go home,' she wailed. 'I don't want to do this any more. Daddy, help me . . .'

Iain took her hand and glared at Noni. 'We're getting you an epidural.'

'Oooh.'

'I don't think so,' Noni said, and heard Jacinta grunt in an undeniable downward urge. Relief swamped her because she knew they'd made it. And just in time, because Iain had finally cracked. Her denial to rush to do his bidding had shocked him.

He blinked. 'Are you mad? I'm telling you she wants one now.'

Jacinta grunted again in that same downward urge. 'Well, she'll have to wait until after the baby is born, then, Doctor, if I'm not mistaken.' She crouched down beside the girl. 'Jaz. What were you feeling with that last contraction?'

Her eyes fixed on Noni's as she tried to transmit the feelings she didn't recognise. 'I have to go to the toilet. I want to push.' She glanced around a little wildly. Lurched on the ball. 'Get me up from here.'

'Okay, sweetie. It's okay. This is the part we talked about, where we can finally do something with the contractions.' Noni leaned down and firmly took Jacinta's hand to help her stand. 'Up you come and I'll sit beside you on my stool. We'll take your bikini bottoms off.'

During the next forty minutes, Iain grew paler with every passing second. He kept glancing at Noni as if to say, *When will this hell end?*

Just like any other male, Noni thought. Or any support person who watched someone they loved working hard, in labour. Noni kept sending him reassuring glances, but they missed most of her intended target, judging by the strained face opposite her.

When Jacinta complained about the pressure, she agreed, and Iain rolled his eyes. 'I know it's hard, sweetie. That sharp, burning feeling is where your body is telling you to push.'

Jacinta grunted and groaned her way through the contraction. 'It's not working. Why is it so slow?' she said through gritted teeth.

'Everything is stretching to make way for the baby. You're doing beautifully. You don't want it to pop out – you want your baby to ease out gently.' Noni wiped the beads of perspiration off Jacinta's brow with a washcloth dipped in icy water.

Jacinta threw her head up and glared at them. 'Drink!'

Noni smiled at the economical request. 'We're getting down to serious business here.'

'Don't you think we should move her onto the bed?' Iain looked to be gauging if he could carry his daughter out of the bathroom.

Noni raised one eyebrow quizzically without bothering to answer. Eventually, she saw the dawn of realisation that Noni was quite content to have his grandchild born in the shower. His voice cracked. 'Jacinta, baby, I think you should get up now and come lie on the bed.'

'I'm not going anywhere. Noni, it hur-rts.' Another huge push later, the first crescent of black hair could be seen.

Noni nodded to herself when she heard Cathy outside the door shifting the infant resuscitation trolley closer to the door. Cathy would have recognised the noises too.

Noni reached behind her and picked up a mirror. She propped it in front of Jacinta. 'Have a look, Jaz. See the baby's head.'

Jacinta glanced up from where she'd been concentrating on the floor and suddenly she saw it. Went still and stared. Her mouth stretched in a stunned oval. 'She's got black hair.' With eyes glued to the progress she could see, she bore down with gritted teeth.

Iain swayed. 'For God's sake, where's Soams?'

The bathroom door opened. 'I'm here, Iain. Looks like you three have been swimming.' The older doctor looked across at Noni with a twinkle in his eye and Cathy waved from behind him. 'Do you need us, Sister?'

Noni smiled and shook her head before concentrating on the girl in front of her. 'Okay, Jaz. Slow it down. Gentle now, and pant. Little pushes. Good girl.' Her gloved hand hovered under the baby's head without touching it. 'Lovely.'

Iain had looked like he'd been having the worst hour of his life. Then, suddenly, miraculously, it changed. His face softened and relaxed as he watched his grandchild's head finally being born, soon followed by the anterior shoulder, and then the other shoulder.

'Reach down and slip your fingers under baby's armpits, Jaz.'

Jacinta's hands came tentatively down to touch her child and, with a final push, the baby slithered out into Jacinta and Noni's hands. Jacinta automatically lifted her child to her chest and cradled her.

Iain sagged against the wall, and for a moment there Noni thought he would fall, but then he straightened and smiled. Like a sunbeam, he smiled. She could tell he couldn't believe the strain and stress were over.

He looked weary. Bone-shatteringly exhausted, and his glance met Noni's as he shook his head. He brushed away the moisture from his eyes and met Noni's smile across the bathroom floor again. He didn't say the words but mouthed them clearly enough for her to understand. 'Nice delivery.'

She pretended to glare at him. He knew she didn't deliver babies – mothers birthed them. He also knew she disliked the word 'delivery', but that was his retaliation and she let him have it. They'd won.

'Congratulations, Jacinta. What have you got?' Dr Soams chuckled as Noni placed a warm bunny rug over mother and daughter to help Jacinta keep the slippery infant against her.

Jacinta stared at the tiny screwed-up face and then tentatively kissed her baby. 'It's over. I did it.' Then she glanced between the baby's legs. 'A girl.' She let out her breath in a big sigh. Then she looked up at Noni and her father. 'What are you two crying about?' she asked in surprise, then she gathered the little scrap closer to her chest. 'You're going to have to go through this one day, kid. But it's worth it.'

Noni looked at Iain as Dr Soams declared, 'Jacinta looks a hundred per cent compared to her father. You look like you've been run over by a truck, Iain.'

Iain looked rueful and Noni stifled a laugh. *So much for the obstetrician.*

Chapter Forty-one

Jacinta

Jacinta couldn't believe that this tiny and precious infant snuggled against her skin was hers. She glanced at the clock on the wall. Two hours ago. How had that happened? It was almost four o'clock in the afternoon. She had no idea where the time had gone. And she couldn't believe the wave of absolute love that surged and swelled so high within her. Then the tiny features blurred as her eyes filled with tears.

OMG. Her baby. Her Olivia. Her arms tightened and the scent of her baby's skin filled her senses. Olivia Winsome Noni Adele – McCloud, of course. Though she hadn't told Noni and Win, yet. She'd been going to put her mum's name second, but when she'd played with the letters it came out OWNA – OWNA home, and that was what she was going to provide for this tiny baby, so she'd never be without a place to come back to. She would show her baby that a girl could do anything, be anyone, and achieve goals that fulfilled them. Her dad would help, but only to get her started.

She'd go to uni, use his backing to set herself up, then she and Olivia would conquer the world. She would be a mother to be proud of – not right now, but in the future – and these early months with Olivia needed to be savoured because the time she had now was so precious.

Then Noni appeared at her door.

'What a beautiful picture – mother and baby tucked up in bed together, resting.'

Noni came to stand beside the bed and Jacinta dragged her dreamy thoughts away from her daughter's future and smiled at the woman who had helped her achieve this miracle. Noni looked more tired than Jacinta felt. She guessed her dad had been pretty exhausting.

Jacinta grinned up at her midwife and friend. 'Isn't she beautiful?'

'No question there. She's gorgeous.' Noni moved closer to the bed and touched Olivia's cheek with one gentle finger. 'Stunning, she is. Though still a little blue around the edges, with her hands and feet, but that will come good.'

Jacinta felt Noni give her shoulder a tiny poke. 'Go you, with that amazing breastfeed in the birthing suite. You were a natural, and so was Olivia.'

Jacinta smiled. It had felt a bit weird, those soft but insistent sucks at her breast, but Noni had draped the sheet so no one could see. And Olivia had stayed there for ages. But yes, it had felt strangely right to see what her tiny little girl could do. Jacinta still couldn't believe her baby had actually shifted and wriggled until she'd put herself on the nipple – just like a puppy would if left alone. And it hadn't hurt. More crazy mother stuff she hadn't thought she'd be feeling.

She looked at Noni and gave the tiniest shrug so as not to

disturb her daughter. 'Breastfeeding isn't so bad. It just felt right for her to be there and to feel her against me.'

Noni's smile made Jacinta feel like a queen. How did she do that? Make her proud to be herself? But then again, she guessed she had done pretty well.

Noni said, 'Sometimes, it happens like that for people who don't think breastfeeding will suit them. As long as you're happy, I think it's wonderful. And Olivia knows what she wants – just like her mother does.'

Good. Because she was going to be in control of her life and so was her daughter. 'I can't believe it's all over and she's mine.' Jacinta stroked the tiny palm until Olivia's fingers curled and grasped her larger one, and another one of those huge swells of emotion rolled over her.

She smiled at Noni. 'I want to show her off. When are Win and Harley coming in?'

Noni glanced at her watch. 'They'll be up after tea when you've had a rest, but maybe they could come earlier. Something tells me you won't be sleeping – you're too excited. You're a very clever girl.' She leaned over and kissed her, then Olivia. 'I know I've already said it, but it's worth saying again. You were awesome in labour.'

Jacinta felt the heat in her cheeks. It embarrassed her, even though she really loved hearing Noni say that.

'It's so exciting to see the both of you here,' Noni continued. 'But I'm nearly ready to head home, Jaz. Do you need help with anything before I go?'

She shook her head. 'No, thanks, Noni.' She just wanted to stare at her daughter. And maybe feed her again when she woke up properly. 'I can ask someone else if we need help.'

'Your father will probably be in before us tonight. Bye, Jaz.'

Noni scooped up her bag from beside the bed and waved as she headed for the door. There was something sad in her voice – but she was gone before Jacinta could ask. Dad was probably being a pain again. Who would have thought he was an obstetrician? And he hadn't told Noni. Jacinta shook her head. *Stupid*. He was so dead.

Then she looked at her daughter and forgot about Noni and her dad. She had a fleeting thought about how she could get anonymously in contact with Pedro to let him know they were both well. She owed him that. But she wouldn't tell Iain or he'd worry.

She could understand her dad's concerns about Pedro and his underworld connections better now. As a parent it was her responsibility to keep her daughter safe from danger and if she had her way, Olivia wouldn't even know that world existed – or that she'd been conceived there. Funny how being a parent changed your views.

Chapter Forty-two

Noni

When Noni arrived home, Iain sat waiting for her on the back verandah.

'Congratulations, Grandpa,' she said in greeting, giving him a plastic smile. He looked startled she'd directed a comment at him. *Keep trying to figure me out, mister.* She didn't stop, and pushed through the door. 'Aunt Win?'

She heard Iain follow her in. 'She said she'd be back soon. She's gone to buy something pink for the baby. So you'll have to talk to me.'

Noni smiled sweetly at him, resisting the urge to poke him firmly in the chest. No way was she touching him. 'I don't have to do anything, Doctor.'

'No, you don't. But I would like you to at least give me a chance to say thank you.' He obviously felt the need for contact because his arms were warm and gentle as he turned her to face him.

She wriggled out of his hold and he grimaced. The feel of him touching her made her traitorous body want to step closer, but she supposed she'd have to get used to that and not give in. He'd lied to her face. He couldn't be trusted. And she wasn't fighting for him any more. Without trust there was nothing.

He was watching her with those blue eyes of his, the sea-blue deeper today, with the emotion from Olivia's birth still in them. She'd almost hugged him back there in the birthing unit when his granddaughter had been born. She'd seen the glint of tears he blinked away, read the release of fear, and saw his tense shoulders drop in relief that it was over and mother and baby were safe. Just a father and grandfather experiencing new feelings. No sign of the distant obstetrician there.

'You're very good at what you do, Noni. I learned a lot today and Jacinta and I are really glad you were there.'

Really. You don't say. 'Personally, I think you're darn lucky I was. Or your daughter might have had an epidural she didn't want, and not realised what she could achieve under her own steam.'

She paused, aware that what she said next was the most important message she could give someone like him who could influence a woman's life as she gave birth. 'Can you see now how a woman can absorb so much faith in her own ability to raise her children from her labour? The decisions she's allowed to make, the respect she's afforded, and achievement of the birth regardless of how that baby arrives – these experiences are so important as lessons to help in the tough times to come. Raising children is harder than labour. It's not just about today, you know. You shouldn't rush to put limitations on a mother unless she asks for help.'

Her words hung in the air, and they both remembered his struggle over allowing Jacinta to choose her own pain management.

'You're right. I was wrong.' Then he raised his hands in surrender and smiled at her. Her resolve wavered further when he said, 'I hear you.'

Noni felt like screaming. Couldn't she just let off steam without him agreeing?

But he went on. 'You were a warrior. Jacinta was magnificent. And I was the fly in the ointment.'

Shoot. He was making this hard. 'Well, you were a mess.' She needed to get out of here before she crumbled. 'Harley will be back from school in a minute and I want to have a shower before he gets home.'

He looked at her and she didn't stay to hear if he had anything else to add. Now she felt mean and that just made her even more cross.

Noni took the stairs two at a time without looking back, but she could feel his eyes on her. He'd lied. He'd pretended to be a stockbroker, then a surgeon when he'd been caught out. He'd brushed off all the times she could have talked to him about her concerns for the maternity unit. All reasons to loathe him.

Still, that had been close. She'd really wanted to ask him why he couldn't have told her, why all the hiding? Maybe even throw herself into his arms. But sometime during the day she'd realised it wasn't going to work. This was where her lack of experience with other relationships came into play. She had no flipping idea how to understand what men meant when they said something.

Iain wasn't going to commit himself fully to her, and she couldn't risk changing her life for the short term if it didn't work out. If she chose to enter a relationship then she was going to do it right next time. Engagement. Marriage. She and Harley couldn't afford to get hurt and abandoned in Sydney after she and Iain imploded in their non-progressive relationship.

At least she could tell herself she had tried to make it work for the last week. Had tried talking to him. It was harder that their attraction had culminated in them making love, but she couldn't regret the bitter sweetness of those memories, because she knew now how it felt to make love with someone you cared about.

In the bathroom, the hot needles of water soothed away the tensions of the night and morning. As Noni slowly rotated under the shower, she knew without a doubt they didn't have a two-sided relationship. She'd been building hope over something that just wasn't there. She'd fallen for Iain before he had promised her anything, so it was no use complaining that he'd misled her.

It had only been six weeks, she reminded herself. The memories would fade. Though it had been long enough to damage her heart. It had been naïve to expect a commitment from a man who didn't even understand her world. She'd been so silly to fantasise about happily ever after, like some sort of Cinderella dream. She knew women who'd had stable relationships for years, had children, and still chose not to have a wedding. Why did she think he'd been talking eternity the few times he'd hinted at a future for them?

Imagine if she'd taken Harley out of school and moved to Sydney with Iain, only then to find out how little she meant to him – how unequal the relationship was. She shuddered. She wouldn't be making that mistake again.

She turned off the shower and stepped out, thoughts tumbling around in her mind.

Iain and Jacinta would be gone by this time next week. *All I have to do is distance myself from Iain and start preparing Harley for their departure,* she decided, and sighed.

If only it were that easy.

*

At the hospital later that evening, after Win and Harley had left, Noni felt exhausted from trying not to catch Iain's eye, and wearied from the emotions of the last eighteen hours. She'd been up since two am – no wonder she felt shattered. Plus, it had been an incredible journey with Jacinta through her labour. She glanced once more at the young woman in the bed nursing her baby as if she'd been holding tiny infants for years. It was so satisfying to share this time with Jacinta, but awkward sharing it with Iain when she knew they were at odds.

Maybe it was just because they sat opposite each other across Jacinta's bed. She gave up and rose from the chair to make her own departure. 'I'll leave you with your dad, Jacinta, and see you tomorrow when I come to work.'

'Noni, before you go.' Jacinta looked straight at her father. 'What happens when I leave the hospital? When were you planning to go back to Sydney, Dad?'

Iain shifted in his seat, looking only at his daughter. 'I expect we'll go back Saturday, once you feel up to travelling.'

Noni had known it would come, but hearing it stated as a fact hit her like a blow to her chest. She looked away from Jacinta but knew the young woman had seen her distress. She gathered her bag, ostensibly to search for her keys, and moistened her lips. Her fingers gripped the keys as if someone were threatening to take them off her and the pain from the metal teeth digging into her hands felt strangely appropriate.

'You two will sort it out. I have to go. Goodnight.' She waved without meeting their eyes and had to force herself not to run out the door.

Chapter Forty-three

Jacinta

Jacinta looked at her father, who had turned his head to follow Noni's retreating figure. She had no idea what he was thinking, but from the way his eyes seemed riveted on Noni's departing figure he was definitely into her. 'Any plans there?'

He turned back to face her, his expression bland. 'What do you mean?'

Jacinta wondered again how he could hide his feelings so easily. Everyone seemed to know when she was angry or frightened or freaked out. And Noni's face said everything. 'You watch her all the time.'

When he didn't reply, she sighed. Was he thick or was he pretending he didn't know? 'She needs an obstetrician and you're one. Did you think of helping her out?'

'I understand Noni has problems. That the hospital here has problems. But no. My life is in Sydney.' His gaze never wavered. 'And I don't want to talk about Noni.'

Jacinta shrugged again. 'Sure. Posh house makes you happy, but it's a shame, that's all.'

'It's not about the house,' he said cryptically, and she raised one brow at him.

Then he said, 'I was proud to be your father today, Jaz.' And diverted by his quiet, emphatic tone, she forgot about Noni. She looked at the truth in his eyes and then her beautiful daughter asleep in her arms. When she turned her gaze back to her dad she smiled with real joy.

'She's amazing, isn't she?'

'You're amazing.' His voice was very low, but she could feel herself blush.

Then she tilted her head and studied him, remembering moments during the birth, which coloured her voice with amusement. 'Labour's pretty intense. You'd think someone like you would have known that.'

He agreed ruefully. 'I had no idea I'd feel so helpless. It's pretty different to what I'd imagined from the support person's side. Probably the worst, most helpless feeling in the world.' He shrugged. 'I don't do helpless well.'

'I thought it was fast.' She shrugged. 'And Olivia's here safe. When can I go home to Win's?'

He looked at her with that strange expression on his face again. 'Don't see why you can't go tomorrow, if you like.'

She nodded. 'Good. Aimee and Kylie are coming tomorrow morning to see Olivia. We could go home after that.'

He lifted his head and stared straight at her. 'We'll go *home* to Sydney when you're ready. Maybe a couple of days after that.'

*

When she carried Olivia into Win's guesthouse, Jacinta did feel like she'd come home, despite what her father said. She couldn't believe she'd only been here for six weeks – it felt like six years. But she did understand that her dad had put his life on hold for her.

First time in seventeen years he'd done something for her, so she didn't feel too bad for him.

As she settled back into the household, she decided it was fun being the person everyone wanted to be with. Not something she had a lot of experience with before this, and she understood Olivia was the real drawcard, but it felt wicked good.

Dressing her baby in her new clothes and watching her sweet, funny expressions were such a joy, and she had to pinch herself that life could be this great. She tried not to expect it all to implode again.

Harley spent a lot of time sitting on the floor near her chair in the lounge room when Olivia was awake. She looked at his bent head as he watched Olivia having tummy time on the floor beside him.

'She can lift her head up way better,' Harley said, and Olivia, as if she understood, stretched her neck and turned her face towards his voice.

'Your mum said to make sure I put her on her belly a couple of times a day so she could use those muscles. I don't want her to get one of those flat-sided heads babies get when they sleep on their back.'

Harley pulled a face. 'One of the kids at school's little brother has a flat head. Can she sleep on the side?'

'If I'm watching her she can. But otherwise she has to sleep on her back in case she chucks.'

Harley wrinkled his freckled nose. 'Why do babies throw up so much? It's gross.'

'No idea. She's not too bad. My friend Aimee's baby spews all the time.'

'Funny how they're different.' His little face turned thoughtful and Jacinta wondered absently what new lightbulb he'd come up with. The kid had a mind like a steel trap.

Then he said, 'Though she's the same as me.'

Jacinta looked at her tiny daughter all dressed in a pink Bunnykins jumpsuit and then the little boy with scuffed knees and Transformer T-shirt. 'How's she the same as you?'

'She doesn't have a dad, either.'

Jacinta thought about that, not wanting to rush the answer. Finally she said, 'Her dad's dead.' And for the first time, she understood why her mother had lied to her. Jacinta couldn't say, 'Her dad's a scum bag', because then Harley might think she was assuming his dad was too. Noni hadn't said that and Harley didn't need to think it.

'But she's got a granddad. And you and Win and Noni, even if we live in a different place to you. That's a pretty good extended family. We'll come visit.'

Harley crossed his arms and narrowed his eyes. 'You should stay here. Iain should stay here.'

Poor kid. 'You know people don't stay here forever when they come to visit at Win's.'

He put down his head. 'I know. But nobody's ever stayed this long or been fun.'

Except for the strain between Noni and her dad. That wasn't so much fun. Even Jacinta noticed how Noni avoided Iain as much as she could considering they were living in the same house. Maybe it would be better for everyone if she and Iain went back to Sydney. She'd miss them all. Even the kid. And it was a little scary to think of having Olivia totally her responsibility without Win and Noni as backup.

Maybe she could stay here and Iain could go back. Just for a while.

She sighed. It would be so much easier if her dad decided to move here.

Chapter Forty-four

Noni

For Noni, Friday arrived slowly, sliding towards her like a snail, without a silver line. She wanted to scream for Iain to leave, even though deep inside she dreaded it, but they all knew Jacinta wasn't in a hurry to go.

The only good news was that a temporary replacement obstetrician had agreed to do a three-month stint at Burra while a last-ditch recruitment drive was carried out. And work had been busy as usual and she was almost glad to be home, despite Iain being there.

She sat on the chair outside on the verandah to slip off her shoes and was wriggling her toes when she heard something that made her look up.

Jacinta pushed open the screen door and sat down next to her. 'Noni? Can I come to classes with you tonight and show off Olivia?'

'Of course you can. I wanted to ask but wasn't sure if you'd be too tired.'

Jacinta rolled her eyes. 'I've been home four days and Olivia's only woken once for a night feed. I even went for a walk today pushing the old pram Win had in the shed. I reckon I'm almost back to my pre-pregnant self.'

Noni hadn't slowed up much after Harley's birth, either. There was something to be said for having babies young. 'I'm sure everyone would love to see both of you. Just remember, everyone's going to ask you about the labour.'

She looked askance at that. 'Not the gory bits?'

Noni laughed. 'Especially the gory bits.'

Jacinta shrugged. 'I just won't tell them stuff if I don't want to.'

Noni smiled to herself this time, then stood up and patted the younger woman on the shoulder. 'Keep that strength. I know I won't have to worry about you. Sometimes, I believe if the things we go through are hard maybe it's because we'll need that experience later. To help us handle anything life throws at us.'

Jacinta screwed up her face as though considering that statement, and rolled her eyes. 'Yeah, right.' She raised her hand. 'Noni, before you go . . .'

Noni stopped with one hand on the screen door.

'What are you doing about your relationship with Dad?'

Noni felt her face stiffen instantly – like melted wax dropped in cold water. She thought of launching into a big explanation. She thought of saying, 'I haven't decided.' Then she looked at the no-nonsense face of the girl in front of her and thought of the truth. What could she do about a man who didn't need her in his life?

Get on with her own.

'Nothing.' She grimaced and looked at the floor. She pulled open the door again and stepped inside, straight into the chest of the man she'd just given up on.

His arms tightened around her for a moment before they fell away. For that fleeting instant she felt better.

They both stepped back. Noni stepped too far and tripped on the screen door ledge, nearly falling through the flippin' door. Iain caught her shoulders to correct her balance, and this time his hands took longer to let go.

Noni closed her eyes briefly before gently loosening his fingers to sweep his hand off her shoulder. 'Thank you,' she said stiffly, and moved past him into the house. She hated that. Why did she have to be the awkward one? The one who almost fell over? It should have been him, though he moved like a cat so she doubted that would happen.

Then again, maybe if the positions had been reversed, she would have let him drop.

Fifteen minutes later Noni came downstairs ready to head out to the class. She found Iain waiting in the hallway.

'Do you mind if I come too?' he asked.

Great. Why wouldn't life kick her when she was down? 'They're your classes, too, although it would have been a courtesy if you'd mentioned your profession to everyone in the beginning.'

'I've apologised for that.' He looked ready to launch into a big explanation and she so wasn't willing to go there.

Noni resisted the urge to scream. 'I don't want to rehash anything, Iain. Don't wallow in it. You're the one who wants to live on the surface of life. Just let me go to my class and do my job without giving me a hard time.'

He didn't say anything, just stared thoughtfully at her until she turned away.

Over her shoulder she asked, 'Is Jacinta ready?'

'We'll take my car.'

She snorted and raised her eyebrows. 'Will you?'

'We should all go in my car.'

She picked up her helmet. 'Right.' She pushed open the screen and strode off to get her motorbike.

When she unlocked the door to the antenatal classroom, she threw the keys on the table so hard they skidded across the top and down onto the floor. Yep. That pretty well summed up her life. Fast lane with two men and then *splat*.

She leaned down to pick up the keys and sighed. At least she had ten minutes to herself before they arrived. She flung open a couple of windows and rearranged chairs with aggressive precision. By the time the room had been organised to within an inch of its life, she felt better. Which was lucky, as people began to gather in the car park.

Paul and Suzie shuffled in, and Noni noticed Suzie held her stomach gingerly. She raised her eyebrows at the couple. 'Having a few pains, you two?'

Suzie breathed out and let go of her stomach. 'They've been coming and going for a few days now. I've still got three weeks to go and it's driving me crazy. Paul keeps trying to shove me into the car to come to the hospital. Talk some sense into him, Noni.'

She glanced at Paul. 'He's just trying to do the right thing.'

He looked nervous and Noni remembered the feeling of not knowing when labour was ready to really kick in from her own experience. Even after all the books she'd read she'd been scared she'd miss the early signs. Boy had that been a dumb idea. Nobody missed that feeling. Though sometimes other people talked you out of listening.

'She'll know when she's ready, Paul,' she reassured him. 'It could take days or even weeks for labour to truly start. You'll drive each other crazy if you worry all the time.'

They both slumped with dejection at that, and Noni tilted her head in sympathy. 'Some people get these pains for ages beforehand, but the good news is it usually speeds up the true labour when it does arrive.' She turned to Paul. 'It's your job to keep the car filled up with petrol for a quick getaway when the time finally arrives.'

Paul ran his hand over his chin. 'Well, can I have one of those cord clamp things? I'm sure Junior's going to pop his head out as we go over the traffic bridge, and then where will we be?'

Noni laughed. 'At least on the right side of the river and the placenta can stay attached. You only need a cord clamp if you cut something. But I know what you mean. It's a worry.' She smiled at Suzie. 'Have faith. You'll know when you need to hit the road. Just wait for her,' she pointed at Paul, 'she'll tell you in no uncertain terms to get the damn car. Now!'

They both grinned at that.

More people arrived and Noni smiled and welcomed them and savoured that feeling of friendship, excitement and satisfaction of helping a well-meshed group of people preparing for a life event. Finally, when everyone was assembled, she said, 'As you can see, we've had our first baby.'

The prospective mothers and fathers *oohed* and *aahed*, much to Jacinta's obvious satisfaction, and Noni smiled to herself. She loved this part.

'Olivia was born on Sunday and I thought we'd ask Jacinta to describe her memories of labour while I draw a timeline on the board. It's a kind of revision for the classes. Is that okay, Jacinta?' The girl nodded.

As Jacinta recounted her own memories, Noni marked the times of changes, progress and options used to gain pain relief on the board. Noni couldn't help noticing Iain's pensiveness. It appeared his own memories were different to Jacinta's perspective on things. She wondered if the whole experience would make him a better obstetrician in the future or if he'd give up obstetrics altogether. She smiled bitterly to herself. Maybe take up surgery.

She hoped he'd change for the better, but she'd never know because he was leaving.

A kaleidoscope of their past conversations; contrasting opinions in class; catching the other's eye and a shared smile flashed through her mind. Moments that twisted and swooped in her chest like a flock of birds doing group ballet in the sky. Her throat closed over and she swallowed. Somehow, she'd get through the evening.

The snap of the last window lock had an air of finality about it. Would this be her last class here? If the maternity unit shut she supposed they could still run classes, except that the families would have to go to the bigger hospitals to actually give birth.

Maybe the new doctor would fall in love with the place and stay. Although, there had been some talk at work today that he might be going to pull out. No. He wouldn't. Everything would stay the same.

'You're dreamin', girl,' she muttered.

'What are you dreaming about?'

She hated that. Why couldn't the guy cough or something? Noni's intake of breath seemed to go on forever.

'Well, Iain, it wasn't you.' She stopped and frowned. 'Though, it could have been now that you're an obstetrician.'

It was his turn to frown. 'I don't understand you.'

Noni gave him a perfunctory smile as she brushed by him. 'So? What's new? Goodnight.' She deliberately pushed past him without closing the door. Or even locking it. One thing she knew about Iain, he wouldn't follow her until he'd ensured the place was shut properly and the lights were off. She didn't want to tie herself to someone like that, anyway.

Jacinta sat in his car with the interior light on as she patted Olivia. Noni waved before she pulled on her helmet. She didn't know why she felt an urgency to get out onto the road before Iain caught up with her. But it was definitely there.

The engine roared to life just as he walked up beside the bike. He said something, but she pointed to her helmet and revved the bike noisily again before she accelerated away from him.

It felt good for the first twenty seconds and then her mood flattened again. She turned left and then right and pulled up beside the river to allow a minute of self-pity to wash over her.

She wished she'd never met Iain McCloud.

She gave a half-laugh, half-sob. That wasn't true. He'd been a window to a place where there was more to life than being a mother, a niece and a midwife. She'd wanted the experience and should be thankful it had held some beautiful moments she could remember one day when it didn't hurt so much. It just seemed such a shame they'd shut that window. And pulled the blinds.

She started the bike again. It was no use staying here to mope. She made a very careful adjustment to prevent the bike sliding sideways. No way was she doing the damsel in distress this time.

When Noni arrived home, she could hear Iain on the phone. It sounded serious and she felt her stomach sink. *No more crises tonight, please.*

She went in search of her aunt. 'I'm going to see Harley and then I'm off to bed. Do you know what time they're leaving tomorrow?'

Her aunt looked worriedly at her. 'They may not be leaving yet. Greg has rung a few times and asked Iain to fill the gap while they try to find the new O and G man. Apparently, the one they'd lined up can't come. Iain must be considering it. He asked if they could stay here another couple of weeks.' She glanced at her niece's face. 'I could say no if that would be easier for you.'

'And have Harley never speak to me again?' Noni bit her lip. 'At least someone will be happy.' She patted her aunt. 'It's okay, I'll stop being a martyr soon.'

She'd see Iain tomorrow at breakfast and that would be soon enough to know if the torture was going to continue.

The next morning at breakfast she found out it was.

'I'm staying for another two weeks.' Iain looked at Noni as he passed the marmalade, but she refused to meet his eyes.

'Great.' *Hell.* 'I'm going out.'

'Stay.' He laid his fingers over her arm. 'I need to talk to you, Noni.'

'Well, I don't want to listen.' She glanced down at her arm and hated the frisson of awareness he could transmit with that light hold. She was a basket case. How was she supposed to last another fortnight?

'Jacinta said she'd mind Harley if you and I go out this afternoon. I'd really like to speak to you somewhere we won't be interrupted.'

'Why would that be, Iain?' This time she did meet his eyes, and what she saw there confused her even more. She didn't think she could ride this roller-coaster much longer.

'Come and find out. Let's drive somewhere and go for a walk. We need to talk. There's something I need to discuss with you.'

Ironically, the weather turned on a glorious autumn afternoon down by the river. Noni could have done with black clouds and lightning.

The weeping willows swept the water's edge, with bright-green ribbons of leaves hanging along the bank. The light shining through the taller gums dappled the grass with shifting polka dots, and birds trilled as if everything was right with the world. Now that was a joke.

In the far distance the constant baaing of sheep drifted on the breeze. This was Noni's favourite spot for thinking, and as usual, there wasn't a soul around. Now, after Iain being here with her, she'd probably ruined her best retreat forever, too.

It felt strange to be with Iain somewhere not related to either of their children or work. Win had insisted she throw a blanket and some nibbles into a bag before she left for her weekend, instructing Noni on where to find the thermos. Iain had just put everything down in a pile under a gum tree and was watching her warily. Well, she was wary too.

They stood for a while, neither of them knowing where to start, then Noni threw a rock into the river. The game that started out as desultory ended up competitive. Iain threw a larger-than-normal rock close to the water's edge and Noni sucked in her breath as the backsplash flooded her face.

'Hey, that wet me!'

Iain grinned with satisfaction and Noni narrowed her eyes and retaliated. The water splattered his chest. He raised his eyebrows and picked up another rock, but she got her next one in first.

'Enough!' Noni laughed and stepped back to wipe the droplets of water from her face. That had been cathartic. There was something steadying about cold water on your face. Funny that. 'So, what do you want to talk to me about, Iain?'

He dropped his next round of ammunition and the stones clattered at his feet. 'Can we sit down first? Please.' He held out his hand.

She stared at his long, outstretched fingers, deciding if she needed the closeness for the cost of the pain, before, reluctantly, she placed her own in his care.

'Thank you,' he said quietly. He squeezed her hand gently and smiled, and she felt the ache in her heart tighten.

Noni couldn't smile back, but for some stupid reason she couldn't look away from his face. Something was different. As if they had both just discovered something new in the other person and magic had crept up on them – despite the fact that she'd already given up.

They walked slowly, careful not to trip without watching their steps, before halting beside their supplies at the tree.

'I'll spread out the rug, shall I?' She looked down at their hands, not willing to be the first to disengage.

He must have been thinking the same thing. 'I suppose I'll have to let you go.' Iain's voice came deeper than usual and she nodded her head, reluctant to agree out loud.

'It's there – isn't it, Noni? It's not just me feeling something between us when we touch?' He stroked his thumb down the edge of her hand and she turned her head to watch the goosebumps on her arm.

She bit her lip. 'Maybe that's our problem.' She looked up at him and his eyes were a deep, startling blue, like a too-deep ocean she wanted to dip into. She was over this horrible teetering. 'Should we go with our feelings instead of talking about it, Iain?'

He opened his arms. 'Will you come here?'

She moved to stand in the circle of his arms, rested her cheek against his shirt and closed her eyes. When he wrapped his arms around her she sighed and listened to his heart *tum-tumping*.

It so wasn't fair. Why did she feel that this man's heart was the one she was destined to beat in time to? Why did she feel suddenly safe when previously safety had never been an issue? They had spent – or wasted – so much time at conversational cross-purposes. Was it really so simple? Stick their bodies together and they stopped creating problems.

'Do many people come along here?' Iain asked quietly.

Noni's cheeks warmed. 'Are you propositioning me?'

He raised those eyebrows. 'I'd like to kiss you, but should we go somewhere less exposed?'

She glanced around. 'It's not a popular place because of the stinging nettles, but we can watch out for that.'

His arms loosened. 'Stinging nettles? You're kidding!'

Such a city slicker. 'It makes good tea.' She pulled him along behind the tree a little way until she found a small hollow free of nettles. It was screened from the path and golden shafts of sunlight from the canopy above danced and flickered on the ground.

'Are you fond of nymphs and satyrs, Iain?' She intended to tease, but after it had been said she couldn't help her own imaginings. She had to smile at the mental picture of Iain with horns and a tail.

'If I have my own wood sprite to protect me.' He glanced around and looked dubiously at the stinging nettles. 'The country can be uncomfortable for we urban dwellers, but I'll have to trust you to save me.'

'I'll make no promises.' Their eyes met again and the undercurrents were understood. She spread the rug and stepped onto it, holding out her hand. 'Welcome to my fairy grotto. Do you dare to enter?'

The blue of his eyes grew dark and dangerous. Deliciously so. 'I love a dare,' he said, and took her hand.

There it was again. She could almost feel his power seeping up her arm. When he kneeled and pulled her down to join him, it seemed natural to lie with him there, under the trees, wrapped in his arms.

His first kiss settled like a gentle feather and brushed her lips for the space of a breath. She sighed and nestled into him, curling her arm around his neck to pull him closer.

'You drive me crazy, wood sprite.' His eyes stared into hers and she could see his intent. Good. That was her intent, too.

'Stop talking and kiss me,' she demanded softly, and he chuckled before claiming her mouth again to meet her needs – and his.

This kiss was a study in slow and deep, an erotic duel of two opposing forces finding common ground. It moved to a faster pace that demanded more passion and fed upon itself before they drew away. The next kiss started slow but filled her body with fierce longings, her mind with swirling sensations and her spirit with a strange freedom. It didn't end until she ran out of breath and she had to pull away. But she went back.

For a while there, the trees and river disappeared, and the world became a gliding, swooping maelstrom of hunger and need. In a blur of sensation, emotion, and need, her hands sought to feel and stroke the strong body beside hers. Savouring the strength of his neck and shoulders, the solid steel of his upper arms and the molded musculature of his chest.

His hands roved her still-clothed body, and everywhere he touched seemed to spring into flames until her needs surged and built and made her plead for more. At the danger point, their hands stilled, and a long, burning look passed between them – the point of no return.

'Enough,' Iain said, though his hand tightened on hers.

Noni knew it could be the last time they ever made love. Why not? As long as . . .

'Boy scout?'

Her question made him smile and pat his wallet. 'Yes, but no.'

She decided she was glad as they held each other until their hearts stopped pounding and gentleness returned and they could do what they had come to do. To talk.

So they lay side by side and finally, to her relief, he asked about her work, her worries and all the things he'd adroitly and not-so-adroitly avoided when she'd wanted to share her worries with him. But he didn't talk about why they were here.

After a while, they fell silent until Noni began to notice the twigs and small stones only partially shielded by the blanket. His eyes were half closed as he watched her fidget.

'Iain?'

'Hmm?'

'This bed has suddenly become quite lumpy.'

Iain half laughed and rolled onto his back to pull her on top of him. 'Let me look at you.' He ran his hands up the sides of her face and cupped her cheeks. 'You are incredible.'

She stared down at this man who had permeated her life with such impact. Yes, she loved him. Probably would always love him. They should be able to work things out. She didn't want to think further than that.

He slid his hand behind her neck and pulled her face down to his for a swift kiss.

'Perhaps, we should devour some of that food instead of each other,' she suggested.

'Sounds good. Where did we leave our stuff?' She started to giggle then sank her cheek on his chest and laughed into the solid wall.

They stepped out from the shelter of the trees and found their supplies. Noni reopened the blanket in a patch of late-afternoon sunlight and unpacked the hamper. They ate, leaning against each other and staring at the ripples in the water. Finally, Iain cleared his throat and broached what he'd wanted to say.

'I don't want to go back to Sydney without you, Noni.'

So, it had come. He did want her with him. But on what terms? Noni waited for her heartbeat to settle back to normal. How easy it would be just to say yes, and not worry about the future or the lies or the risk. It was hard to imagine Iain not being there, but she had more to fight for.

'Some things would have to change,' she said. 'I've lived in the same house with you for the last six weeks and I still know very little about you. I could live with you for a year and still not know you.'

'What do you want to know?'

'Lots of things.'

He picked up a blade of grass and tried chewing it. 'Shoot.'

'If I shoot you I'll never know.'

'True.'

So, she asked the questions she wanted answers to. 'Tell me why you lied to me, for a start.'

He took the grass out of his mouth and threw it away.

She went on. 'I'd like you to explain your reasons for keeping me at a distance. I'd like to know where you met Jacinta's mother and I'd like to know about your family.' Now that she'd started, she found it hard to stop.

He reached out and lifted her fingers to rest them in his palm. 'All of that and more, eh?' He squeezed her hand. 'I'm not particularly proud of the deceptions about my job, but I do think that's all part of my defence against a particular blonde-haired mini-bombshell that I was trying to stop myself from racing off with.'

He leaned his head back and stared up at the branches overhead as if marshalling his thoughts. Then he looked back at her. 'You see, here I was, finally meeting my commitment to my long-lost daughter, and there you were, distracting me. It was very disconcerting.'

He spread his hands as if asking her to understand. 'Then there was the hospital-staff shortage, which I knew I could help with but I wanted to avoid a situation where you knew I was an obstetrician. I didn't want to fight about it. I'm not a general practitioner who can turn my hand to all. To be honest, your one-horse town hospital is a little out of my comfort zone. I'm used to having a back-up emergency team and I didn't want to put myself out there for litigation if I stuffed up. But I see it's not like that here. And I didn't need the team. I might be rusty at some things I haven't done since my training but I could re-learn the rest. So to lie to you was wrong.' He shook his head. 'To do it twice was lunacy and I'm sorry. I guess it's true that one lie leads to another.'

He sighed. 'As for keeping you at a distance – again, that was self-protection. I haven't had much long-term success with the women in my life. And most of it has been my fault.'

She tilted her head and looked quizzically at him. 'This doesn't sound like the Iain I know.'

'As you said before, you don't know me well. Perhaps I'm afraid that if you did know me you might not like what you see.'

She tilted her head to study him and then said tongue-in-cheek, 'You could be fine with a few minor adjustments.'

His eyes dared her. Promising her a run for her money if she thought she could change him. 'And you think you're up for it?'

'I might be.' Noni said it sedately. 'Tell me about your childhood.'

He laughed once. 'What's there to tell? My father walked out and left me with my mother when I was very young. But at least he left us very well provided for. Unlike Jacinta.' He twisted another blade of grass between his fingers. 'I vowed I would never do to my children what he did to me. But it seems I did. Only worse.'

Noni felt his pain. 'You didn't know about Jacinta.'

'That doesn't make it right.' His sigh came from the depths of his chest and she wanted to stroke his arm. But if she touched him . . .

'Tell me about your mother,' she said. They needed these conversations more than she needed to touch him. Just.

'This is a far-reaching discussion.' He looked up at the sky again as if for inspiration. 'My mother . . .' He ran his fingers through his hair, taking a few moments, as though he didn't quite know how to start. 'I didn't understand my mother,' he began. 'And never will now that she's gone. Such a bitter woman. I had quite a few "uncles" who didn't stay in the picture long, and I don't think I learned how to have a long-lasting relationship. The women I fell for, the relationships I tried, most were a dismal failure.' He ticked them off his fingers. 'Jacinta's mother. Well, I was young. Seventeen and just finished school. A year early. I'm rather smart,' he said smugly.

'Smart alec,' she corrected.

'Tsk. As I was saying, my mother disliked me, and I was about to dive into my medical training when I met Adele. It wasn't planned. I was waiting for my results when I saw her. Just saw her walking in town one day and followed her home. Adele was so funny and sweet. So different to anyone I'd met. Her age only intrigued me more.'

'Precocious child.'

'Look who's talking.' He fondled a twig he'd picked up, staring into the distance. 'She was such a stunningly beautiful woman and I think to start with she felt amused that I'd fallen for her. I can see now I was infatuated. I asked her to marry me numerous times during those crazy few months, but she always laughed and refused.'

He took a sip of his coffee she'd poured from the thermos, seeming to savour the taste. 'Then, one day, she changed. It was as if she couldn't stand the sight of me and eventually, I stopped trying to see her. She gave me the impression that she had a new lover, although I never heard of anyone with her. Obviously, now, I realise she was pregnant.'

He sighed for the lost communication he should have had. 'Not long after that I went away to uni, and proceeded to skip from one disastrous relationship to another until I'd had enough failures and simply abstained. Five years later I met my wife, Wendy, a nurse at King George Hospital, and we were married in haste to repent at leisure. The ironic part about it was Wendy couldn't have children. It's hard not to wonder if our marriage would have been different if we'd been able to be parents – or if Adele had told us of Jacinta's birth.' He drained his cup as if he deserved the bitterness, and stared into its empty centre.

Noni squeezed his other hand. 'Perhaps Adele felt it would have ruined your life – or tied her to a man she had nothing in common with.'

He looked up. His gaze narrowed. 'Are you condoning her behaviour?'

Frustrated that he couldn't look at it from Adele's point of view, one that gelled with Noni, she volleyed back at him, 'Are you damning her without knowing the full story?'

They glared at each other across the rug until they both saw the damage. How had they got into this after what they had just been through? It was almost as if they were on a self-destruct mission.

Noni knew she should be steering the conversation away from this topic. Or she could just get it out in the open.

Iain looked as if he was over telling his past. He was focused on the future. 'Are you coming to Sydney with me or not?' *Back to his own agenda.*

Talking just didn't work for them. But she had to clear the air before they went any further. 'That's a big ask, Iain. I'm not so sure now it would work. There are so many things we still don't know about each other.'

He grimaced. 'Like what? I've just spread out my whole sordid early life for you.'

'And me? You've never asked about Harley's father.'

Iain sat back. The look on his face said that was because he didn't want to know. 'I guess I assumed he was dead.' His tone said he hoped so.

Was he jealous? Of someone she'd slept with more than five years ago?

'Well, you assumed wrong. He was a one-night stand.' She met his eyes. 'And I never told him about Harley, just like Adele never told you.'

She saw the shock. The ripple of distaste crossed his face as if Iain couldn't believe what he was hearing. 'So, there's some guy out there who could waltz into your life and claim half your son? Claim you?'

Men. Seriously? 'What? If I fancied him once I could do so again – is that what you're thinking? That's a pretty big leap.' She could see he definitely didn't want to hear this. And she wasn't happy with his assumptions. He really did need a lot of work. She hoped her instincts were right that he'd be worth it.

But she directed her answer to his main question. 'That wouldn't happen.'

'How can you be so sure he won't find out?'

'Because even if I did know where he was, I wouldn't tell him.'

Iain winced. 'Just like Adele.' She saw it all rise up in front of him, all the pain he'd felt at his exclusion from Jacinta's younger years. Saw him realise he'd picked the wrong woman, again. Saw him consider his options, weigh the negatives, and felt her own loss. Maybe there was no future for them. No future for her with him. He still wasn't listening. He wasn't trying to see her reasoning.

Iain said, 'What if something goes wrong for you, like it did for Adele? Are you going to dump Harley in his father's lap out of the blue?'

'No. Aunt Win's lap.' Noni stood up and splashed the contents of her cup onto the grass. He couldn't push past his own bitterness. 'You don't want to hear my reasons, do you?'

She gathered up the rest of the picnic and shoved it willy-nilly in the bag. She looked at the man who had infiltrated her protective wall and her heart with far too much ease and called herself a fool, again. She shook her head. 'You're not perfect. You're willing to offer me a temporary arrangement because that's convenient for you. It's safe and if it doesn't work out then you can blame your mother for not teaching you about long-term relationships. That way, you're not compelled to take the rough times with the smooth. Don't you know that the more you put into a relationship the more you'll get out of it?'

She picked up her bag, hoisting the strap over her shoulder.

'Well, that's no better than if I'd trapped the man who was Harley's father. He wasn't interested in a relationship with me, he told me that. And I'm telling you I'm not interested in one with you. I'd really prefer if you'd find somewhere else to stay for the next fortnight until you go back to where you came from.' It was spiteful, but she was hurting.

Now he was angry too. 'How convenient for you if I move out. But I'm still allowed to work the next two weeks to save your precious maternity ward,' Iain said cynically and brushed himself off.

Noni turned and walked back to the car. At least she hadn't slept with him today, she told herself, but somehow, that only made her feel worse.

Chapter Forty-five

Noni

When Suzie and Paul went in to have their baby, they couldn't believe their luck.

'Imagine Iain being the doctor on call and you the midwife. That's great.' Paul was grinning.

Noni smiled weakly and ushered them into the birthing suite. The last fortnight had been horrendous. Iain and Jacinta had moved to Dr Soams's house and the whole hospital was gossiping about the tension between Iain and Noni. The rumours she'd tried to quash she'd tracked back to Penelope Soams.

The worst part of it all was Iain acting so damn nice. His crooked smile as he followed the midwives in their less interventionist methods warmed her undisciplined heart, and she acknowledged how well he had adapted to the more holistic care Burra provided for their maternity patients.

Surprisingly, he was working hard at giving her his full attention whenever she had to speak to him. She knew it was all a strategic game, but she couldn't figure out the rules and she so wasn't interested. It was too little too late, as far as she was concerned. And too painful.

He made no effort to discuss any of the personal issues they'd disagreed on, or even tried to see her out of work hours. Not that she would have gone. Although, he still coached Harley's cricket team.

She kept telling herself it would be over soon if the tension didn't kill her. It was harder to work together than to live in the same house. If Noni had to have another polite conversation with Dr Iain McCloud in the maternity ward she'd surely scream.

At least Suzie's labour progressed quickly and kept her mind occupied. It could have been the classical music that did it. Noni found out that Paul was a violinist in an orchestra and they'd been playing the music for baby during most of the pregnancy.

Noni completed an examination and Suzie's eyes were closed after a particularly strong contraction. 'You're eight centimetres dilated, your cervix is very thin and almost ready to open all the way.'

Suzie looked up with the first threads of panic in her eyes. 'I don't know if I'm ready to do this.' She reached for her husband's hand. 'I thought I'd have the baby late tonight. It should be slower with my first child.'

'Not after all those Braxton Hicks.' Paul squeezed her hand in return. 'Remember the transition and the "frantic" feelings Noni talked about? That might be what you're feeling now.'

Noni nodded. 'I think so, too, and this is the first time I've had someone complain about their labour being over too soon.' She laid her hand on Suzie's arm and smiled reassuringly. 'It was all that practice your uterus had before coming into labour. That annoying stopping and starting has done great things.'

'Nice to know it had an upside.' Paul looked more exhausted than his wife did. 'We haven't had a decent night's sleep for weeks.'

'You'll both probably be too excited to sleep tonight.'

'Here comes another one. Ooh.' Suzie hunched forward on the birth ball and Paul rubbed the small of her back in a slow, circular motion.

'You guys are doing brilliantly. I'll give Iain a ring and let him know how you're going.'

Noni closed the door behind her and leaned back on it. She sighed to relax her shoulders before straightening up and pushing herself off the door. She had to force herself to go to the desk and pick up the phone.

'Dr Soams's surgery. Hold the line, please.' Penelope's voice grated on Noni's ears and she rolled her eyes as she waited.

Finally, the woman came back on the line. 'Can I help you?'

'It's Noni Frost. Can I speak to Dr McCloud, please?' Noni's voice was brisk and she acknowledged that she didn't feel this way with any of the other doctors' secretaries. She really should get over Miss P.

'Dr McCloud speaking.'

Noni watched the hairs on her arms rise, and closed her eyes. How could he do that to her with just his voice? She realised she hadn't answered and opened her eyes. 'It's Noni.'

'Noni. What can I do for you?' His voice softened and her mind threatened to wander again before she pulled herself up smartly.

'Suzie and Paul are in labour here, and chugging along at eight centimetres. The baby's head is fairly low in her pelvis. I don't think you'd better hang around when I ring to say she's in second stage because I think she'll be quick.'

'Foetal heart's fine?'

'Yes, Doctor.' *Why wouldn't it be?* He was so tuned for disaster it drove her crazy.

'I'll see you soon, then.'

But soon you won't. You'll be gone, and this torture will be over. 'Thanks.' She hung up.

As she turned to go back to the birthing suite, the sound of Suzie's moan travelled up the corridor. It had that special tone that made midwives everywhere rise from their seats with a smile.

Noni pushed open the door and grabbed the odd-shaped birth stool from behind the curtain.

'I want to push,' Suzie said as soon as Noni walked in, and Paul looked at her with fervent relief.

'I know. It's great. Sit here, Suzie. You can hang onto these handles and bear down when you have the pain. Now that you have something to do with it, use your contractions.'

Noni put her hand on Paul's shoulder after she'd settled his wife, and steered him onto a chair behind the stool. 'Suzie can lean back into your arms.'

Suzie wailed, 'I think it's coming!'

Noni pressed the nurse-call buzzer once. She settled herself on a footstool in front of the birthing stool and lifted Suzie's gown.

'Yep. I can see the hair. Do you want a mirror?'

'I don't want to see it but Paul wants to.'

'No worries. We'll just angle it towards him and get on with it.'

Another midwife poked her head around the comer. She met Noni's eyes and they both smiled. 'Want me?'

'Give Dr McCloud a ring and tell him now. Thanks.' Noni's voice was matter-of-fact, and Suzie and Paul relaxed at the lack of tension in the room.

The other girl nodded. 'Will do. I'll be back.'

'Here comes another one.' Suzie strained with her body's urging and the circle of dark hair spread wider with each push.

Noni's voice was calm and quiet. 'You're doing beautifully. Gently does it and lean back on Paul when it's done.'

The muted sound of classical music and Suzie's steady breathing were the first sounds the little ears heard as the head was born. Just then, the door opened and Iain came in quietly as the baby's shoulders rotated and, with a gush the rest of the body arrived. Noni lowered the little boy onto the pillow between his mother's feet and wiped the infant's body with a warm towel. Then she gestured for Suzie to lift up her baby.

Suzie wrenched her gown over her head to bare her skin, reached down, and lifted her baby son to her chest. The baby mewled and Suzie hugged him to her breasts. 'Our baby.'

Tears ran down Paul's face as he reached around and cradled his family. 'Darling, he's beautiful.'

The cord could wait. Noni sat back. She looked up and caught Iain's eyes on her, and suddenly she too felt like crying. It hit her then that she and this man could have shared a similar moment to this as parents. If only . . .

'Could you pass me another one of those warm bunny rugs, please, Iain?'

When he handed it to her, Noni laid it over the baby's back and around Suzie's shoulders before sitting down again on the stool.

The umbilical cord ceased pulsation. Noni placed two clamps on either side of the area to be cut and offered the scissors. 'Would you like to cut the cord, Paul?'

He swallowed once before shaking his head. 'I would, but I think I need to take a few deep breaths at the moment.'

Iain caught Noni's eye. 'Perhaps, you had better do it, Sister.'

'Maybe.' Noni looked up at the mother. 'What about you, Suzie? You've done everything else.'

Suzie flicked her hair out of her face and grinned at Noni. 'Take a picture of this, someone.' She shifted the baby to her left arm and took the scissors. The thick, rope-like connection between mother and child separated with a firm snip. She handed back the scissors.

Suzie frowned suddenly and groaned. 'Hey, you said the pains would go away after I had the baby, and I've got another one.'

Noni smiled. 'You needed one more, to finish the fabulous job you've done.'

A few seconds later it was over. Noni placed the dish on the bottom of the trolley and helped Suzie tidy herself.

Paul sighed quietly and closed his eyes.

Noni looked up. 'Can I hold baby for a minute, Suzie?' She wrapped the rest of the bunny rug around the baby and quickly stood up and out of the way. 'Iain. Fainting father over here,' she said as Paul slid sideways off the chair onto the beanbag beside it.

Iain raised his eyebrows.

'Please.'

Iain gave her a crooked smile and then shrugged. He stepped over to the casualty.

'Sometimes it's just too much. Come on, old mate, I'll get a wet washcloth for your face.'

Paul opened his eyes. 'What happened?'

'It's time you went out for some fresh air. Bet you haven't eaten all day.' Iain helped him to his feet and smiled at Paul's wife. 'He'll be back in a minute. He'll be fine.'

Noni and Suzie watched Iain help Paul stagger out the door and both tried hard not to laugh.

'Poor Paul,' said Noni. They grinned at each other.

'Let's get you up on the bed and settled with this little man before he comes back.'

When Suzie was settled in bed with her baby nursing gently at her breast and the room returned to tidy, Noni let out a breath of relief.

'I'll slip out and see if I can find Paul.'

'Before you go, Noni.' Suzie hugged the little body to her. 'Is Iain really leaving tomorrow?'

Noni stopped and met Suzie's eyes. 'Yes. Why?'

'It's sad. I thought you two might be good together.'

Noni had thought so, too. 'Sometimes things don't work out, but it's not the end of the world.' She forced a smile to her face and then turned towards the door. 'I'll go look for that husband of yours.'

Chapter Forty-six

Noni

Noni woke early on Saturday morning, strangely relieved that it would soon be over. She dressed and steeled herself for one more day of pretending all was right in her world, but when she opened her front door Iain stood on the verandah as if he'd been about to knock.

This hard-eyed stranger wasn't the caring doctor she'd seen for the last fortnight at work. He'd gone. In his place stood a furious consultant ready to tear strips off her. She couldn't think of anything she'd done wrong.

'Iain? What's wrong?'

'You. You're wrong. Not content with me missing the first seventeen years of Jacinta's life, are you? So, how long have you two been cooking this up?' His voice hissed out, colder than she'd ever heard it, and he examined her through narrowed eyes. She'd never seen him so angry and she didn't like it.

Time out. Her eyes scanned the front yard for inspiration but found nothing that cleared the mystery. Jacinta wasn't in the car, so she must still be at Dr Soams's house. 'Come in. I'm not doing this here. Come into the study.'

He stepped inside and then halted to gesture sarcastically for her to precede him down the hallway.

Once she'd entered the study, she sat sedately on the lounge trying to still her agitation. The dark cloud had certainly followed him in and the tension kept building. 'Don't tower over me.' She gestured with her hand for him to sit, and waited.

He opened his mouth and then shut it again before he walked angrily around the room. Apparently too furious to speak. *Good grief.*

'Cooking what up?' she prompted him, keeping her voice even, despite the agitation that rose inside.

Win appeared, and Noni heaved a sigh of relief. Aunt Win would calm him down. Win looked from one to the other and her face turned grim. She sighed and crossed her arms over her ample bosom.

'It's my fault,' Win said. 'Jacinta just rang and asked me if she could stay here for a while with Olivia, instead of going back to Sydney with her father.'

Noni began to see the light. 'And you said . . .?'

Win looked at Iain, lifting her chin. 'The same as I said to you, Noni. Of course I said yes.'

Iain snorted. 'Spare me. Do you think I'm going to believe she,' he gestured to Noni, 'knew nothing of this? You're both in this together.' He threw a cynical glance at Noni. 'Well, I'm leaving today. That's what you want, isn't it? Without my daughter. My sympathy goes to Harley. He has to live with the scheming lot of you.'

Win glared at him. Noni sucked in a breath and held her tongue. From experience, she knew that when people were this angry they couldn't hear you, anyway. And Iain was livid.

An hour later he arrived back, deposited a subdued Jacinta

on the footpath, and refused to come in. Boy was he going to eat humble pie when the truth came out. Noni could admit to a degree of infuriation that she'd been blamed for the whole fiasco. But she would have said yes as well so it was a moot point.

It was a very sombre crew that watched the Lexus pull out of the driveway for the last time. As if on cue, Olivia began to cry and Noni felt like going out in sympathy. *Not like this*, she kept thinking. How had it ended like this?

Finally, she touched Jacinta's hand and squeezed it in question. 'So, what is all this about, missy?' Her voice emerged calm and quiet, in contrast to how she felt inside.

Jacinta shrugged, a little sheepish now, and Noni suspected the ulterior motive. 'It wasn't any fun with him in Sydney before and I'm not sure what I want to do. It is okay that I stayed, isn't it?'

Noni half laughed. That was rich. 'A bit late now but, yes, it's fine. Can I ask: do you have a more detailed long-term plan for you and Olivia?' She suspected that Jacinta had more going on behind those blue eyes than anybody guessed. She crossed her fingers behind her back that she was right.

Jacinta nodded and met Noni's eyes with a glint of determination. 'When Olivia's older I'll see about uni. I'm going to study medicine.'

Noni nodded, satisfied. She'd thought so. No grey shades there. And her father's help would come into play because it would be crazy not to, and Jacinta was nothing if not practical. 'Right, then. Let's go and fix your room properly.'

Noni's brain and her heart ached. Nice to know someone had a plan for the future. She and Harley had just had a wobble put into their worlds but she was happy for Jacinta.

She turned to her son, whose heartbreaking loss shone clear on his small, pinched face as he stared along the empty road. His hero had hastened away and her heart sank again. 'Harley. Darling. Iain will visit.' She hoped. 'Try to remember the good times and how much you learned while Iain was here.'

'You could have asked him to stay.' Harley turned and stared accusingly at his mother. His eyes glinted with unshed tears and Noni felt stabs of that hurt twist her chest. Then he turned and ran into the house.

Noni rubbed her temples.

'I'll stay home this weekend,' Win said. 'We'll all try to cheer Harley up.' Noni had forgotten Aunt Win had been standing there through the whole fiasco. She didn't need Noni's dramas either and Noni decided she felt as miserable as Harley looked.

'You sure? You'll have much more fun away from the sad bunch here.'

Win nodded with her own resolve. 'And I'd worry all weekend. No, I'll stay. But I might go out tonight with Greg. He's been trying to take me to tea for a couple of weeks now and tonight's the night.'

Noni blinked. There was something in her aunt's voice. 'At least that's a good change now that he's retired.' She glanced at her aunt. Saw her face soften with a wistful expression before it was bustled away from view.

What was that look? 'Are you still having Sunday lunches?' Noni had been so absorbed with all the Iain and Jacinta dramas she'd paid little attention to her aunt's life. *Selfish niece.*

'Yes.' Another soft smile that seemed to light her aunt up from within. 'I enjoy Greg's company.'

Noni heard the subtle change. Had she thoughtlessly relied

on Win to be there as always? What if Aunt Win was on the verge of change, too? What if Aunt Win was considering a huge change?

The thought brought a tinge of panic and she stuffed it down. She had no control over other people. Certainly not over Iain. Or Jacinta. Just herself, and Harley for the time being. She'd learned that from the dear woman in front of her. And more than anything she wanted Aunt Win to be happy.

Noni looked at her aunt and comprehension dawned. Her aunt's life had been put on hold for hers. 'And he obviously enjoys your company,' she said softly.

'Apparently.' Her aunt actually blushed. Noni couldn't remember the last time she'd seen that, and despite her distress for the way Iain had left, the sight made her mouth twitch.

Noni stepped back and looked at her aunt. 'And apparently, there's more afoot here than I've paid attention to.' Her eyes narrowed and she studied her aunt from head to toe. She saw a magnificent woman, big bones, warm, soft eyes, a generous mouth and her long white plaits. And a blush. Her wonderful Aunt Win was in love. And she hadn't noticed.

She shook her head slightly and smiled with a strangely bitter-sweet but very honest happiness. 'When did this happen?'

'What?' Aunt Win pretended innocence.

'You know what I mean. Dr Soams "connecting" on a more formal – or rampantly non-formal – basis.'

Win's eyes twinkled. 'Greg has always been my friend.'

Noni realised that was true. She'd rarely seen Dr Soams when he hadn't asked after her aunt. More in the last two years since his wife had died, certainly. But before that, too. If she thought about it, he was a good-looking, eligible widower, who had always been her aunt's friend. Though admittedly, he did have a stay-at-home daughter who had never been Win's favourite. Noni suspected Penelope hadn't hidden the fact that she looked down on Win's niece. That wouldn't go over well with Aunt Win.

She said gently, 'Things have changed for you and I haven't noticed. I'm sorry.' This time she was the one who hugged her aunt with extra fervour.

'Has he asked you to marry him?' A horrible thought occurred to her. 'You haven't said no because of Harley and me?'

Chapter Forty-seven

Win

Win felt the tears prick her eyes. *Dear Noni.* She hadn't said no to Greg, only because the chance hadn't arisen, but she'd thought about it. Had thought she'd put him off tonight.

'No.' It didn't come out sounding as definite as it should have.

Noni narrowed her eyes at her. 'You said he's been trying to take you out for a while. Do you suspect he's carrying a ring?' Her hand covered her mouth, but it kicked up at the corners. Then more seriously, she said, 'You're the one who said life owns its own directions, and we're just here for the ride. Goodness. This is a chance for a whole new adventure you haven't had!'

Win felt like crying, which wasn't like her. But Noni saying all the things she knew to be true made her want to cry, and laugh. Her darling niece was being so brave and loving, but how could she leave while Noni's heart lay bruised and battered? She could box that Iain McCloud's ears for having a tantrum and blaming Noni. She had no doubt he'd see reason, but seriously? He needed a good woman to take him in hand. Noni would sort him out if she had the chance.

Win blew out a breath and brushed away her emotions. 'There's no rush. Let's recover from all this tumult before I think about it.'

'No.' Noni kissed her cheek and stepped back. 'Winsome Frost, go into that house and phone the man you love and arrange your dinner date. Then prepare yourself to say yes. Your wedding will be the perfect diversion to lift all our spirits. Maybe Harley could be in the wedding party.'

'He could give me away.' Win chewed her lip, but deep inside the tiny ripple of excitement gathered momentum, louder and faster, like approaching the rapids on the river in her kayak, being drawn towards the inevitable rush of splashing speed, the spice of danger and the balance needed to stay upright in her craft.

Could she do it?

She lifted her head. Maybe.

Was she being timid? Probably.

Did she love Greg? Had done for years.

Noni was right. She had to take the challenge. Risk it. She'd ring Greg and just maybe . . . She'd say yes, tonight.

That evening, Noni helped her dress. She wore a ruby-red skirt that fell to the floor and swirled with bands of deeper velvet; a white peasant blouse that Noni said made her look soft and feminine; and her cashmere wrap. Not that it was cold, but the wrap settled around her shoulders like protective angel wings – just there. Flat shoes – she only owned flat shoes – but for a fleeting moment she wished she'd had at least one pair of mid-heels she could have worn.

'You look perfect,' Noni said.

Jacinta nodded her head in agreement. 'Bad.'

Win blinked. 'Bad?'

Noni raised her eyes at Jacinta. 'Bad means good. Doesn't it, Jacinta?'

'Absolutely. Awesome. Wicked.'

Win laughed. She didn't mind looking wicked. Her outfit wasn't conventional. She hadn't wanted to be something she wasn't. But it was feminine and even trendy in a vintage way, and she hadn't been on a proper date for centuries. At least it felt like it.

Tonight, Greg would come for her. And they wouldn't rush home. She felt like a teen waiting to go to the school dance. *Ridiculous.*

'I am very happy for you,' Noni said softly. 'Everything will work out perfectly.'

Win wasn't so sure about that, but Noni had convinced her that two unhappy people did not make things better, which was very sensible. She should have seen that herself. Silly. Let alone Greg's feelings in the matter. Her little stream of excitement burbled away underneath the veneer of a well-dressed woman. The grandmother clock began to chime in the dining room in a silvery benediction.

Someone knocked at the door and her heart bumped with an extra fillip of excitement. 'I'll go. I won't have him come in. Goodnight, girls.' She glanced back at her niece and blew her a kiss. 'Thank you.'

When she opened the door, Greg's beautiful eyes widened in admiration. There was no mistaking the pleasure in them. Then they darkened into something more delightfully disturbing that she didn't expect. *You devil.* She smiled to herself, and then at him.

'You look beautiful,' he said.

'Thank you, kind sir.' She held out her arm and he tucked it into his own and escorted her to his car.

Chapter Forty-eight

Jacinta

Jacinta saw the shine of tears in Noni's eyes as the door shut after Win.

This was all her fault. She'd thought her dad would just turn around when he cooled down but that hadn't happened. How had she got it so wrong? She'd only been trying to keep them together. Had she made it worse?

This was ridiculous. She slipped out of the hallway and up the stairs to her room and shut the door. He would have to have calmed down by now. Surely. She stabbed his number in on the phone he'd given her.

He picked up on the first ring. 'Iain.'

He sounded normal. How could he be normal when they were all so miserable? 'It's Jacinta. Are you sane yet?'

Her dad pretended to growl. 'Grr. Getting there, oh disloyal one.'

She could feel the relief roll over her with his teasing. At least someone was amused. 'I'm not the mean one here. Why haven't you rung Noni? I don't know what's was wrong with you. We all know you love Noni. Don't you?'

There was a pause and Jacinta thought for a moment she'd got it wrong. Maybe Noni was right?

'Yes. I love Noni.' There was no doubting the sincerity in his voice and she sagged a little in relief.

'And you know that Noni loves you, right?

'I believe she has feelings. Yes.' Less sure.

Before he could say anything else, because seriously, she was so over his faffing around, she continued. 'She knows what she wants, so how come you don't know what you want?'

'Jacinta.' Iain tried to break through her explosion of words.

She sucked in her breath, telling herself to settle. 'So, are you coming back?'

'Yes, Miss Fix-it. I'm coming back. But you can't say anything yet. I have to extricate myself from a whole world down here. I'll finalise my work commitments Monday and the apartment Tuesday. I'll be back Wednesday afternoon. Dr Soams arranged an interview with the hospital for Friday, and I have to spend the next couple of days arranging the change from a Macquarie Street specialist to Burra Hospital's new obstetrician.'

Jacinta felt relief roll over her. She hadn't ruined everything. 'That's good.'

'I'm glad to hear it.' His voice dropped to a soft and urgent tone. 'How's Noni?'

'Not happy, though Harley's worse. He's making all our lives hell.'

'I always knew he was a good boy.' She heard the smile in his voice.

It was Jacinta's turn to laugh. Her relief was making her silly. But she needed to stay quiet because she didn't want Noni to hear that she was happy if she couldn't tell her why. 'You're a rat.' Then she remembered the glint of tears she'd seen. 'Why haven't you rung Noni? She's sad.'

'I wish I could.' She could hear the uncertainty in his voice and that was strange. He was never uncertain. 'I can't just phone her. I blew it badly, Jaz. I was terrible to her. I need to apologise in person. A couple of days and I'll be back, but I don't want you to tell her either. I'd be a wimp if you did my dirty work for me.' He paused, then said, 'She doesn't like wimps.' The smile was back in his voice for a moment.

She rolled her eyes even though he couldn't see her. 'Well, hurry up.'

'I'm glad you miss me,' he teased.

'Noni misses you. I just want someone to hold Olivia while I shop.'

He laughed and she knew he got that she missed him too. It looked like her daughter would get that extended family they all seemed to need – if they could survive till Wednesday.

She went back downstairs. She found Noni in the library, tidying the shelves as if she needed to keep her hands busy. 'Hi Jaz.' Her voice was very bright. Fake bright.

'Thanks for letting me stay, Noni. I'm sorry Dad was angry with you when it was my fault. It makes me sad that he upset you.'

Noni shrugged and pushed a book firmly up against another. 'It's sad he thought I'd scheme against him to keep you here but that's not your fault. So don't you be sad. You've birthed a beautiful daughter and have your plans for the future. Plus, I'm hoping we'll have some really good news when Aunt Win comes home from her dinner date that will cheer us all up.'

More change for Noni, Jacinta thought. 'It's been a busy couple of months for you, hasn't it, Noni?'

Noni lifted her head to meet Jacinta's eyes, then smiled. Even though it wobbled a bit, it was genuine. 'I met you, and Olivia. And despite his mistakes your dad is a very nice guy. So yes, it's been busy, but I wouldn't have missed any of it.'

That's what Jacinta couldn't get. Noni was just so awesome.

Chapter Forty-nine

Noni

Wednesday morning, Noni slipped away to go to work early before her son woke up. She hoped Harley would cheer up by the time the weekend came. He'd barely eaten over the last few days and most of his ill temper had been directed at his mother because she'd 'made Iain leave'. There was enough truth in it to hurt and Noni felt bereft of Harley's love as well as Iain's. She'd even offered him another visit to Cath's house but he just shook his head.

She rubbed her temples to relieve a low-grade headache. She'd had an uncomfortable feeling of disquiet, lingering like a scent, all night and when she woke up this morning it was still there. The sky hung full of grey cumulus clouds, so maybe it was just the barometer blues from the impending storm.

Thankfully, Jacinta had been spending as much time as she could to divert Harley's sulks, asking him to hold Olivia when she was awake, get her a nappy or extra wrap, or read his kindergarten reader to both of them.

Jacinta had turned into a joy. Lucky someone had. Though to be fair, Aunt Win had a special glow since Sunday, but she wasn't sporting a ring. Noni suspected she and Dr Soams were holding their official news for a week to let the household settle.

She smiled as she tucked away her bag, greeted her shift buddy, and cooed over the babies in the ward that had come back from the base hospital. The ward was still open for pre- and post-natal care despite the ban on births until they found a doctor – thankfully, three mums had been to Wagga Base Hospital and returned to Burra to rest. Things would settle. She hoped.

By the time the shift ended, the afternoon had turned dark and damp with the impending downpour. Storm warnings broadcasted to the patient TVs and on the radio in the nursery warned of heavy rain to come. A flash flood had ripped through one of the creeks up in the mountain village two valleys away and Burra was on alert for a deluge that just might close some roads.

The first raindrops fell as Noni climbed onto her bike and turned the key. The scent of rain and wet grass hung in the misty air and she breathed deeply. Even the sheep were quiet. Harley would be damp when the bus dropped him home. Aunt Win would make him hot chocolate to cheer him up – she'd done that for Noni many a time and it had helped to lift her mood. If only it were that easy. Maybe she would ask for hot chocolate when she got home, too. With marshmallows. Harley loved marshmallows.

The drizzle turned into rain, and rain into needles that stung her arms, and she ducked her head to stop them flying down her neck. At least Harley should have been home before the heavy rain. It was a relief to glide in under the carport and shake off the drops.

Instead of the smell of hot chocolate and the serenity of home, the sound of a distraught baby crying greeted her. She stripped off her wet-weather gear as she walked through to the lounge, expecting to find Jacinta or at least Win tending to her, but Olivia lay red-faced and sweating, alone, and Noni's disquiet turned to the beginnings of alarm.

Frowning, she scooped up the baby, soothed her and swiftly changed her soaking nappy before turning back the way she'd come.

'Hello? Anyone home?' She walked swiftly into the hallway and up the stairs. Olivia bounced on her shoulder, at peace now, snuggling into Noni's warmth and she hugged the infant closer.

'Noni!' Aunt Win's voice broke the silence from downstairs and the thread of anxiety turned into fear. Noni's nerves tightened. Aunt Win was never flustered.

'I'm here.' She descended quickly. 'What's going on?'

Aunt Win swallowed, lost for words or catching her breath, and Noni's disquiet multiplied, the dread in her gut building alarmingly.

'Harley didn't go to school today. I put him on the bus and the bus driver said he went in the yard.' Aunt Win's gaze met Noni's. 'But one of his friends just rang and asked if he was all right. He thought he must have been sick.' The distress spilled out with the words. 'He's not anywhere. I think he ran away this morning instead of going to school.'

'Because Iain's gone,' Noni whispered, and her head spun as she fought through a cloud of panic that seemed to drain the light from the room.

She blinked several times as if clearing the fog from in front of her face. One part of her tried desperately to think like a five-year-old boy and work out the most likely place to hide or run. The other wanted to throw herself on the floor and scream.

The baby squirmed in her arms. She breathed deeply and slowly, battled the horror that rose with the fear. 'Where's Jacinta? Why was Olivia here alone?'

Win gestured towards the door with her hand. 'It was only for two minutes. I spoke to the teacher and she said she hadn't seen him at all. Thought we'd forgotten to call. Jacinta walked to the shops to see if anyone had spotted him and she didn't want to take Olivia out in the rain.'

As she finished speaking, Jacinta skidded to a panting, bedraggled stop at the front door. 'Nobody's seen him,' she puffed, bending over to drag great gulps of air into her lungs. Not bad for a young woman who'd birthed three weeks ago. 'He has to be hiding somewhere here.'

Noni sank onto the hallway chair and the baby squirmed as she unconsciously clutched her tighter as if to keep her own child safe. In the next instant, she bounced up again. 'I'll check his room. He must be in the house, hiding.'

Win opened her mouth and closed it again. 'Here, give Olivia to me.' Win reached out and Noni blinked as her shock faded, and she handed over the infant.

She ran up the stairs following Jacinta and they split up while Noni checked every cupboard, under every bed, spending the longest in Iain's old room, looking under the bed, in the wardrobe and behind the curtains.

Lightning flashed and thunder rattled the windows as the rain fell in great sheets now onto the high roof and poured from the overloaded gutters. 'We'll try the carport again.' She had to raise her voice so Jacinta could hear her over the rain.

Noni shuddered to think of her baby huddled outside

somewhere. Alone. Or worse. What if someone had taken him? Or he'd accepted a lift? She closed her eyes, but her brain stayed sluggish with terror and shock. She had to get a grip and move fast. 'Think, think.'

All she could think about was Harley, lost and frightened, and Iain five hundred kilometres away when she needed him. The thought of Iain sharpened her mind.

'Right. Let's get back to Aunt Win,' she said to Jacinta.

Aunt Win was still standing in the hall, clutching Olivia, looking more shocked than Noni had ever seen her. Noni's voice shook as she tried to speak calmly.

'You phone the police, notify Sergeant Rodgers of his disappearance. He'll know what to do.' At least in a small town, the police instantly knew each family and who they were looking for. 'I'll phone Iain on my mobile, grab some stuff and I'll drive around in your ute after that.'

'I'll come.' Jacinta's eyes were huge in her face. 'Please, Noni.'

Noni wiped a distracted hand across her face. 'Jaz, what about Olivia?' Noni knew she had to act quickly. He'd been gone all day!

'I could mind Olivia here. We'll be fine. I'd be happier if you had someone with you, Noni,' Win said as she moved away to phone Sergeant Rodgers.

Noni tried Iain's mobile, but it went straight to message bank. Was it off, engaged or out of service? She thumbed urgently through the address book for the landline number he'd given her when he'd left for Sydney. She couldn't believe Harley could have done this to her. She couldn't believe she was such a bad mother that she hadn't realised what he was going to do. She found the number and punched it in. It rang and rang and finally she heard Iain's voice.

'Iain! It's Noni.' The voice continued talking. 'Stupid answering machine.' She felt like throwing the phone against the floor and took a deep breath to regather her wits. 'Iain, if you're there, this is an emergency. Pick up the phone!'

The voice finished and the phone beeped.

'Iain, when you get home ring me on my mobile.' She gave her own number and disconnected. They didn't have his work number. Of course. That would have given away his true profession. A spurt of frustrated anger blurred her vision for a minute before she snapped herself out of it.

'He's not home,' she said unnecessarily to Jacinta.

Win reappeared. 'The police want a photograph and will send someone around to pick it up. I'll give them the one on the mantelpiece.'

Noni thought she was going to lose her control then. She bit her lip with a grinding ferocity and fought back the fear that clutched at her stomach. This wasn't happening. She squeezed away tears and tried to stay sane. *Sane!*

'Jacinta can come if you think you'll be all right with Olivia,' she said to Aunt Win, her voice cracking.

Aunt Win nodded vigorously. 'We'll be fine. I'll ring your mobile when she needs a feed. Go. I'll phone Greg. He'll come here in case we need him.' Win put her hand over her mouth as Noni looked at her. Then she said, 'I need him.'

It took three long minutes to grab torches and leave. Noni barely spoke as she tried to block out images of her son, lost and crying. Wet and cold. Forlorn and frightened.

The worst was the drum of the rain as it rushed through the gutters and pelted the roof of the car. Searching was made harder by the darkness and poor visibility from the storm, even though it was still only four-thirty in the afternoon.

She couldn't allow herself to think he'd been taken. Or bobbing, drowning in a rushing stormwater drain or one of the swelling creeks. She kept picturing Harley crouched somewhere in the rain, waiting for her to find him. Desolate and drenched. Doubting his mother would come.

'Try the cricket field.' Jacinta's voice broke into her thoughts and Noni swerved to avoid a fallen branch.

Terror closed her throat again and her voice faltered. 'We have to find him soon.'

'We will.' Jacinta's voice shook and then steadied. 'He's probably holed up somewhere warm and dry, eating his play lunch.'

'Please, God. If someone's taken him . . .' She couldn't say it. She swallowed the lump in her throat. 'I have to find him.' She gripped the wheel tighter, the pain in her heart so fierce she could barely breathe. Harley was her world. The joy of her life. A series of memories flashed behind her eyes as she drove. His shining eyes when he asked a question. His enthusiasm for any type of ball game. His love of Olivia. His dirty knees and boundless curiosity.

She needed help. She needed Harley. 'Why hasn't Iain phoned us back?'

Chapter Fifty

Jacinta

'Dad doesn't know yet,' Jacinta soothed. 'How can he know until he finds out you rang him. He'll come as soon as he gets the message.'

Jacinta wanted to scream. She knew her father was coming, permanently. But this changed everything. He needed to be here *now*. Guilt weighed her down. If she'd told Harley her dad was coming back he would never have run away. But she hadn't known he was going to run away. If she told Noni now that would be a distraction she didn't need. Dad had to ring back.

An hour and a half later, Noni and Jacinta passed two police patrols as they turned for home. It was futile in the semi-dark, driving from place to place. The rain continued to fall as if a flood was on its way and the mobile phone between them stayed silent. It had been growing darker by the minute. They'd have to go home. Olivia would need feeding. Jacinta glanced across at Noni and she could see tears running down her cheeks, silver in the light of the street lamps as she drove.

They passed a small bridge over a creek, and they both looked at the rushing water. Fresh fear rose like a monster in Jacinta's throat as the headlights reflected the volume of water surging powerfully into the creek. *Surely, he wouldn't hide in a stormwater drain?* Now she felt sick.

'Aunt Win might have news.' Noni's voice cracked as she spoke and Jacinta nodded vehemently. *Please.*

They drove into the carport, and as the ute rolled to a stop she heard Noni drag in a big breath as if preparing herself for the worst.

Inside the guesthouse, one look at Aunt Win's face as she huddled under Greg's protective arm telegraphed the lack of progress in the search. She had no good news.

'The local radio is alerting everyone to the search and state emergency workers are dividing the swampland into a grid for a foot patrol.'

Chapter Fifty-one

Noni

Car headlights shone into the driveway and pulled into the carport. They all turned to look and Noni felt the tears well up.

'It's Iain!' Noni was out of the door and into his arms before the car had barely enough time to stop. He squeezed her tight and she burst into tears from the fear and trauma of the day. It was the last thing she wanted to do but couldn't help herself.

Iain's arms squeezed her tighter still. Hugging her against him with one arm, and stroking her hair with the other. 'Hey. It's okay, darling. Settle down.'

Noni pulled herself back off his chest and wiped her nose with the back of her hand. She sniffed and caught her breath. 'It's Harley, Iain. He's gone. He's run away.'

Iain's face drained of colour and he squeezed her shoulders. 'Come inside. How long has he been missing?'

'He didn't go to school. We didn't know who to call when we couldn't reach you.' She was tripping over words, trying to tell him everything at once as he ushered them back towards the house.

'Slow down, my love.'

Noni turned around to look at him, confused.

Iain said, 'It's okay. We'll talk about it all later. Just know I'll do anything you need to get Harley back.'

Her brain refused to think so she said, 'Thank you for coming, Iain.' She took another steadying breath. 'I've driven and looked everywhere. The police and volunteers are out looking for him. They think he might have been washed out onto the flooded swampland. Why haven't they found him?' Her voice was desperate. She stood in the centre of the lounge with Iain's arms around her and shut her eyes. Where was he? Harley had been on his own for hours. She shuddered.

'Win's made sandwiches. Please, have one.' Jacinta appeared at her elbow, her eyes huge in her face, a tray of food shaking in her hands. She held it out as if she were scared someone would bite her as she offered the plate.

Noni waved them away. 'I couldn't eat anything. He must be hungry and cold, Jaz. I don't think I can sit here all night, waiting for the phone to ring.'

Jacinta looked grim. 'There must be something I can do to help.' She offered the plate again. 'Try to eat something.'

Noni nodded distractedly.

A few minutes later there was a knock on the door and they all looked up. Noni put her hand to her throat and Iain strode across to answer it.

It was Sergeant Rodgers. The tall man looked grave. His normally genial features were set with worry. 'No luck on our side, yet.' He took Noni's hands and steered her towards the chair. 'Sit down, Noni.'

Noni sat, with her hands clasped together as her head screamed with anxiety.

Sergeant Rodgers's voice penetrated. 'Can you think of anywhere else that he could have gone?'

Noni racked her brain. She'd tried everywhere. They'd tried everywhere. It was a small town, with wide tree-lined streets, an oval, and paddocks with sheep once you left the centre of town. They had a small shopping centre, which the police had canvassed door to door, but nobody had seen him.

Painstakingly, the policeman spent the next half hour talking about where they'd looked and planning where they would search next. Then he asked about new friends, his school mates, his cricket friends, anyone he could have slipped away and gone to despite the fact that they all knew nobody would have kept him after dark without contacting them.

Before Sergeant Rodgers left, he asked Noni to stay home so she would be there when they brought Harley home. When Noni would have protested he put his hand on her arm. 'It's more important you're here where we can find you with any questions we might have. And for when we bring him back.'

There was little to say to that and Noni stared blindly at the mantelpiece where the framed photo of Harley had stood until this evening. The laughing little boy in the silver frame, missing – like her son.

Vaguely, Noni heard her aunt as she stuck her head around the door. 'Anyone seen Jacinta?'

Iain looked up. 'She was here a minute ago – maybe she's gone upstairs.'

'No.' Win sighed heavily as if she didn't want to add to their burdens. 'I checked. She fed Olivia and put her down, and now she's gone. And so is your car, Iain. I think she's gone out to search for Harley.'

Iain looked on the coffee table for his car keys, then groaned in frustration. 'Why couldn't she tell us what she was going to do?'

Noni sighed and slowly shook her head. She faced him doggedly – she couldn't go out – Jacinta had heard that and gone in her stead. 'She knew we'd try to stop her. Don't underestimate your daughter, Iain. I don't. Maybe she has an idea, though I would have preferred to hear it than find her gone.' She clasped her hands again, realised what she was doing and stood up to pace. 'I just hope she knows how to drive your car.'

Iain raked his hair and glanced at the rain sheeting down the window. 'She shouldn't be out in this.'

Noni sighed again. 'She's probably driven in worse. She's more streetwise than I am and I admire that in her. And she knows things I don't know about hiding on the streets. I'll take her help if it brings my son back.'

Iain glanced at his watch and hugged Noni to him. 'I don't like the idea of her driving in this, and it's not about my car, but you're right.' He stared at the rain pouring in rivers down the window. 'She's probably slept in more unusual places than we could imagine. Maybe she's thought of somewhere like that.' He took a deep breath and straightened his shoulders. 'I wish she'd come back, but I'm proud of her, looking for Harley. I wish I'd been there to look after her when she needed me.'

Noni felt the tears prick her eyes and she reached out for him. 'I think we both need a hug.'

The minutes stretched into an hour and Harley's photo flashed on the television screen. Every mother and father's worst nightmare. Aunt Win gasped and took off to the kitchen with Greg following her. Noni put her head in her hands and sobbed while Iain held her. She closed her eyes as his arms tightened around her. 'I'm so scared,' she whispered, but scared didn't even begin to describe her feelings.

His warmth enfolded her and she drew as much energy as she could from him until she felt she could go on again.

Another hour dragged by and Noni stared at the phone, willing it to ring. It wasn't the phone that rang, but the door opening slowly.

'Mummy?' said a tiny croaking voice she'd feared she'd never hear again. Harley stood there. Bedraggled and pinched with cold. His shirt soaked and torn, his red-rimmed eyes seeking his mother, and his shaking white hands outstretched with pleading. In the door-way, an equally bedraggled Jacinta stood behind him.

Noni stumbled to fling herself to him and snatched him into her arms. Nothing had ever felt as good as his small, cold and very wet body as she cradled him against her.

She hiccupped a sob and Harley burst into tears. His little arms clung to her neck in a stranglehold. She put her other arm out and drew Jacinta into the hug.

'Where was he?' Iain's arms came around the three of them.

Jacinta stood with a huge grin on her face. 'Asleep under a bench at the railway station. I missed him the first two times. He was tucked away really well.' Jacinta's voice was muffled under the group hug and she squeezed out of it. 'I've slept under railway benches heaps of times. The good news is he didn't know how to catch the train to Sydney.'

Noni closed her eyes and hugged the dishevelled absconder closer. 'Come on. We'll get you into a hot bath. And you into the shower, Jacinta.'

On cue, Olivia began to wail from the bedroom upstairs as if she'd heard her mother's voice, and Jacinta turned and jogged up the stairs. Iain made all the phone calls and Win and Greg minded Olivia while Jacinta showered.

After she had helped Harley bathe and dressed him in his pyjamas, Noni sat with him asleep in her lap. The tears had dried on her face and her world slowly edged towards righting itself, but the fear would linger for a while, yet.

Jacinta had been thanked so many times she had uttered, 'Spare me,' and gone to take her baby to bed.

'Why don't you go to bed, Noni?' Iain came up behind the lounge chair and massaged her neck.

She rolled her shoulders under his hands, moved her head from side to side and sighed with bliss. She'd always known he had beautiful hands and she needed that human touch for healing her frightened heart.

'I'll never sleep, but I will have to move. My legs have gone numb under Harley.'

'Here. Let me lift him. Would you like to sleep with him tonight in your bed?'

'Put him in his own bed and we'll leave the door open. I'll hear him if he wants me. I need your arms around me tonight, Iain. He won't mind me sleeping with you – though he might come in in the morning.'

Iain laughed softly, dropped a tender kiss on her lips and lifted the boy easily out of her lap to carry him up the stairs.

Chapter Fifty-two

Noni

Half an hour later, Noni had showered and was sipping the hot chocolate Iain had insisted she needed.

He came back into the room, sat down and slid his arm around her. 'This wasn't quite the situation and setting I'd planned, but I do have something to say.'

Noni put down the cup and tried to calm the sudden thumping in her heart. She looked into the face of the man she'd come to love and knew, without a doubt, that she had to stay with him despite the dilemmas they hadn't resolved. It wasn't just Harley who'd been heartbroken that he'd left.

'First of all, I'm sorry for accusing you of knowing Jacinta was planning on staying with you. On Saturday, it took me until about fifty kilometres south of Burra to realise that of course you hadn't known she planned to stay behind. I think I always knew you'd never stoop to underhanded methods to arrange that change of plan.'

He sighed. 'It was all Jacinta's idea, although for the life of me I couldn't understand why she left telling me until the last minute.'

He grimaced and squeezed her shoulder. 'I was so disappointed in her lack of loyalty, I blamed you. And I was over the top about it. I'm sorry.'

Noni ran her finger along his jaw. 'I understand that. Before she went to bed, Jacinta told me she wanted to make sure we still saw each other. That she could see we were good for each other if we could hang in there. She stayed so we would still keep in contact.'

'She's a stubborn young woman.'

'Just like her father.' Noni took a deep breath and hoped the offer was still open. 'But I can see what she means. I will take you on your terms, Iain. I think we should try to make a life together, and it's no good Harley and me staying in Burra if our hearts are down in Sydney with you.' She expelled her breath. There. She'd said it and she meant it.

He took her face in his hands and kissed her gently. 'Ah, Noni. You're too much for me. Thank you for your typically brave offer, but let me finish. Where was I? Oh, yes. I'm not stubborn, by the way!

'It only took another five kilometres to realise I didn't want to leave Burra, either. The challenges of a country practice might be the answer to rejuvenating my interest in obstetrics. But it's you, not the town, which is drawing me back. If you'll have me.'

Noni was lost now. 'What are you saying, Iain?'

'I'm saying . . . I love you. I want to marry you. I want to live with you, be a part of your family and you be a part of mine, in Burra if you want to, for the rest of our lives.' He took her hand in his and kissed her fingers.

'Say that again,' Noni whispered. She couldn't believe it.

'I love you. The first time I saw you it was as if I'd been searching for you my whole life. Or maybe we've connected before in one of Win's other lives.' He smiled and stroked her hair. 'I don't know what it was. I loved the way you stood up to me despite the fact that you only come up to the top button of my shirt. I love your empathy with the pregnant mums and fathers-to-be, your huge well of love for Harley and the rapport you have with Win. I love your kindness and the non-judgemental attitude you have with Jacinta that's helped bridge the gap between her and me, that I thought was insurmountable.' He kissed her again.

Noni couldn't believe it. Today had been the worst day of her life, and yet . . . the best. She almost couldn't take in such extremes of emotion. 'Why didn't you ring me and tell me you were coming back?'

'I wanted to. I swear I did. But it was the coward's way. I spoke to Jacinta on Sunday night and she blasted me for leaving. I'd already started the ball rolling but I needed to talk to you properly, and beg your forgiveness in person. I was pretty harsh with you when I left and I thought you deserved a face-to-face apology. It was going to be a good one. I have flowers in the car.'

She remembered the last time he'd gone to Sydney when he hadn't phoned her at all. She supposed she could forgive him, but she would have to break him of that ridiculous habit. 'I'll have to set you up with email if you ever go away. I can't stand not hearing from you.'

He laughed. 'I had hoped distance would make your heart grow fonder by the time I arrived back, and I planned to explain it all then.'

'Well, for goodness sake, don't do it again. We'll make a contingency plan.' She couldn't believe how good it was to be talking to Iain like this again.

'I'm sorry. I wanted everything sorted and under control before I came back.'

'Of course you did. We need to talk about that. You're like one of those universal remote controls – trying to run everything from the one handset. Stop. Please.'

He smiled at her and the expression on his face made her throat close with happy tears. 'I'm sorry. I love you. Can we go back to you being my instructor?'

Noni reached up and kissed him. 'I think that's a very good place to start. Do you need instructions on how to carry me up to my bed?'

'Not at all. I have past experience of that. And the rest we can work on together.'

Epilogue

Noni

One year later

Noni woke to the sound of not-so-secret whispering. She squeezed her eyelids together, but sleep had skedaddled and her smile snuck out. Judging by the light around her lashes, it was time to greet the intruders.

Iain's hand eased from her breast, a discreet shift in their position in bed to keep it clean for the kids.

The whispering came closer and she opened one eye. Harley stood near the bed, about six inches from her nose, Jacinta behind him, and the smell of burnt toast gave away his surprise. His tray held a full glass of orange juice balanced too close to the edge.

Jacinta's quick hand swooped in and caught it as it began to slide. 'We'll just put the juice on the bedside table.'

'Surprise! Happy Mother's Day!' Harley leaned forward to kiss her and the rest of the contents crab-walked towards the edge of the tray.

Noni sucked in a breath. 'Thank you, both. That's so sweet.'

Jacinta steadied the tray then hoisted the baby on her hip, who squealed and pulled at her mother's hair. Noni mouthed 'thanks' for preventing a disaster.

Harley moved closer, the dishes rattling ominously, and Noni scrambled to sit up before the whole tray ended on her chest. Iain's shoulders shook beside her, which wasn't helpful. He redeemed himself by stacking her pillows and she eased back against the support. His wicked smile, a well-known friend since their wedding, showed his appreciation of the view from his angle next to her. She twitched the neckline of her nightdress and admonished him with her eyes. But she couldn't help smiling, too.

She took the tray with relief. 'Thank you, Harley. This is lovely. Breakfast in bed. Wow.'

'I made toast and cereal, and your special tea,' Harley catalogued as if Noni couldn't see what was there.

Her baby. He'd grown so big in the last year. Even more independent and eager to learn everything Iain and Jacinta could teach him. Her son learned so fast it was scary. He'd miss Jacinta when she went.

'Thank you, darling. It's beautiful.' She smiled at Jacinta. 'And such a wonderful surprise. It's your Mother's Day, too, Jaz. Someone should have given you breakfast in bed.'

Jacinta patted her baby's bottom. 'Olivia will do it for me one day. Plus,' with a glance at her father, 'Dad said he's taking us all out for brunch, with Win and Greg, so I'll have breakfast then.' She screwed up her nose. 'I hate crumbs in my sheets.'

With the tray parked safely on his mother's lap, Harley looked hopefully at the space between Iain and her on the mattress. Iain patted the spot and Harley bounded around the bed and climbed over his stepfather, making strange crackling noises that seemed to come from inside his pyjama jacket, until he was snuggled next to his mother.

Noni managed not to spill her tea.

'I have presents.' Harley wriggled again while Noni steadied her cup with both hands. She could hear the quiet rumble of Iain trying not to laugh at her balancing act.

From beneath his pyjamas, Harley produced a roll of papers. One he gave to Noni, and the other he proffered smugly to Jacinta. 'I drew these for you,' he said in a boy-are-you-lucky voice.

Noni examined hers with suitable reverence. 'It's a drawing of a room full of babies. Look how many there are. And I have a big smile on my face.'

Harley leaned towards the picture. Pointed with a vegemite-smeared finger. 'That's you at work.'

Noni tried not to laugh. 'It's beautiful, Harley. Thank you.' She kissed his cheek. 'I'm glad it's not me at home,' Noni spoke quietly with a sideways glance at her husband and a pat of her rounded stomach.

Harley licked the vegemite off his fingernail. 'I've got a drawing for Aunt Win, and this is Jacinta's.' He handed the other picture to his new stepsister.

'Wow. One for me. Wicked.' Jacinta studied it, and Noni could see she was pleased. The thought warmed her. Then comprehension creased Jacinta's cheeks and she laughed. She turned it until Noni and Iain could see from the bed.

It required a small stretch of imagination, but Noni could make out Jacinta, astride Noni's motorbike, apparently with Olivia on the back wearing a tiny black helmet.

'Harley! You just outed me.' Jacinta lifted her chin, but the mischief in her eyes showed them all she wasn't worried. 'Guess I may as well tell you, Dad. I passed my motorbike learner's test.'

'Why am I always the last to know?' Iain asked the room in general.

Noni shrugged as much as she could with a tray on her lap. 'Your daughter is as stubborn as her father.'

'Oh, I know that.' His tone sounded grim. 'The perfect revenge for missing the first seventeen years.'

Jacinta hitched Olivia higher and her voice drawled with that I-know-best tone she did so well. 'Now that Noni's pregnant, someone needs to keep the bike turning over.' A mischievous smile spread across her face as she rocked her baby and pretended to sway dreamily. 'I love the speed and the wind in my hair.'

'Spare me.' Iain put his hands over his ears. 'I know when I've lost.' He looked down at the little boy between Noni and him. 'Harley? Are we outnumbered?'

Harley stole a piece of toast from his mother's tray and nodded. 'Yep.'

Noni raised her glass of juice in a salute. Iain was getting good with his child- and teenage-daughter-wrangling skills. 'You love it. Jacinta has booked her provisional licence for next weekend. We were going to tell you soon because you paid for it on your visa card.'

Noni waited for the explosion. Jacinta jiggled her baby.

Iain gave up the lost cause and blew a kiss at Olivia. 'I suppose your poppy will have to get you a sidecar.'

Noni smiled at her husband. 'See how far we've all come in only a year. Brilliant negotiations on all flanks.'

Noni appreciated Jacinta's tactics, smiling and confident with Olivia on her hip. A young woman full of plans for her daughter, plans for her own future in medicine, and plans to tease her dad more every day.

Noni savoured the warmth of Harley, blithely nestled between Iain and her, bouncing out of his skin to grow big and strong like his new dad, the man who was her husband. Her lover. Her greatest fan. Her partner in life and doting father of the baby to come. How had she been so fortunate?

As if he'd connected silently, he whispered across Harley's head, 'I feel incredibly lucky, you know.' He blew her a kiss. 'Thank you for my family, my love. Happy Mother's Day.'

Acknowledgements

Many years ago I wrote a short medical romance called *Midwife Under Fire*, which was basically an abridged version of Noni and Iain's story. Set in the nondescript town of Burra, it held tiny glimpses of the women you've just spent time with.

The characters in that story, and the fun I had describing the antenatal classes, have stayed with me. Actually, they teased me with a bigger story for years. Although some of the medical practice has changed since then, the fundamentals of midwifery remain the same. The character of Jacinta was inspired by the amazing young mums in our local TIMTAMs class (that's a weekly antenatal session for teens, Teenage Information Mornings Teens As Mums) and I'm still in contact with many of those inspiring and incredible mothers today fifteen years later.

That story was my favourite until I began writing for Penguin Random House and had more space to really explore interactions between women. This wonderful freedom allows me to touch on social issues and their impact on families, along with the romance (which is fun, but not nearly the whole story I want to write!).

ACKNOWLEDGEMENTS

After I wrote *The Homestead Girls*, I knew I loved exploring friendships between women of different ages, and I was thrilled that my publisher agreed Noni's story was something I should develop. I relished the opportunity to share Aunt Win's perspective as well as the amazing life of Iain's surprise daughter, Jacinta, with her experience and world view as a teen mum. Iain's viewpoint went out the window, which I think is funny, although my husband's not sure if he agrees!

I wanted to make Burra into a real place in my mind, so I was lucky enough to spend some time in the beautiful valleys of the Riverina, NSW. I thank my dear friend and fellow writer Bronwyn Jameson, who lives near Wagga Wagga, for her company. Many kilometres and photos later, both on her sheep station and as she drove me around, I fell in love with the lovely Riverina towns, and especially Cootamundra.

One of my Aussie Midwives, Lisa Ferguson, introduced me to Bianca Jones, who was at that time a student midwife in Cootamundra's real maternity ward (not the one in my mind), and Bianca helped me understand the logistics of a maternity unit that was even smaller than the one I worked in, so I could bring Noni's workplace to life. Thank you, Lisa and Bianca.

The descriptions of Burra Hospital in this book are based on the original but decommissioned hospital building further down the street in Cootamundra. The on-call demands and special skills of a country GP, and how much midwives love their profession, are not exaggerated.

I'd like to thank my publisher, Ali Watts, and my editor, Amanda Martin, from Penguin Random House, for their faith in my writing and for their fab input at the let's-stand-back-and-see-what-you've-done stage. I love working with you both.

Thank you to my agent, Clare Forster from Curtis Brown, and to Alex Nahlous and Beth Hall for their work on the manuscript. Thank you also to the amazing publicity team at PRH, who are taking me on my first book tour with two other authors. Yay!

Thank you to my writing friends and mentors – there's nothing like having your own tribe to feel nurtured in.

And of course, I thank my darling husband, Ian (not Iain), who has to live with me through all the incarnations a book has as it grows. Thank you for your patience, my hero.

Most of all I'd like to thank you, my readers, who have supported me, bought or borrowed my books, sent amazing emails and handwritten letters to say how much you enjoyed my characters – such comments that make my ordinary days shine like stars. Thank you!

I hope you enjoyed *Mothers' Day*, which celebrates all mums, as well as nanas, aunties, friends and midwives who help mother the mothers when they need it. If you haven't already done so, I hope you give it to your mum or your mum person, because I just love this new, big story and I hope you do, too.

With warmest appreciation,
Fiona